It Started With Jasper

A PORTHGARRION STORY

by

Suzie Peters

Copyright © Suzie Peters, 2024.

The right of Suzie Peters as the Author of the Work has been asserted by her in accordance with the Copyright, Designs and Patents Act, 1988.

First Published in 2024
by GWL Publishing
an imprint of Great War Literature Publishing LLP

Produced in United Kingdom

Cover designs and artwork by GWL Creative.
Watercolour illustrations by Tonia Tkach

Apart from any use permitted under UK copyright law, this publication may only be reproduced, stored or transmitted, in any form, or by any means, with prior permission in writing of the publishers or, in the case of reprographic production, in accordance with the terms of licences issued by the Copyright Licensing Agency.

All characters in this publication, with the exception of any obvious historical characters, are fictitious and any resemblance to real persons, either living or dead, is purely coincidental.

ISBN 978-1-915109-39-2 Paperback Edition

GWL Publishing
Chichester, United Kingdom

www.gwlpublishing.co.uk

Dedication

For S.

Chapter One

Anna

"I know it's Sunday, but I really don't feel like a roast."

"Then don't have one."

I look up at Stephen, and he smiles, his hazel eyes sparkling. Other people often remark on how different we look, but we never do. Maybe because we know we're half-brother and sister, and that I got my colouring from my mother, while he got his from our father. It's something we have to explain often enough to make it boring, but there's no-one to explain it to today, so for now I return his smile.

"In that case, I won't. I'll have the gammon steak."

"With egg or pineapple?" he says, trying not to smile.

"That's not even a serious question."

"No, it's not. I'll order it with the pineapple."

"Don't you dare."

He chuckles, getting to his feet, and wanders to the bar while I sit back and look around. The Harbour Lights is the only pub in Porthgarrion, which I suppose makes it my local, although I don't come here often enough to give it such a name. I don't go anywhere, really, other than to the office, and home again, making occasional visits to the baker's, the general store, and the pharmacy. It's the kind of village where you can get just about everything you need, if your tastes are fairly simple… which mine are.

We're seated by the one of the windows that overlook the harbour in the distance, and the terrace immediately outside, although there's no-one foolhardy enough to be sitting out there today. Spring might be just around the corner, the sun reminding us of the warmer months to come, but the wind is making its presence felt. I guess that's why it's so busy in here. People are sheltering and enjoying a convivial Sunday drink… or lunch, like Stephen and me.

"What are you having?" I ask as he sits down opposite me again.

"Roast Pork and everything that comes with it."

"Including crackling?"

"Naturally."

I wonder if I made the right decision, except the thought of such a heavy meal at this time of day doesn't appeal, no matter how much I like pork… and crackling.

While I sip on my dry white wine, Stephen takes a gulp of his mineral water, because even though it's Sunday, he's on his lunch break, and can't afford to go back to work with alcohol on his breath, or a stagger in his step. He's the manager of the Seaview Hotel, which explains the smart, light grey suit he's wearing, and the darker grey tie, all of which looks a little out of place amidst the jeans, thick sweaters, and walking boots adorning most of the other people here, including myself. I'm proud of what he's achieved in his thirty-four years, but I wish he'd take some time off… or just learn to relax a little. As it is, the moment he puts down his glass, he checks his phone, just to make sure it's switched on, and then looks up at me with another of his smiles.

"Sorry. You know what it's like."

"I thought Sundays were your day off."

"They are, but we're so busy I'm having to go in just so I can catch up all the things I'm not getting done during the week."

"You could have cancelled lunch, if it would have made things easier for you."

He shakes his head. "No. I needed to get out. Besides, it feels like ages since we've done this."

It has been ages, but it's not his fault. Not entirely. "Why is it so busy?" I ask. "Christmas is a distant memory, and Easter's a few weeks away yet. Surely it should be quiet now, shouldn't it?"

"Hmm… it should be," he says with a roll of his eyes. "But Head Office have just informed me we're supposed to be implementing a new computer system next week."

"And that's a problem?"

"It is when the hardware hasn't been delivered yet, and nobody's had any training."

"Ahh… I see how that might be an issue."

"On top of which, we'd only just integrated the system for booking the weddings, so…"

"Oh, yes. I remember you telling me about that. How's it going?"

"Not too bad. I think we're going to be rushed off our feet in the late summer and autumn, and as for next year…" He lets his voice fade, rolling his eyes.

"That's good, isn't it? It was your idea, after all."

"I know. It's not the weddings themselves that are the problem. Although they've certainly kept us busy."

"Why? Surely you employ people to manage them, don't you?"

"I've employed extra people to work behind the bar, and in the dining room, and kitchens. What I haven't found yet is anyone who can help with the admin and general organisation. Which is why it's been so chaotic."

"I see. And that's all that's wrong, is it?"

"Isn't that enough?"

"Yes. I suppose. But what I meant was, is it something more personal that's bothering you? Something clearly is, but I'm guessing it might not be work related?" I say, and he sighs yet again, shaking his head.

"You always could read me like a book, couldn't you?"

"I could. And on this occasion, I'd say your problem is that you're sick of being the bridesmaid and never the bride."

He chuckles. "I suppose that's one way of putting it. Not the one I'd have chosen, but…" He sits forward a little and lowers his voice. "I feel like I'm surrounded by people who've found their one true love."

"You believe in that, do you? You think there's only one person in the world for each of us?"

He frowns, studying me closely. "Not necessarily. I know plenty of people who've found love a second time around. All I'm saying is, I'm sick of other people's constant good cheer. Honestly, if it isn't couples coming to the hotel for a romantic weekend, or to tie the knot, it's my assistant."

"You mean Laura?"

He smiles, his frown disappearing in an instant. "I keep forgetting she's your landlady."

I roll my eyes at him, as only a big sister can. "How? You introduced us."

"I know, but I'm tired. It makes me forgetful."

"It makes you grumpy, too. How can you resent other people's happiness… especially Laura's?"

We're interrupted by the arrival of our food, and although the waitress puts my plate down first, I'll admit my eyes are drawn to Stephen's. His lunch looks delicious, and the aromas wafting their way towards me are divine.

"That looks good," I say, and he smiles, clearly pleased with his choice.

"Yours doesn't look bad," he replies and I glance at my gammon steak, a perfect fried egg perched on top, and lovely, fat crispy chips piled on the side. There's a salad garnish, but even so, it's hardly a slimming lunch, or a small one… although it's smaller than Stephen's.

"You were saying about other people's happiness," I remind him, as he cuts into a crunchy roast potato, and I stab a chip.

"Hmm… I don't resent it."

"You'd just like some of it for yourself? Is that it?"

"Yes. Is that too much to ask?"

"Not necessarily, although I don't think happiness is a right."

"Neither do I, but did you know I haven't dated anyone since I moved here? If I'm not careful, I'll forget how."

I smile at him, shaking my head as I sip my wine between mouthfuls of delicious gammon. "That's hardly surprising, working the hours you do. Where would you expect to find the time for dating, let alone an actual girlfriend?"

"A girlfriend? Remind me, what is that? It's been so long since I had one, I can't remember."

"I'm sure you can."

"That's half the problem. I can remember only too well."

I can empathise with every word he's saying, but I'd prefer not to think about what it was like to feel loved. Stephen isn't talking about love. To my knowledge, he's never been in love. What he's talking about is having fun, and they're two different things. At least, they are in my experience.

"And what's the other half of the problem?" I ask, before I start to dwell too much on my past.

"That you're right. I never seem to be able to find the time. If a minor miracle happened, and I found a free hour or two to take someone to dinner, I'd never be able to follow through, would I? Something else would be bound to get in the way."

"You need to prioritise. And maybe stop worrying about it. Just let it happen."

"Is that your philosophy for finding a boyfriend? To sit back and wait for it to happen?"

I can feel the heat in my cheeks, and I turn, staring out of the window, the waves picking up in the harbour. It looks like there's a storm brewing and I gaze at the view for a while before turning back to Stephen, who's still focused on me, his eyebrows raised, like he's waiting for an answer.

"We're not talking about me."

"No, but I think we should, don't you?" he says, putting down his knife and fork. "You've been living here for nearly eighteen months now, and I haven't noticed you getting out that much... not with anyone of the opposite sex, anyway."

"Do you blame me?" I raise my voice just slightly, and then cough, wishing I'd kept quiet. "Do you blame me?" I repeat in a whisper. "After everything that happened, do you seriously think I want to get involved again?"

Stephen sucks in a breath, his chest expanding, before he releases it again. "Not every man is going to be like Fergus, you know?"

Fergus is the very last person I want to talk about. Even now, it still hurts just thinking about him, and although I'm grateful to Stephen for everything he did at the time, it's a subject I'd rather avoid.

"Maybe not. But I've got Jasper now, and I'm happy with him."

"Jasper's a dog," he says, shaking his head as he starts eating again.

"Don't let him hear you say that. He's convinced he's at least half human."

"In which case, why didn't you bring him with you today?"

"Because I took him for a long walk this morning and he was asleep when I came out."

"Oh. He sleeps, does he?"

I narrow my eyes at him. "Of course he does. And before you tell me he's not a substitute for human company, I have to point out that I've got the same problem as you."

He frowns, like he doesn't understand. "You've forgotten how to date?"

I shake my head at him. "No. I'm busy. Work's crazy at the moment. I've even got to go in early tomorrow."

"I hope Ben's making it worth your while."

"I'm sure he will."

He smiles just as his phone rings and he rolls his eyes, putting down his knife and fork again, before picking up his phone.

"Yes?"

He's quite abrupt and I focus on my gammon, rather than him, barely recognising my own brother as he tuts a couple of times, then lets out a loud sigh.

"Okay. I'll be five minutes."

He sounds very grumpy and I look up again as he puts down his phone, without bothering to say 'goodbye' to whoever was on the end of the line.

"I take it you're not happy?"

"No, I'm not." He shakes his head, wolfing down his food. "Honestly. Is it too much to ask that I be allowed to have Sunday lunch in peace?"

"I guess so."

He polishes off the last of his pork, leaving the broccoli and peas, and pushes his plate aside, gulping down his water.

"I'm sorry, Anna. I've got to go."

"It's okay." He reaches for his wallet, but I hold up my hand, halting him. "Don't worry. You can pay next time."

"You're sure?"

"Positive." I can see how keen he is to leave, despite his complaints about the interruption to our meal.

"I'll call you," he says as he stands and turns towards the door.

"Okay."

I don't even get to say goodbye to him before he's gone, and I sit for a moment, marvelling at the whirlwind that seems to surround him before I get back to finishing my lunch at a slower pace.

The chips are especially good, and I dunk them into the egg yolk, smiling to myself at one of life's simplest pleasures.

It doesn't take me long to polish off my meal and I sit back, letting my lunch go down while I drink the last of my wine.

There are clouds scudding across the blue sky, but despite the wind, the sun is making a sterling effort at showing its face, which bodes well for Jasper's afternoon walk. He isn't keen on strong winds, but he'd rather have sun than rain… not that he's fickle. Heaven forbid.

Thinking of Jasper, I suppose I ought to get back and check he's okay, and I get up and make my way to the bar, shrugging on my coat as I go.

Ed looks up as I approach, giving me a friendly smile. I may not be a regular here, but I know him fairly well. I walk Jasper past the pub every day, and if he's outside, we often stop to talk.

"It's unusual to see your brother in here on a Sunday lunchtime," he says, putting some clean glasses back on the shelf above his head.

"He's had to rush back to work, unfortunately."

"He's always dashing somewhere, isn't he? Never seems to settle for more than ten minutes."

"No." I can't think what else to say, other than to ask for the bill, which he fetches, handing it over to me. I pay in cash, telling him to keep the change, which makes him smile.

"Thanks," he says. "Have a nice afternoon."

"You too."

He smiles. "I'm heading upstairs soon, once the lunchtime rush is over, and I can't wait."

Ed and his fiancée Nicki are getting married soon. I've had an invitation to attend, which surprised me, and I surprised myself even more by accepting, although I'm too shy to ask whether his afternoon will be filled with wedding plans, or with putting his feet up in front of the television. Either way, he doesn't seem to mind, and I smile and nod my head, unsure what else to say, as I fasten my coat and head for the door.

The walk back to my flat is short. All I have to do is turn left out of the pub and walk up Church Lane to the row of houses opposite the police station.

The wind is behind me, coming in off the sea, and I decide that a scarf and hat might be in order for taking Jasper out this afternoon. I didn't need to wrap up just to walk to the pub, but Jasper could do with a good run, and I hate getting cold.

I let myself in, smiling at the hug of warmth that greets me. It's followed by Jasper, who bounds over from his basket, jumping up. I'm reliably informed that cocker spaniels are renowned for being friendly, but I'm trying to stop him from leaping up at everyone he meets. Dogs aren't to everyone's liking, and he needs to learn that… somehow.

"Down," I say in a firm voice, and he calms a little. "Good boy." My praise makes him jump up again, and I crouch down to his level. "When are you ever going to learn?" He nuzzles in to me, making me smile, and then laugh as he almost pushes me over. "Enough, Jasper."

He stops, looking up at me with his wide, dark brown eyes. His coat is a lustrous black, and I stroke his floppy ears, which are so soft to the touch.

"Come on." I get up and he steps back, his tail wagging so fast his body struggles to keep up with it. "I need a cup of tea, and once I've had that, I'll take you for a walk."

With a lot of dogs the mention of that four letter word would have them bolting for the door in anticipation, but Jasper seems to understand every word I say, and he makes straight for the kitchen, looking up at the kettle, like he knows there's a method to this, and that before he can get his walk, I need to make the tea, and to make the tea, I need to boil water.

Like I said to Stephen, he's at least half human.

And he's mine.

Chapter Two

Seb

One of the best things about living in Porthgarrion, other than the views, and the harbour, a fabulous pub, and the house that I live in on top of the cliff, is that the weather is usually fabulous.

At least, it is when the wind isn't blowing a gale.

Okay, so 'gale' might be an exaggeration, but it's blowy enough that I can't go out sketching, which is how I'd intended to spend my Sunday morning, and I have to admit, I'm a little disappointed by that.

I've spent the winter cooped up, unable to go out and enjoy the views, or consign them to canvas, and when the forecast said today was going to be sunny, with a temperature well into double figures, I rejoiced in the news, and the prospect of a little fresh air, and planned to spend it out on the harbour, drawing.

What I failed to notice, or pay the slightest attention to, was the wind.

And that's unfortunate, because it's way too strong for me to consider doing anything out of doors that involves paper.

So much for making plans…

It makes me reluctant to say I'll try again tomorrow… but I will.

I know tomorrow will be Monday, which makes it a work day, but over the years, I've developed a habit of getting up early on lighter mornings, and finding somewhere to sketch for my own amusement. It can sometimes be the only chance I'll get in a day, and I treasure it… especially as early mornings are often so quiet and peaceful, and the light can be magical.

Still, that doesn't resolve what I'm going to do with the rest of my Sunday, does it?

I could work, I suppose, and a part of me even thinks I should, regardless of the weather. I'm nearly at the end of my latest project, and a few hours in the studio would give me a head-start before next week's final stretch.

But it's Sunday. It's supposed to be a day of rest, and even if the wind is blowing a gale of sorts, the sun's shining, and I don't feel like being hemmed in by walls, or work, or deadlines.

I feel like going out.

I get up from my seat at the island unit in the kitchen, before my conscience can talk me into staying behind, and make my way through the formal living room, and into the hall.

The black-and-white floor tiles in here always strike me as a little stark, but I've softened the look with some paintings, which I've hung on the bright white walls. They're my own, some of them recent drawings and watercolours of the local views around here, while others are cityscapes of the area where I used to live, in Oxford. I like them, even if I say so myself.

Grabbing my coat, I put my keys in my pocket and open the door, deciding at the last minute that a scarf might be wise. My long blue one is hanging from the hook, and I wind it around my neck before I head off, pulling the door closed behind me.

My car is parked over by the wall, but I don't need it, and I turn to the left, heading along the driveway which eventually leads to the road. I'm not going that far, though, because there's a footpath which forks into the trees. If you didn't know it was there, you could easily miss it, but I was fortunate enough to discover it the first weekend I was here when I was exploring my new surroundings, and now I often go for walks this way.

The woodlands are not as quiet as usual, thanks to the wind gusting through the trees. There are no leaves for them to catch onto yet, though. The gnarled branches are bedecked with buds, which will burst into life in the next week or so, I imagine, and in the meantime, the noise is limited to a kind of crackling, rather than a rustling.

It's quite a pleasant accompaniment, especially as the trees provide a little shelter, and I trudge through the undergrowth, keeping to the left wherever the path divides, because I know that will bring me out to my destination…

The top of the cliffs.

Leaving the woodland is like stepping from night into day, so bright is the spring sunshine, and I stop and look up at the clear blue sky, ignoring the occasional scudding cloud, and admiring its brilliance before I walk forward to the cliff edge and let my eyes drop to the sight of the white horses, cascading over the surface of the churning turquoise sea.

The wind is even fresher up here, and initially it's a struggle to catch my breath. I manage it, though, reluctant to turn away from the exquisite view. There's a sense of freedom up here that I don't feel anywhere else. In fact, I'm not sure I've felt anything like it in my life.

I know a part of that is because there's literally nothing around me. The woodland is a distant memory, and as I turn, looking both right and left, I can't see a thing other than sea and sky.

It's perfect.

Or it would be if I could just feel a little more at home.

I know why I don't… or, to be more precise, why I can't.

It's because the house I'm living in isn't my own.

Which means I can't settle. I can't put down roots.

When I first contemplated moving from Oxford last year, my main priority was to find somewhere completely different. I was looking for a change of scene, having lived in the city all my adult life, and while I'll always love its dreaming spires, I wanted something new... something to inspire me, I suppose.

I'd visited Cornwall on holiday several times over the years, and it seemed like the ideal solution... a mix of rugged landscapes and seaside villages. What could be more picturesque?

What could be more complicated, as it transpired, because even after extensive online research, I still couldn't decide exactly where I wanted to live within the county. So, I came down for a two week fact-finding mission.

And found that I was none the wiser.

There were pros and cons to almost every place I visited, and every property I saw.

I found a remote farmhouse, but ruled it out on the basis that there's remote... and then there's remote, and I wasn't sure I was ready for that level of seclusion.

There was a smart town-house with the ideal space for a studio on the top floor. But it was in the middle of Falmouth, and while Falmouth is delightful, I wanted something a little more out of the way than that.

I saw over twenty properties during my stay, all available for sale, but I couldn't find exactly what I was looking for... until I happened upon this beautiful cliff-top residence.

The problem was, it wasn't for sale. The owner wanted to rent it out, and would only offer a tenancy of six months. I was devastated, but just looking at the particulars was enough for me to want it all for myself. I wasn't put off by it being such a big house. Why would I have been? It had plenty of space, and a lovely room overlooking the sea, that I knew would make a fabulous studio for me to work in. Not only that, but it offered the best of both words. The convenience of a nearby village, with the privacy of a fairly remote property.

I decided to see it, knowing I'd probably regret that decision… and I did. Because the moment I stepped through the front door, despite the black-and-white tiles, and the strange, almost floating staircase, I knew it was perfect for me.

Even if I could only stay for six months, it would be six months well-spent.

That was what I told myself when I signed the tenancy agreement.

I also tried to convince myself that I might be able to persuade the owner to let me stay on longer… and maybe even to buy the place.

The staying on longer hasn't been a problem. At the end of the first six months, he agreed to let me continue as his tenant for a further term, with no fuss whatsoever.

As for buying it?

Every enquiry I've made of the letting agents has been met with a resounding 'no'. The house is most definitely not for sale.

That's a shame. Although it won't prevent me from enjoying my time in Porthgarrion. I might not be able to put down any roots, but that's only because there's nothing of permanence to my presence here.

Yet.

Because even if I can't acquire this most perfect of houses, I'd like to buy somewhere else. The problem is, where? Properties around here are like gold dust, but as long as I've got a roof over my head, I'm willing to wait for the right house to come along. It would need to be somewhere close by… perhaps even in the village itself. It's a lovely place, and although I haven't been here very long, I've grown attached to it. The locals have made me very welcome, too. When I first arrived, I half expected to meet with some of that resistance you hear of, when people move into a small village like this, but there's been nothing of the sort.

That said, I suppose I am pretty good at keeping myself to myself.

I like it that way, and even if I lived in the middle of the village, I can't see that I'd be any different. Except I'd have to get by with a lot less space than I have now.

And that wouldn't be too hard, I suppose.

The house is enormous. It's far too big for me. But I wouldn't mind somewhere smaller, if it was right, and if it were mine. After all, what middle-aged, divorced man, with no dependents, needs a house with more than one bedroom, anyway?

Not this one, that's for sure.

I keep my eye on the property guides, and every time I pass the estate agents on the harbour, I stop and glance in the window, just to check what's available.

Admittedly, I don't pass there very often, but so far, nothing has come up. If it does, I'll take a look, and in the meantime, I'll make the most of what I've got.

I'm a lucky man, after all.

I can afford to live in splendid luxury, which makes me a lot more fortunate than most.

My good fortune didn't come from an inheritance, or winning the lottery, or speculating on the stock exchange. I worked damned hard for it... and I suppose there are a lot of people who'd say I've paid a price for that.

I shake my head, unwilling to think about that, and set off along the headland, refusing to let the clouds of my past intrude on the relatively sunny outlook of my present.

I let myself back into the house, my cheeks prickling a little from the wind, and I unwrap my scarf and shrug off my coat, leaving my keys on the hall table before I make my way into the kitchen.

It feels lovely and warm in here, and I put the kettle on, and open the fridge, inspecting what's inside. I went shopping yesterday at the supermarket, about five miles outside the village. The local stores are well stocked, but every so often, I make the journey in the car, and get the bigger things… washing powder, toilet rolls, dishwasher tablets. All the boring stuff. I always think it seems silly not to fill the fridge and freezer while I'm there, and I stand for a moment, trying to decide between cheese on toast and a sandwich. The sandwich wins, and I pull out a loaf of bread, some ham, and a pack of tomatoes, leaving them to one side, while I make the tea.

I'm a stickler when it comes to tea, using fresh leaves in a warmed pot, and once it's prepared and sitting on the side to brew for at least four minutes, I get on with making my sandwich. I'm less fussy about that – as I am about preparing most foods – and it takes no time at all to slap some ham and roughly sliced tomatoes between two slices of buttered bread, cut them up and put them on a plate.

My tea has brewed long enough, so I give it a stir and use a strainer to pour it into my bone china cup, carrying that and my sandwich to the island unit, where I sit, reaching for my phone, which I left here when I went out.

That was intentional. I didn't want to be disturbed. But I suppose it can't hurt to catch up with the news, and maybe check my messages, although hopefully there won't be any. Not on a Sunday.

I go to my e-mail app, taking a bite from my sandwich while it opens, and then let out a groan. I only have three messages, two of which are from shops where I've recently bought clothes. One is offering me a discount off my next purchase; the other asking for a review. There's nothing wrong with that. It's the third message that's the issue.

It's from Rodney. He's my agent, and I put down my sandwich again, wondering why I didn't leave my phone alone… or just look at the news, and ignore my messages for a little longer.

The subject is 'Need to talk', which is worrying, but even so, I'm tempted to ignore it. I mean, why ruin a perfectly good weekend? And what's wrong with the man? Doesn't he have a life?

I munch on my sandwich again, still staring at the unopened message, wondering what to do. I know if I open it, my day will be overtaken by work. Equally, if I don't, I'll just fret about whatever it is Rodney wants to discuss.

I decide to at least read the message and put myself out of my misery.

'*Seb,*

Hope you're okay.

Just wanted to touch base to find out how you're getting along with the illustrations for the Dastardly Dinosaurs book? The deadline is Friday, so can you let me know if there's going to be a problem?

Also, I need to speak to you about a new project. It's for the same publisher, but a different author. A new one. Louis hasn't given me much information yet, except that it's a book about rainforests. Ideally, I need to talk it through with you, so wondered if you're available for a chat.

Let me know.

Rodney.'

I take a sip of tea, shaking my head as I replace the cup on the island unit.

Why?

Why do I do this to myself?

Or more to the point, why do I let Rodney do it to me?

I love my job, don't get me wrong. Illustrating children's books is fun, even if there are times when I'd rather paint and draw whatever I like, instead of having deadlines hanging over my head. But as jobs go, illustrating dinosaurs or witches, or a hiccuping hippo is nothing to complain about. It's how I earn my living, and it's a very good living, too.

Even so, there's no way I'm talking to Rodney on a Sunday.

Working at weekends was one of the mistakes I made when I was married, and although I'm very much a single man now, I don't want to get back into that habit again.

I put down my phone and take another sip of tea, along with a deep breath, wondering what Rodney will make of my silence. He's one of those people who expects instant responses to everything… whether that's a text, an e-mail, or a phone call. The word 'impatient' was invented just for him, I think, and it occurs to me he might decide to call when he doesn't hear from me.

And that's the last thing I need.

I grab my phone again and return to his e-mail, hitting the 'reply' button, and typing…

'Rodney,
We'll talk tomorrow.
Seb.'

I know I could answer his questions, but I don't want to even start down the road of a conversation. Dismissing him seems like the best bet, and I put my phone down again, feeling pleased with myself… until it beeps, almost straight away.

This has to be a joke.

I pick it up, rolling my eyes when I see Rodney has replied already. Was he waiting for my response, with his phone in his hand?

He must have been.

I click on the message and read…

'*Seb,*

Thanks for getting back to me.

Sorry. I'm in meetings all day tomorrow. Is there any chance you can spare ten minutes now?

Rodney.'

"Bloody hell," I say out loud, wishing I hadn't bothered to reply at all now.

If I'd left it, he'd probably still be sitting at home, or in his office, or wherever he is, waiting for me to get back to him. As it is, I don't see that I have much choice.

I press 'reply' and type the simple word, '*Okay*'. It's blunt enough to let him know I'm not happy, although he's clearly not bothered by my mood, because my phone rings immediately, Rodney's name appearing at the top of the screen.

I answer, putting it onto speaker and let it rest on the surface in front of me.

"Hello?" he says, like there's some doubt in his mind I'll be here.

"Hi."

"How are you?"

"I was fine until my Sunday was interrupted."

"Oh? What by?"

"You, of course."

He chuckles, like I've said something amusing. "I know you don't mind, really." As it happens, I do. But he's got skin like a rhinoceros, so there's no point in trying to make him feel guilty. I've tried it before and it doesn't work.

"What do you want, Rodney?"

"First, I need to check how things are going with Dastardly Dinosaurs."

"They're going absolutely fine. I've just got the triceratops and stegosaurus to finish, and then it's done."

"So you'll have it all completed by next Friday?"

"Of course."

I hear a satisfied sigh on the end of the line. "That's good, because, as I said in my message, I've already got the next job lined up for you."

It feels like he wants a fanfare of pipes and drums and maybe a twenty-one gun salute, just for doing his job. Which is unfortunate, because he's not getting any such accolade. He takes fifteen per cent of everything I earn, and that feels like more than enough reward to me.

"What's involved?" I ask, pretending an interest I don't currently feel.

"All I know at the moment is that they require twelve full-page illustrations, plus the cover. It's not just about rainforests, but about the animals that live there, and they want the style to be similar to the one you used in that book about the sleepy sloth. Do you remember?"

"No. I make a habit of forgetting my commissions the moment they're done. Of course I remember."

"That's good."

I hate the fact that sarcasm is so lost on him.

"What's the deadline?" I ask.

"I don't know yet. I've got a breakfast meeting with Louis on Friday, so I should have more information for you by the end of the week."

"Don't agree to anything silly, will you? I'm not in the mood for slaving over my drawing board in the wee small hours of the morning."

"Don't worry. I'll look after your best interests, just like I always have."

I'm not sure that's strictly true. It seems to me Rodney's done a fairly good job of looking after his own best interests, but I can't complain. In doing so, he's kept me in steady work for the last fifteen years, and I've got the bank balance to prove it.

"Was there anything else?" I ask, wondering why any of this required a phone call, and couldn't have been said in an e-mail that I could have attended to in the morning.

"No, I don't think so."

Fabulous.

"Okay. I'll hear from you when you've got more information about this new project, then."

That's my way of saying don't bother me again before Friday.

"That's fine. Enjoy the rest of your weekend."

I'm not sure I can now, as I end the call and sit back, feeling disgruntled.

I don't know how Rodney does it, but even during the most innocuous of calls, he always makes me feel like I should – or at least could – be doing more.

Not only that, but my tea's gone cold.

I get up, taking my cup and plate to the sink, and then, as though I'm on automatic pilot, I head for the stairs.

They're set into the wall, with nothing apparently supporting them on the other side, and I'll admit, I was nervous about walking up and down them to start with. I'm used to it now, though, and I climb up, going straight into my studio.

Sunday or not, now I know more work is in the pipeline, I won't settle until I'm truly on top of these last illustrations. I meant it when I said I'd have them ready by Friday, but I can't forget the fact that, even before my call with Rodney, I was feeling the need to get a head-start on next week.

And it's not as though I had anything better to do today… or that I mind spending time up here. I don't. I like this room. Not as much as I like my bedroom, but I like it. The views are spectacular, and it's practical for drawing, with excellent light.

It was once an office, the wall opposite the window housing a large fireplace, either side of which is filled with bookshelves. That's hardly a surprise when you realise that the owner of this property, and former incumbent of this delightful room, was the novelist, Sean Clayton.

I imagine when he was living here, the shelves would have been stacked with copies of his novels and all kinds of reference books, although they're a lot less impressive now.

I have books. I even read them, but I don't for one second imagine I have as many as he would have done… or that they're as thought-provoking.

The empty spaces are useful, though, for storing pencils, paints and brushes, so it's not all bad.

I don't know where Sean Clayton went when he moved away from Porthgarrion, but he left behind most of his furniture, including his dark wood desk, which was over by the window. There was a sofa in front of it, facing the fire, and while I've moved the desk to the side of the room, I've left the sofa where it was. Every so often, when I need a break, I'll lie out on it. I've even dozed off up here, especially on warmer, less windy days, when the windows are open, and the sound of the sea lulls me to sleep.

When that happens – which isn't very often – I put it down to overwork, refusing to admit that my advancing years might have anything to do with my need for a siesta.

I replaced the desk with my drawing board, positioning it so I can work with my back to the view. If I didn't, I'd never get anything done, and I wander over, looking at the illustration that's currently taped down. This is the one of the triceratops, and it's almost complete. The stegosaurus needs more work, but all I've got to do here is finish the pattern on the dinosaur's frill, the shading on the rocks in the background, and get the sky right.

There are a couple of pictures taped to the top of my desk, for reference, and I study them as I sit down, thinking about the colours I want to use for the frill. My pallet is right beside me and I mix a little Perylene Green with just the slightest touch of Cadmium Yellow, glancing back at the picture before adding in some Terre Verte. The colour looks about right, and I try it out on a scrap of paper, nodding my head, before applying it to the illustration, filling in the circular patterns on the frill. Later, when that's dry, I'll add a touch of black to the colour to dot in some texture over the top.

The clouds need looking at next, and I turn around, glancing at the sky for inspiration. That's a mistake, because my eye is immediately drawn to the sea and I sit and stare for a moment, absorbed by the waves as they rise and bob.

I love being outdoors, and I still regret not being able to make it down to the harbour this morning to do some sketching. That said, there's a beautiful garden here at the house, and before last summer, I might have been tempted to work out there, rather than up here… no matter how good the view. I've done it before in previous properties, and always enjoyed it.

That all changed, though, when I discovered a mole on my back.

It was new and felt strange to touch.

I couldn't see it very well because of where it was, but I panicked, like most people would, and even though I wasn't registered with the local GP, I went down there, made quick work of filling in all the forms and then I made an appointment to see him.

I remember he studied me closely, perhaps wondering about my tan.

"Do you work out of doors?" he asked once I'd explained the problem.

"Not all the time, but I do in the summer, if I can."

He frowned. "What do you do for a living, then?"

"I illustrate children's books."

"I see. Will I have heard of them?"

I knew he was trying to make conversation, to put me at ease, but it wasn't working.

"I don't know. Do you have children?"

"No, but we have a few books in the waiting room."

"Well, I've done a humorous series about different animals. There was one about a terrified tiger, and another about a hiccuping hippo."

"Oh, we've got that one."

I nodded my head. "And my favourite is a book I did for a lovely lady from Dorset. It's called *Atticus the Ant*, and it's just marvellous."

"We've got that one, too," he said with a smile.

"In that case, you know who I am, and what I do."

"You draw exceptional illustrations," he said, and I felt myself blush.

"Thank you."

"And you sometimes do this outside, do you?"

"Yes. In the summer, in my back garden."

He frowned. "And you don't wear a t-shirt, or a top of any kind?"

"Not always."

"I see. And how long might you be outside for at any time?"

"Hours," I said, letting out a sigh. "I know that's not good, especially as I don't wear sun cream, but it's so easy to lose track of time when you're working."

"It is," he said, understanding, rather than admonishing.

I knew I'd made mistakes, but it was too late to worry about that.

He did his best to sound reassuring, and referred me for urgent tests.

Waiting for them to take place was torture, and having an over-active imagination, I went through every possible scenario in my head, before even seeing the consultant.

Of course, seeing him didn't resolve anything. There was even more waiting involved, while they discovered that there was absolutely nothing wrong with me.

I was relieved, obviously. But I haven't forgotten that fear, and I've resolved not to work out of doors in the summer anymore.

I'll enjoy the garden, and sit in the shade with a t-shirt on, but I won't work out there. As I said to the doctor, it's too easy to lose track of time, and forget that you're in the full heat of the sun… and have been for hours.

In the autumn, once I'd recovered from being scared out of my wits, I found I quite enjoyed just pottering around in the flower beds, which is another sign of old age, I suppose. I never thought I'd be someone who found pleasure in gardening, but I'm not bad at it, even if I say so myself.

I glance down at my hands, surprised that my fingers aren't turning green. They're not, although my tan's fading a little now. Still, what does it matter? Like everything in life, it's transient.

As I know only too well.

Chapter Three

Anna

How can I already be exhausted?

All I've done is get up, take a shower and get dressed, but just thinking about the week ahead has left me weary. How am I going to feel once my Monday morning actually gets started?

It doesn't bear thinking about.

I know the reason, though. It's because I'm due for a ludicrously busy few days, and I'm not looking forward to it.

As I said to Stephen yesterday, my boss Ben asked me to come in early today. In fact, he came to see me before I left work on Friday and perched on the corner of my desk, which is almost always a sign that something's wrong.

"Sorry to interrupt," he said, as I finished typing my last letter of the day, and I looked up at him. He's a tall man, probably around six foot three, with brown hair that's only greying at the temples, and nowhere else. I'd put his age at somewhere around fifty, but he could be a few years older, or a few years younger. It's hard to tell when I only ever see him in a smart suit. I always think it's easier to judge a man's age when you see him wearing the clothes he prefers to relax in. Jeans say one thing. Smart trousers say another. But suits tell you practically nothing.

"Is something wrong?" I asked and he let out a sigh, letting me know there was.

"Would it be possible for you to come in early on Monday morning?"

"How early is early?" I wasn't willing to commit without knowing that much, at least.

"An hour before you usually do?" he said, sounding doubtful.

"Oh, that's fine." From his expression, I'd half expected him to say something significantly worse.

He nodded his head, smiling now. "Thank you."

"Is this because we're so busy?"

"It is."

I wasn't surprised. He'd exchanged contracts on two conveyancing matters that morning, both with completions set for next Friday, and I'd seen some correspondence come in about the ongoing dispute between two neighbours in a village further along the coast. Ben's representing one of them, although to be honest, the whole thing could probably have been sorted out over a cup of tea, if the two parties involved hadn't become so entrenched about it. As it is, they're both spending a fortune lining solicitors' pockets, and at the moment, getting nowhere.

The thing that I know is causing most headaches for him, though, is a divorce he's handling.

Mr and Mrs Green aren't from Porthgarrion. They live in Padstow, and the basis of their case is that Mr Green has left his wife to live with another woman. She is an old schoolfriend of Mrs Green's, and while her husband claims not to have been aware of the connection, it's impossible to believe that her friend was ignorant of it. The hurt must be enormous. Unsurprisingly, Mrs Green wants a divorce, and while her husband is being represented by a lawyer close to where they live, who I believe is also a personal friend, Mrs Green has come to Ben. She found him online – or that's what she said when she called to make her initial appointment – and I know Ben didn't feel as though he could turn her away, even though he hates dealing with divorces.

Aside from the adultery, and the nature of it, which is bad enough, this one is even more complicated than most, from what I've seen. Not only are Mr and Mrs Green at loggerheads over just about everything, the matter is further complicated by them having two children under the age of ten, as well as a house, a jointly owned business, and an interfering mother-in-law.

Simply put, it's a mess.

With all of that on Ben's plate – not to mention countless other matters that aren't so pressing, but still need his attention – I couldn't possibly say 'no' to him.

It wasn't as though he was asking the earth of me, and in any case, he's a nice man.

I've worked for him ever since I arrived here in Porthgarrion, and he's been a fabulous boss. He was especially kind when I asked how he'd feel if I got a dog, and brought it into the office every day.

"I'm sure it'll be fine," he said, smiling up at me. "As long as it's well-behaved."

At the time, I didn't know what kind of dog I was going to get, but I was thrilled by his response... until I got home and remembered I lived in a rented flat... a very immaculate rented flat. I don't know how I'd forgotten that, but I had. Anyway, I checked my lease and found it made no mention of pets at all, so I spoke to my landlady... Laura. She gave me roughly the same answer as Ben, and although I couldn't be sure how well-behaved my dog would be, I thanked her, and went to the rescue centre the following weekend.

The lady who was showing me around warned me that cocker spaniels can be headstrong, but I'd already fallen in love with

Jasper by that stage. There was no way I couldn't have him, and when I drove him home a few days later, I just hoped he'd buck the trend of his breed, and be a calm, well-behaved little dog, and not a crazy canine that ran around and wouldn't sit still, or keep quiet for more than a few minutes at a time.

I was nervous on the first day I took him in to work, but I didn't need to be. Jasper charmed Ben straight away, sitting obediently by my chair while he was introduced, and then settling in a basket under my desk. Being half human, it seemed he'd realised straight away that, when he was at the office, he had to be good. What I hadn't expected was that, by the middle of the afternoon, Ben would have coaxed him out from under my desk, and suggested moving his bed to the space near the filing cabinets.

"It can't be very comfortable for him, beeping cooped up under there, in the dark," he said, reaching for the basket. He carried it over, then called to Jasper, who glanced up at me with a smug expression on his face, before he trotted over and sat down, looking very pleased with himself. By the next lunchtime, Ben had installed a jar of dog biscuits on top of the filing cabinet. Jasper seemed more than pleased with life, and things have carried on like that ever since.

I just hope he doesn't mind me working a longer day today. It's a lot to ask, but I don't have any choice.

"Are you ready?" Jasper looks up at me from his basket, tilting his head, like he's confused. "I know it's earlier than usual, but needs must."

I clip his lead onto his collar and he gets the message that, regardless of whether he'd rather sleep on for another hour, we're going for a walk.

I'd have preferred another hour in bed myself, but now I've got my coat on, I feel a little less jaded. Hopefully, the sea breeze will blow away any residual cobwebs, and I smile, feeling grateful that the wind has died down since yesterday. Today is positively calm by comparison, and as I pull open the door, I realise I won't need a scarf to keep warm. It's surprisingly mild, and the sun is shining already. It looks like it's going to be a lovely spring day, which makes it even more disappointing that I'll be spending so much of it cooped up in an office.

Still, that's the life I've chosen, and I'd better get on with it.

I close the door as Jasper turns right, setting off for the harbour. He knows the route we take and trots along happily, stopping occasionally to sniff at something that seems different. It might be a lamppost, or the corner of a building, but once he's satisfied there's nothing untoward, we move on.

We're not used to being out quite this early and, as we turn out onto the harbour, I'm struck by how much quieter it is. Normally, there are a few more people around than this. We often say good morning to the shopkeepers who are getting ready to start their day, and they make a fuss of Jasper. Sometimes we see Ed at the pub, watering the flowers that grow in tubs outside the front door. Or we might just pass someone, who Jasper takes a liking to, and who'll comment on how handsome he is. He can take any number of compliments like that, and I smile when I look down and see him glancing around, as though he's wondering where everyone is.

Most of the shops are still closed, with no sign of life in them, other than at the baker's. Just the thought of a bakery makes me think about crusty bread, with lashings of butter and jam, my tummy rumbling, and only getting worse when my thoughts turn to cream cakes. I really need to learn a little more self control, although who can, where cream cakes are concerned? My waistline is a constant reminder that the words 'cream' and 'cake' shouldn't really be used in the same sentence… if they should be used at all, but somehow I can't get excited at the prospect of a fruit salad.

As we move further along the harbour, I turn and gaze out to sea, wondering why I'm even worrying about my waistline, or what I eat anymore.

I used to fret about it when I was with Fergus, and I let out a sigh, remembering how he'd occasionally drop a hint or two.

"Should you really be having that?" he'd say, eyeing whatever was on my plate, whether it was a burger, or a portion of apple pie, or even a salad… probably because the blue cheese dressing was poised, about to drop onto the otherwise uninspiring plate of food.

I knew what he meant without having to ask. Sometimes, I'd push the food away, terrified of losing him if I didn't conform to his idea of perfection. Other times, I'd rebel and tell him I'd eat whatever I liked, thank you very much… and I would, although I wouldn't enjoy it half as much, knowing I was being watched and judged. Still, Fergus was a liar and a cheat. What right did he have to an opinion?

Regardless of his comments, and my memory of them, I'm not unhappy with how I look. I'm never going to be a catwalk model, but who needs that in their life? Who needs the pressure of trying to look perfect? So what if I'm a little overweight? I'm fit. I'm certainly fit enough to trot along the harbour at the crack of dawn.

Okay, so it's not quite that early. It just feels like it when it's this eerily quiet.

I glance up, noticing a man who's sitting alongside the harbour wall, with an easel set up in front of him. It strikes me as an odd time of day for sketching, or painting, or whatever it is he's doing, but each to their own, I suppose, and I pull Jasper back, knowing that, given the chance, he'll probably knock the poor man flying, along with his artistic endeavours.

That's the problem with Jasper's first walk of the day. It might be earlier than usual, but having been cooped up all night, he can be a little boisterous once he gets the scent of fresh air in his nostrils, and the wind in his floppy ears.

I wonder for a moment about crossing the road to avoid the man altogether, but I'm intrigued by what he's doing, and why he's doing it at this time of the morning. Is it something to do with the light? Or maybe he's trying to capture a particular scene and doesn't want too many people here while he does it. Perhaps he's new to the art world, or isn't very good, and doesn't want any witnesses. Either way, I'd like to see for myself, and I pull Jasper's lead a little tighter as we approach.

We might still be a few feet away, but I can see already that the man is sketching, not painting. As for not being very good, nothing could be further from the truth. The drawing on his easel is a breathtaking view of the harbour, and I have to stop, a few feet behind him, admiring the way he's captured the scene, somehow injecting a depth to his sketch that I wouldn't have thought possible without the use of colour.

"I'm aware you're there," he says, his voice low and grumpy. "You don't have to stand so far back."

I know I'm blushing. "S—Sorry," I mutter and he turns, frowning up at me, before his eyes drop to Jasper. He sucks in a breath and holds out a hand to my dog, who steps forward and sniffs at him, letting the man stroke his head. At least he likes dogs, even if he doesn't seem so keen on humans… at least not on me, anyway.

I raise my eyes, studying his face, while he continues to lavish attention on Jasper. He might be abrupt, but he's very good looking, I'll say that. He's wearing pale jeans, a thick shirt and an olive green jacket, with more pockets than should be feasible in one garment. There are paintbrushes sticking out of two of them, and I realise the jacket is perhaps more practical than fashionable. Either way, it suits him. And unlike Ben's suits, his clothes make it easier for me to say that this man is probably in his mid-forties. He has a thick mop of salt-and-pepper hair, and a much whiter beard. He's not competing with Father Christmas. It doesn't drag down to his waist, or anything like that. It simply hugs his square jaw, neatly trimmed, and distinguished. I lick my lips, wondering why I suddenly feel so hot, and as Jasper jumps up at the man, I focus back on him. He's tanned, which is surprising for this time of the year, although I suppose he might have been on holiday. Whatever the reason, the colour of his skin seems to highlight the piercing blue shade of his eyes, which catch my breath as he slowly raises his head, looking right at me.

"Why are you apologising?" he says. "You have a perfect right to walk along the harbour. You even have a perfect right to stop, if you really feel you must."

"I know I do." I smart at his rudeness, which takes me aback. "Come on, Jasper."

I tug at my dog's lead and he comes, thank goodness, giving up the man's attention in favour of continuing his walk. I'd have been mortified if he'd wanted to stay… because staying with that man is the last thing I need.

Honestly. How arrogant.

Does he think I need his permission to stop and admire his sketch?

I huff, feeling angry with myself for being so bothered about it, and cross over, heading up Bell Road.

There's some activity at the hotel. It's some guests leaving, by the looks of things, although there's no sign of Stephen. It's too early in the day for him to be at work. At least I hope it is. I hope he's not burning the candle at both ends, because the place will function without him. I just wish Stephen would realise that for himself, sometimes. That way, he might have a life of his own.

Not that I can talk…

I startle, hearing female laughter coming from an open upstairs window at the doctor's surgery. It's his home as well, and I smile to myself, remembering the rumour I heard recently that Doctor Carew and his receptionist had become engaged to be married.

I don't know either of them very well. I've only been to the doctor's twice since I moved here, but he's always been kind, and it's nice to think that love works out for some people… even if it didn't work out for me.

We get to the top of Bell Road and Jasper stops. I can't blame him for that. We usually double-back on ourselves now, retracing our steps along the harbour. The problem is, I'm not in the mood for facing that obnoxious man again, so I turn left. Jasper hesitates, following me, although he looks up every so often, like he doesn't understand.

"Don't worry," I say. "We can still get home this way. I just don't want to see that nasty man again."

He frowns… as only Jasper can, because the man wasn't 'nasty' to him, was he?

But honestly, all I did was stop to see what he was doing. Why did he have to be so disagreeable about it?

Because he's a man, I suppose.

Chapter Four

Seb

Why did she storm off like that?

I shake my head, looking back at the sketch I've been working on for the last hour or so. It's gone well, but I'm feeling troubled now.

Okay, so my words came out all wrong just then. I didn't mean to snap at her, but I wasn't expecting anyone to come up to me at this time of the morning.

When I first acknowledged her, I didn't know whether the person standing a few feet behind me was male or female. I was just aware of someone watching. When I turned and saw her, I'll admit, it was a surprise.

She was dressed in a straight grey skirt and white blouse, with a short, thick black jacket over the top, although it wasn't done up. I guess that's because it's milder today than it has been for ages. The wind has dropped, and the sun's out. All in all, it's a lovely day, and I presume that's why she was out walking her dog. He was a friendly dog, too. Very friendly…

Unlike his owner, who was bristly, to put it mildly.

I know I sounded abrupt, but it wasn't intentional. All I meant to say was that she didn't need to apologise for interrupting me. That's not how it all came out, though.

Why was that?

Because I was distracted, I think.

And not by her dog.

It was the sight of her hourglass figure, revealed by that open jacket. That was enough to grab any man's attention, and in my case, make him tongue-tied. I might have been sitting, but I didn't have to raise my head that much to take her in from head to toe, because she can't have been more than five foot four in height, and when I allowed for her slight heels, I imagined her to be maybe two inches shorter than that, in bare feet. When my eyes reached her face, though, I was captivated. I've never been a man who's admired long hair on women, so hers was perfect, cut short in a kind of feathered, layered style. Describing it is beyond me, other than to say it was the colour of Demerara sugar with what I think were natural golden honeyed highlights. You see... colours I can cope with. Style is beyond my pay grade.

As for her face. What can I say?

Her skin was pale, but flawless, and I'd have said devoid of make-up. Her eyes were a dark chestnut brown flecked with tints of hazel, and her lips were full and glossy. She must have licked them, because I don't think there was anything artificial about that effect.

She was beautiful. Distractingly so... and that was my only reason for being as abrupt as I was. It's not a great reason, but it's all I've got.

Is that an excuse for her to have rushed off like she did?

I don't think so. She could have stayed and talked. I'm not an ogre, after all.

Still... it's just like a woman to over-react

I pick up my pencil, trying to get back to my sketch. Except the view's different now. The light's changed and in any case, I've lost the incentive.

"Typical," I mutter under my breath.

There's no point in staying here anymore. I might as well pack up and head for home. I've got a full day's work ahead of me, and I stand, folding my chair and resting it against the harbour wall, while I pack away my sketch book and easel into their carrying case. It all fits in neatly, but weighs quite a bit and I wish I'd brought less equipment with me today. As the weather is so glorious, I'd planned to stay until about eight, or eight-thirty, when the harbour gets busy, but as usual with the best laid plans, something always gets in the way.

And that 'something' is normally a woman.

At least in my experience, anyway.

I trudge back to the car, which I left in the pub car park, and put everything into the boot, closing it with a loud bang, and getting in behind the wheel.

I'm feeling disgruntled now, and it's all that woman's fault. If she hadn't come up to me looking so perfect, none of this would have happened...

I stare down at the picture of the stegosaurus and shake my head. I've only been working on the background today, but it's all wrong. The mountains look different from the ones in the other illustrations, and as for the trees…

I shake my head. They look more like the work of a five-year-old.

It's a disaster, and I put down my brush and turn around in my chair, gazing out of the window. The sky is changing colour, from the cerulean blue that it's been all day to something with hints of mauve at the edges. It must be later than I thought, and I check my watch, which I always leave at the side of my drawing board, surprised to find that I've worked right through lunch, and it's approaching five o'clock.

I hadn't expected that, but now I know I've skipped a meal, my stomach rumbles and my throat feels dry. I haven't drunk enough, and with one last glance at my stegosaurus, I pack away my paints for the evening, wash out my brushes, and trudge downstairs.

The kitchen feels a little chilly, but that's probably because I opened the window while I was having breakfast, and didn't close it when I went upstairs. Still, I close it now, and wander to the kettle, switching it on before going over to the fridge, to see what I've got for dinner.

The contents are less than inspiring, and thinking about it, I'm not really in the mood for a cup of tea, either. I'd prefer something stronger, and I reach for the bottle of wine in the door, before I stop myself.

Drinking alone is never a good idea… especially when I've had a bad day. It usually leads to over-indulgence, which in turn leads to a hangover, and yet another bad day. It's a vicious circle I remember only too well, and before I make the same mistake again, I close the fridge and turn off the kettle, striding to the front door, where I grab my keys and jacket.

My car is parked in its usual place, exactly where I left it this morning, when I came back from the harbour. However, if I'm going to have a drink, I should probably walk. Besides, the exercise and fresh air will do me good. I've been cooped up in my studio for far too long today.

I nod my head, even though there's no-one here to see me, and close the door firmly behind me, setting off down the track that leads to the main road.

It's fairly dark beneath the trees, even though the sun is above the horizon, and I'm pleased I brought my coat. The darkness makes it cold. Cold enough to plunge my hands into my pockets, where I find a couple of sable brushes. There's a number six and a number ten, and I stop and stare down at them for a moment. That's strange. I went through my pockets when I got back home this morning, taking out anything that didn't need to be there. These two must have been left behind, and I shake my head.

As well as falling asleep in the afternoons and taking up gardening, it seems I'm getting forgetful. Old age really is kicking in hard.

I put the brushes back in my pocket and continue on my way, getting to the main road in no time at all. The walk to the town is downhill most of the way, and only takes just over half an hour, which is a blessing, as I'm dying for a drink now.

The harbour is busier than I'd expected, but I make straight for the pub, where Ed is serving behind the bar. He looks up, giving me a smile.

"We don't often see you in here this early."

He's quite right. I enjoy coming to the pub, but it's something I tend to do later in the evening. "Let's just say my day hasn't gone according to plan."

"Can I get you anything that might help with that?" He's got a wry smile on his face, because he knows the answer to that question already.

"I'll have a pint of Cornish Best and a whisky chaser." I eye up the whiskies while he waits. "Make it a Talisker."

"Single, or double?" he asks and I tilt my head to the left and then the right.

"Double, please."

He smiles. "You really haven't had a good day, have you?"

"It started badly, and got worse."

"Oh dear. And it's only Monday."

"Exactly."

He shakes his head, turning to get my drinks, and I glance around the pub. The harbour might be busy, but it's relatively quiet in here, which is a relief. I might not want to drink alone, but I'm not in the mood for too much noise tonight.

"There you go."

Ed pushes a pint glass and a tumbler across the bar and I hand him my debit card, although I immediately pull it back again.

"Actually, I think I'll stop for dinner." That's not unusual for me, either, even if it is earlier than I'd normally eat… my excuse being that I'm starving.

"Do you want me to set up a tab?"

"Yes, please."

I put my card back in my wallet, shoving it into my coat pocket, and grab a menu from the pile on the bar. When I first moved here, Ed used to take my card and keep it until I was ready to leave, like he would with any stranger. But now I've become a regular, and he's got to know me, he doesn't bother… which is nice, and another one of those signs of having been accepted here.

"Just let me know what you want," Ed says, and I thank him, sliding the menu under my arm, and picking up my drinks before I step away from the bar, and make my way to one of the tables at the far end of the pub, which overlooks the terrace. The view's nice from here, and although I could catch up with the news on my phone, I think I'd rather just gaze out of the window, and maybe indulge in a little people-watching. I might even make a few sketches. There's usually a small pad and pencil in one of my many pockets. I rarely leave home without at least some means of drawing, just in case I'm struck by something inspirational.

At the moment, though, the only inspiration that's really giving me pause for thought is food.

I take a sip of beer and open the menu, my eyes alighting on the minced venison cottage pie. It's one of my favourites, and I don't bother even looking at anything else. My mind's made up, and I return to Ed, placing my order. He doesn't write anything down, but nods his head.

"One of these days, the chef will take that off the menu," he says. "What will you do then?"

"Go somewhere else," I joke, and he smiles, shaking his head, because he knows I wouldn't dare. He has to serve another customer, and I make my way back to my table, settling in my seat.

I haven't touched my whisky yet, and to be honest, I'll probably leave it until after I've eaten. The beer's good, though, and I sip at it while I'm waiting, shrugging off my coat, and putting it over the back of the chair.

I was right. There's a notepad in one of the voluminous inside pockets, and I pull it out, along with the pencil that's also hiding in there, and flip it over to a blank page, sitting back and resting it on my bent knee, as I quickly outline the scene beyond the window.

I ignore the pub terrace, which is an empty shell of tables, and folded down parasols. Instead, I focus on the harbour and the houses on the other side of it. They were on the edge of the sketch I was making this morning when that woman interrupted me. I'd been concentrating on the small boats in the harbour, rather than the periphery, but their colours make them interesting… even for a pencil sketch.

"That's fantastic." I look up, a little startled at the sound of a female voice right beside me, and find myself staring at a dark-haired woman, probably in her mid-thirties, who's holding a plate in her hands, which she's protecting with what appears to be a white serviette.

"Thank you."

I sit back and let her put down the plate, closing my sketch pad at the same time.

"Can I get you anything else?" she asks.

"No, thanks."

She nods her head, giving me a smile before she departs, and I turn my attention to the dish before me. The smells are incredible, and I grab a knife and fork from the pewter tankard on the table. They're wrapped in a bright red paper napkin, which I place over my lap, leaving the knife on the table, as I fork some of the delicious venison into my mouth. It's just as good as I'd hoped, and I let out a sigh, all the worries of the day drifting away on a tide of satisfaction.

While I eat, I flip back through my sketch pad. It's quite small, but I don't let that limit me. Most of the drawings date back to last summer, when I had the chance to get out more, but there are pictures in here of all kinds of places… from scenes of the headland above the house, to the shops on the harbour. There are, even a few people, in between the landscapes. I've drawn the man who owns the café. I don't know his name, but he's always struck me as an interesting character. He smiles at his customers, and sometimes passes the time of day with them, but when he's by himself and not 'putting on a show' for anyone else's benefit, he's the saddest looking individual I've ever seen. I've captured his desolate expression, and I have to say, the picture is haunting… and heartbreaking. It makes me wonder what made him like that.

A woman, probably.

I close the book and glance out of the window as I continue eating. It's definitely dusk now. The lights have come on along the harbour wall, and although there are still people out walking – or should I say strolling – it's much less busy than it was earlier.

"How was everything?" Ed asks, coming over, just as I finish the last morsel of mashed potato topping.

"Every bit as good as I expected."

He glances out of the window, just briefly. "It's been a lovely day – at least in terms of the weather."

He's obviously remembered what I said about my day not going very well, and I smile up at him. "I can't complain… not about that, anyway."

"Here's hoping it stays like this until the Easter holidays."

I take a sip of whisky, feeling the warmth in my throat as I swallow it, and I put down the glass, just as Ed's fiancée Nicki comes up behind him. For a moment, I'm reminded of the woman I met this morning… not because they look similar. Nicki's colouring is very different. Her hair is much darker and longer, and she almost always tucks it behind her ears.

No… the reason I'm reminded of that fickle woman, is because she and Nicki are around the same height, which is accentuated when Nicki links her arm through Ed's and tilts her head back so she can look up at him. The height difference is significant… almost ludicrous, in fact. Not that either of them seems to mind. They're both gazing into each other's eyes, and smiling, although Nicki quickly turns to me.

"I'm sorry to interrupt, Seb," she says.

"It's okay."

"What's wrong?" Ed asks, which makes her smile, and she glances back up at him, her eyes twinkling.

"How do you know something's wrong?"

"Because it's not like you to come down here at this time of the evening."

She nods her head. "No… but we've got a problem."

"Okay." He sounds very calm. "Want to tell me about it?"

Nicki lets out a sigh. "I've just had a call from Laura to say they're going to have to change the dessert we ordered for the reception."

Ed frowns. "You heard from Laura? She's still working?"

"Yes. She's trying to iron out the problem with our dessert, evidently."

Ed smiles again. "Rory will be pleased."

"Maybe he will, but can we focus on the problem at hand? We need to choose something else for our guests to eat… and we need to do it now."

I can hear the slight panic in her voice, although Ed turns to face her, putting his hands on her shoulders. "It'll be fine. Have they given us any choices, or are we supposed to come up with something?"

"No. They've given us some choices. Four or five of them, I think. Laura's e-mailed them through."

"Okay. So, what you're saying is, you need me to come upstairs and take a look. Is that it?"

"Yes. I know you're busy, but…"

"I can spare ten minutes to look at desserts," he says, bending to kiss her forehead. He turns to me as he straightens and rolls his eyes, although he's grinning. "Duty calls."

Nicki slaps him playfully on his forearm, and the two of them turn and walk towards the bar, Ed putting his arm around Nicki as they go.

I watch them, recalling my own wedding and the few last-minute hiccups we had. Pippa had a meltdown about every single one of them, and I remember how reliant I was on my best man, Dominic, to keep me sane and smooth the waters.

If only I'd known…

I take another sip of whisky, looking up as the pub door opens, and almost choking when I see the person who's walking in. It's the woman from this morning… the one who was so easily offended. She's dressed in exactly the same clothes, and is talking to someone behind her, who follows her through the door. It's a man… a suited man, who I'd say is at least ten years her senior.

Although I don't know why that's so remarkable. I'm probably ten years her senior, too.

They both seem quite happy together, and she doesn't look around, or wait for him to close the door, but heads straight for the bar, taking several attempts to jump up onto a stool. He catches up, but doesn't help her, which surprises me, although she comes across as an independent woman, who'd probably slap any man who held a door open for her, let alone one who offered to help her sit on a stool that's nearly as tall as she is. Still, I guess her boyfriend's worked that out for himself already, no doubt from bitter experience.

Okay… so maybe I'm exaggerating. The guy doesn't look brow-beaten, and I doubt she's really that bad. She's not that short, either. But if she were my girlfriend, I'd help her. That's all I'm saying.

At least, I would if she'd let me.

The man stands beside her, rather than sitting, so she has to crane her neck to look up at him as he raises his hand to get the barmaid's attention. He orders for both of them, and only now do I notice her dog, sitting obediently by her feet. She's holding his lead in her hand, but I'm not sure she needs to. He seems perfectly happy, just lying there.

She doesn't look in my direction, and even if she did, I doubt she'd remember me, which is just as well. The last thing I need is for her to point me out to her boyfriend as the man who made her angry, or upset, or whatever she was when she stormed off. I sit back a little, deciding I'll stay for a while longer… either until she goes, or until I can find a convenient moment to pay my bill and slip away without her noticing. That might mean I'll have to sit here longer than I'd intended, but it's not a problem. What have I got to rush home for?

Their drinks arrive. He's having something clear and sparkling in a tall glass. It could be water, or it could be a vodka and tonic. Who knows? She's got a glass of white wine, and they clink them together, smiling at each other as they talk, quite animatedly. They seem happy, and despite the difference in their ages – and heights – they make an attractive couple.

I'm surprised by the pang of jealousy that stabs at my chest. I know the feeling and what it means, because I've felt it before… with just cause. Why I should feel it now is beyond me. It's not as though I even know this woman, and nor do I want to, although I can't deny he's a lucky man. She still strikes me as stunning. Exceptionally so. Regardless of her attitude.

Would I want her for myself?

Maybe… but that's not an option, is it?

She's taken, and besides, experience has taught me that relationships are overrated. There's no way I'm going down that road again. Why would I? I like my life.

Most of the time.

The man startles, and I hear the vague sound of a phone ringing through the throng of voices and the tinkle of background music. It's his, and he puts it to his ear, which strikes me as rude. It's something Pippa used to do, and it drove me crazy… back in the days when I cared what Pippa did.

The woman looks away while he talks, glancing around, and inevitably her eyes find their way to me. I don't know whether it's that she doesn't recognise me, or she's choosing to ignore me, but either way, she glosses over me like I'm invisible, turning in the other direction. I ought to feel affronted, but I don't, although I can't seem to take my eyes from her, which strikes me as odd. It's not like I'm interested in her. She's beautiful, but so what? There are plenty of beautiful women around, and I'm sure a lot of them don't come with the same attitude as this one.

She sips her wine, only looking back up at the man when he finishes his call, returning his phone to his coat pocket. They talk some more, but before long, they both gulp down their drinks, smiling at each other, and then they leave. He holds the door open for her this time, and I smile to myself when she lets him, laughing as she passes through. I thought I might have overestimated her independent streak, and it seems I was right. Maybe she's not so bad, after all.

Either way, I guess they've got somewhere else to be… or something better to do, and once the door has closed on them, I get up at last, making my way to the bar. Ed's back, and I step over to him.

"Are you off?" he says.

"Yes."

He doesn't ask, but just turns, going to the till, and returns within moments with my bill. I don't need to check it, but just wave my debit card, and he fetches the machine.

"Did you sort out the dessert situation?" I ask, as he inputs the details.

"We did." He smiles. "I can sleep easy tonight. Until the next catastrophe, that is."

I chuckle, because he sounds as though he knows what he's talking about. Although he doesn't seem to mind.

I tap my card on the machine and wait for the receipt, thanking Ed for my meal before I leave the pub.

It feels chilly now, and I fasten my coat and set off up Church Lane. I'm in no particular rush, but because of the cold, I make it home in no time at all, and once I've removed my coat, I head upstairs.

It's later than I'd expected, because of my enforced wait at the pub, and I want to go down to the harbour early tomorrow, like I did today… only hopefully with no interruptions this time. With that in mind, I need an early night, but before I go to my bedroom, I pop into my studio, switching on the lights and sauntering to the window. The sea is inky blue, the sky just a shade or two lighter, and there are a couple of lights flickering on the horizon. It's calm, and I take a deep breath, soaking in the view before I turn around and look down at the stegosaurus.

It's awful. Absolutely awful.

I reach out, ripping it from the drawing board, the page tearing in half.

I'll just have to start again tomorrow.

But that's okay. I'm good at starting again.

Chapter Five

Anna

We already had a lot to do.

I was expecting it.

That was why I took Jasper out for his walk so early this morning, bumped into that obnoxious man, and went home to have three slices of toast and marmalade, instead of my usual two.

I had an extra cup of tea as well, although I had to gulp it down, or risk being late for work.

When I got to the office, Ben was already there, and it was clear from the pile of letters on my desk that the postman had been.

None of them were opened, and once I'd settled Jasper in his basket, I sat down and got on with it.

Most people communicate via e-mail now, but there are still a few solicitors who insist on everything being done the old-fashioned way, and I put the correspondence to one side, and the mail-shots into the waste-paper basket, before quickly checking my e-mails, and taking a moment to draw breath.

This is an old building, and the interior of this office reflects that. The walls are painted white, and left plain, the only adornment being a clock above the door. Thick carpets line the floors, and there are three chairs along the wall opposite my desk. Beyond those is a bank of filing cabinets, where Jasper has his basket, and on the far side of the room is an alcove, in which Ben has set up a small kitchen area, just big enough for us to make a cup of tea or coffee. Behind me is a large window, which overlooks the harbour and lets the sunshine in.

It's a pleasant place to work… but admiring the scenery wasn't achieving anything, so I got up and wandered into Ben's office.

The door was open, but I knocked on the frame and he called out, "Come in," sounding weary already.

"Are you all right?" I asked, putting the post into the tray on his desk.

His room is similar to mine, except the walls feature a few certificates showing his outstanding qualifications, and rather than filing cabinets, he has a row of bookshelves, filled with legal tomes. I'm sure he could look up anything he needed on the Internet, but the books are more impressive.

He didn't even glance up as I entered, but continued to stare at his computer screen, shaking his head as he let out a long sigh.

"I've had a message from Pamela Green," he said.

"Oh, yes?"

"She sent it on Friday evening, not long after we'd gone home, saying she thinks her husband has been siphoning money out of their company."

I leant against the side of his desk, folding my arms across my chest. "Are they still working together?"

"No. He won't let her into the building, evidently."

"That's a problem in itself, isn't it? The company belongs to her, just as much as it belongs to him."

"It's another bone of contention. Put it that way."

"You mean, along with his mother demanding separate access to the children, Mr Green insisting the marital home has to be sold, and threatening to stop the mortgage payments if Mrs Green doesn't do everything he demands?" I recited just some of the issues, ticking them off on my fingers.

"Exactly," he said, running his finger around the inside of his shirt collar.

"Is he still maintaining that his girlfriend has the 'right' to be there when his children come to stay at the weekends?"

"He is. Or at least he was when I last spoke to Mrs Green about it." He frowned. "I'll have to call her and set up a meeting, if I can."

"Okay."

I left him to it, going back into the reception and across to the kitchen to fix us both a coffee. It seemed we were going to need it.

"She's coming over." Ben's voice made me jump, but I hadn't expected his call to be so short, and I turned around to find him standing in his doorway.

"Today?" I asked, the milk carton in my hand.

"This morning." He rolled his shoulders, looking stressed. "She said there's something else she needs to talk to me about."

"Something else?"

"Yes. She didn't want to talk about it over the phone, and as I was asking to see her anyway, she said she'd tell me about it when she gets here. The problem is, I was going to focus on that blessed boundary dispute today, but it looks like the Green case will have to take priority."

I nodded my head. "Has anything new come in on the boundary dispute?"

"Yes. We had an e-mail from the other side on Friday, saying their client has found a document showing they have right of way."

"Have they? I mean, does it?"

"I don't know. That's what I was going to look into." He stepped a little closer as I added milk to our coffee and gave both cups a quick stir. "I don't suppose you could…?"

"You want me to take a look?"

"If you don't mind."

I handed him a cup and gave him a smile. "Of course I don't mind."

He smiled. "I'll forward you the e-mail. The document's attached."

"Okay."

He took his coffee and disappeared back into his office while I sat at my desk.

From then on, the day just got busier. Mrs Green arrived about forty-five minutes later and went straight into Ben's office, where she remained for nearly two hours. I spent that time going through the document he'd forwarded to me, and fielding the calls that came in for him, answering queries where I could, and taking messages where I couldn't.

When Mrs Green left, Ben saw her to the door, and I couldn't fail to notice that she'd been crying. I wondered how he'd handled that, but kept my eyes focused on my screen as he said goodbye to her, trying to sound reassuring.

Once the door had closed, he came and stood by my desk

"How did it go?" I asked.

"She's finding it very difficult."

"I'm not surprised. Is there any substance to her claims about him embezzling the money?"

"I don't know yet. She's given me copies of the company's most recent bank statements, and…"

"Mr Green won't like that," I said, interrupting him, and he smiled.

"Mr Green can lump it." He sounded very gruff, and I turned in my seat, looking up at him.

"What's he done now?"

He perched on the corner of my desk. "Mrs Green decided to give in to his requests – or at least try to meet him halfway – and let him have the children for the weekend, providing his girlfriend wasn't there."

"Was that wise?"

"No, and I wish she hadn't done it. At least, not without consulting me first, so we could have set up something more managed. But she said it was a spur-of-the-moment thing that he talked her into. Anyway, it was all arranged that he'd pick them up at seven-thirty on Friday evening, and drop them back no later than four, yesterday afternoon."

"What went wrong?"

"Not only did he cancel Friday evening, and not pick the children up until Saturday lunchtime, but he didn't bring them back until late last night."

"Seriously?"

"Yes. Then he claimed it was all her fault."

"How?"

"Can you believe, he said that, because she's not at the office anymore, he'd had to work late on Friday?"

"But he's the one who won't let her anywhere near the office."

"I know. It's completely illogical." He sighed, shaking his head. "Needless to say, it led to another argument on the doorstep. She told him he couldn't get the children home that late again, and he said he'd do whatever he wanted with his children. So, she said she'd have to think twice about letting him have them for an entire weekend in future, and he told her he's decided to apply for full custody."

"Oh, God. Is this what she wanted to talk to you about?"

He nodded. "She's distraught."

"He won't get it, though, will he? Full custody, I mean."

"It's highly unlikely. To be honest, I don't for one minute think he's remotely interested in having his children come to live with him. I think he's just making threats to get what he wants."

"Which is?"

"The best of both worlds. He wants to have the new life he's chosen, *and* bring with him the parts of his old life that he wants, whenever he wants them."

"Can I assume his girlfriend wasn't there at the weekend?"

"I don't know. Mrs Green seems to think that was the actual cause of the problem with him collecting the children on Friday evening. I'm inclined to agree with her, bearing in mind his reasons didn't make sense. Mrs Green said her husband also revealed something in the heat of their argument that suggested his girlfriend wasn't happy about having to stay somewhere else for two nights… hence he didn't collect them until Saturday."

"I see. Well, that's something, I suppose."

"It doesn't feel like it to her… especially not when it comes on top of this hole in the company's bank account."

"I'm surprised he hadn't shut her out of that."

"I don't think he dared. Keeping her out of their offices is one thing. Locking her out of the company altogether would make him look like the bad guy."

"You don't think he does already?"

He shrugged his shoulders. "As it stands, he can claim to be keeping her away for the benefit of their staff, to stop their marital problems from spilling over into the workplace."

"And that would wash?"

"You'd be surprised how things can be spun."

"But not embezzling money?"

"Not if that's what it is, no."

"What else could it be? I mean, how much are we talking about?"

"One hundred and seventy thousand pounds."

I stared up at him. "Wow."

"I know. Mrs Green hasn't been out of the loop long enough that she wouldn't have been aware of any upcoming capital expenditure on that scale."

"Precisely."

He stood up. "In which case, I'd better get on with finding out what Mr Green has been doing." He started for his office, but stopped and turned back. "How are you getting on with the boundary dispute?"

"I don't think the document is worth the paper it's written on. It's certainly not evidence of title, or right of way. I was about to draft a letter back to the other side, pointing out the flaws in their argument."

He smiled. "That's great. Send it through to me when it's done and I'll check it over."

I nodded my head. "I'll forward your messages while I'm about it."

"You can forward them. That doesn't mean I'll be answering any of them."

I chuckled, and he did too, both of us seeing the funny side.

That was just as well, because our day didn't get any easier. The phone rang incessantly, the e-mail kept pinging, and between us, we barely had time to think.

By the end of the day, I'm exhausted, and I think Ben is too. We've got enough to do that we could easily stay on for another few hours, but he comes out to my office, switching off the light in his, and making it clear it's time to go home.

"I've had enough, and so have you," he says, pulling on his coat. It's one of those woollen, knee-length ones, in dark grey, which is just as anonymous as his suits, and tells me nothing about him.

"I certainly have."

I turn off my computer, the sound of which alerts Jasper that we're leaving. I squeezed in a walk with him at lunchtime, calling at the baker's to pick up some sandwiches for Ben and myself, so we didn't starve.

"I don't suppose you can come in early again tomorrow, can you?" Ben asks as I pull on my jacket.

"Of course. Jasper seems to have managed okay staying here for the extra couple of hours."

"Jasper takes everything in his stride, if you ask me."

"He does." Or it feels that way, at least.

"Do you think he'd take a visit to the pub as lightly?"

"The pub?"

"Yes. I was wondering if you'd like to come for a drink. I'm not in the mood for going home yet… not after a day like that."

I can see his point, and after just a second's hesitation, I nod my head.

"That would be lovely."

He smiles, opening the office door, and holding it there, while I gather my things and exit ahead of him.

Jasper seems keen to be outside, and tugs on his lead, just a little.

"It's good to know he's not always perfectly well behaved," Ben says, nodding towards him.

"He's very far from that."

It's as though Jasper understands exactly what's being said, and he stops being so boisterous as we cross the road and head for the pub, Ben opening the door.

"I'm sure that's not true," he says.

"He latches on to every word you say, so be careful. He'll be getting ideas above his station."

Ben chuckles, and I join in, making my way to the bar. It's a struggle, but I sit up on a stool, waiting for Ben to join me, although he doesn't take a seat, making it clear our drink will be a quick one. I'm not complaining. I still need to take Jasper for his walk and make something for dinner. Heaven knows what. Something that cooks in no time at all would be good.

"What can I get you?" Ben asks, raising his hand to get the barmaid's attention. She's working by herself, and although it's not that busy, he has to wait for her to come over.

"A dry white wine, please."

He nods his head, placing the order for that and a vodka and tonic for himself, which she brings over in no time at all, taking the twenty-pound note Ben offers, and bringing back his change.

We clink our glasses together, and both take a long sip, smiling at each other as we put them down again.

"I needed that," he says.

"Hmm… me too. It's been one of those days."

I glance down, just to check Jasper's all right. He seems quite happy, lying at my feet, and I turn back to Ben.

"Here's hoping tomorrow will be better," he says, taking another gulp of his drink.

"I don't think it could be much worse, could it?"

"Don't tempt fate." He frowns. "It never used to be like this, you know?"

"No, but I don't think people were as litigious as they are now. That neighbourly dispute would never have happened in the past, would it?"

"I doubt it. I can remember when people just settled their differences over the garden fence, with a cup of tea or a pint of beer in hand. Nowadays, they all want their day in court."

"You shouldn't complain. It's how you make your living."

He smiles. "I know, but sometimes I wish we could go back to when it was simpler… to when people were kinder."

I can't disagree with that sentiment, and I sip a little more wine.

"What do you think makes people the way they are?" I ask, and he tilts his head, like he's considering my question.

"I don't know. Maybe it's seeing adverts on television for solicitors who'll sue just about anyone for just about anything, on your behalf. Or maybe it's social media…" He stops talking, startling slightly at the sound of his phone ringing. "Sorry," he says, pulling it from his coat pocket and glancing down at the screen, a smile forming on his lips. "I'd better take this."

I nod my head, turning away as he connects his call. His voice is much softer than I've ever heard it, and it doesn't take very much imagination to work out that he's talking to a woman.

"Oh, really?" I hear him say, even though I'm trying my best not to listen. "Why couldn't they have let you know earlier in the day? Honestly… if we'd realised your class was going to be cancelled, I could have come over after work." There's a silence while I glance around the pub, and then he adds, "No. I'm just drowning my sorrows in the pub with Anna. We've had a horrible day, and despite Anna's optimism, I can't see tomorrow being a lot better." He waits, smiling, and then says, "That sounds lovely. I wish we could have done something tonight, but if you're offering to cook for me, I'll definitely be there."

I turn in the other direction, my eyes alighting on that man I saw this morning… the one who was sketching on the harbour. He's sitting by himself, near the window at the back of the pub, and although he seems to be staring in my direction, I think his attention must be fixed on something behind me. Either that, or he's looking straight through me. It seems about right for him. He doesn't have time for lowly people like me. And why would he?

His gaze is intense, nonetheless, but rather than make anything of it, I pretend I haven't noticed him, and look away in the most nonchalant way I can, as though I'm simply admiring the scenery.

"See you tomorrow, then," Ben says, his eyes sparkling now. He's a completely different man to the slightly morose, disaffected character who came in here with me just a few minutes ago, and as he ends the call and replaces his phone, he blushes slightly. "Sorry about that."

"It's not a problem."

"That was… well, I suppose I have to call her my girlfriend."

This is news. I've always been convinced Ben was a confirmed bachelor.

"I wouldn't let her hear you say that, if I were you."

He frowns at me, and then his face clears, and he smiles. "Oh. I see what you mean. You're probably right. I doubt Gabriella would like to hear me refer to her like that, although I didn't mean it in the way it came out. It's just… well, I'm going to be fifty next year, and Gabriella is only three years younger. It seems silly to call ourselves 'boyfriend' and 'girlfriend' at our age."

"I suppose it does, although there isn't a mature alternative, is there? Other than 'partner', I suppose."

"That always sounds like someone I'd be associated with on a professional level," he says, looking a little wistful. "Maybe it'd be easier if I proposed…" I stare up at him, watching as he slowly comes to his senses. "Sorry. I hadn't intended to say that out loud."

"That's okay."

He leans in slightly. "I'm not acting on a whim, you understand? And it isn't really about what we call each other. I've been thinking of proposing for a while now."

"But you're nervous?" I ask. This isn't how I'd normally speak with Ben, but somehow, after the day we've had, and in a setting like this, it feels okay. In fact, it feels quite natural.

"Not nervous, no. I suppose I'm just wondering if it's too soon."

"Why would it be?"

"Gabriella and I have only been seeing each other since just before Christmas."

"And you think that makes a difference?"

He frowns. "I don't know. Does it?"

"You're asking me?"

"For a woman's perspective? Yes. If you'd only been seeing a man for a few months, would you take his proposal seriously?"

"If I loved him, yes, I would."

He smiles, his eyes shining. "So you don't think it's a problem?"

"I can't say how Gabriella would feel, but it wouldn't be an issue for me."

He lets out a sigh. "I rather wish I was going over there tonight now, instead of having to wait until tomorrow."

"Because you want to propose? You want to strike while the iron's hot?"

He chuckles, picking up his glass. "No. I think I'd like to buy the ring first, but it would be nice to see her."

"Is there a reason you can't?"

"Only that we've made our arrangements now."

"So? Arrangements can be unmade, can't they?"

He pauses, his glass halfway to his mouth. "Hmm… they can indeed."

He swallows down the last of his drink, and I copy him, jumping down from my stool as he steps away from the bar, his decision clearly made. He's like a different man, with a spring in his step, and a sparkle in his eyes, and for a moment, I envy him that.

He holds the door open, waiting for me to join him, Jasper in tow.

"You're a good influence, Anna."

I laugh. "I don't know about that."

He follows me outside. "I do. Thank you."

I can't think what to say, so I say nothing at all, and we both wish each other, "Goodnight," at the same time.

With Jasper tugging slightly at his lead, I watch Ben walk to his car, which Ed allows him to park here at the pub. It's a convenient arrangement, and a necessary one, as there isn't anywhere else on the harbour for him to park, and then I set off along the harbour wall, Jasper's walk long overdue.

"You've been very good today," I say, and he looks up at me, although he's quickly distracted by a lamppost, and stops to sniff at it. While I'm waiting, I look out beyond the harbour. It's too dark to see anything now, and as Jasper seems to be taking his time, I turn back to the pub, noticing the man who I saw earlier – the man who was sketching here this morning – is just leaving. He can't have been waiting for me to leave first, can he? No… that's a ludicrous thought. Why would he do that? And in any case, he doesn't even look up to see if I'm still here; he just strides off up Church Lane.

I have to say, he's taller than I thought. Of course, I've only seen him sitting down until now, but he must be well over six feet tall, and he lowers his head, pulling up his collar as he disappears from sight.

He must be going somewhere further up the hill… but heaven only knows where.

Not that I'm interested.

Jasper tugs at his lead, letting me know he's finished with that lamppost, and we move along. Fortunately, the other street furniture doesn't seem as interesting, and we get to the end of the harbour in no time at all. It's chilly now, and Jasper looks up at me as though to say he's had enough of being outdoors. I can read his expressions quite well now… or I think I can.

"Do you want to go home?" I ask, and he turns around, making me laugh. "I get the message."

We re-trace our steps, going back the way we've come, and although it's not the longest of walks, I'll make up for it tomorrow morning.

It'll be another early start, and I've still got to feed him and have dinner myself yet… although I'm not really in the mood for cooking anymore.

What I am is cold, and we pick up the pace, getting home in no time at all.

The moment I open the door, Jasper makes straight for the kitchen, standing by his bowl.

"I get it. You're hungry," I say, taking off my coat and following him. He stares up at me, wagging his tail as I prepare his food, and he dives into it the moment I put it down for him.

I could do with something just as quick myself, and I open the freezer, finding a chicken tikka masala I bought a while ago, buried near the back. It's not what I'd normally eat, and I can't even remember why I bought it now… but I'm pleased I did, and I check the instructions on the back, relieved to discover it can be cooked from frozen in nine minutes.

Thank heavens for that.

I think even I can wait nine minutes.

Just…

Today feels even warmer than yesterday.

It's like spring has really sprung. The wind is almost non-existent, and the sun is shining. Even at this time of the morning, it feels warm, although I'm still wearing my coat. A little sunshine can't fool me into thinking I can go without that extra layer.

We leave the house a bit earlier than we did yesterday, and make our way straight out onto the harbour, where we stop for Jasper to sniff at the wall, and for me to suck in some fresh air.

There's something very invigorating about sea air, and I fill my lungs before turning, and stopping in my tracks, when I see that man is sitting there again, just like he was yesterday.

Admittedly, he doesn't have an easel with him today. Instead, he has a large sketch pad, which he's balanced on the harbour wall, and he seems to be focusing on the houses which line the far side. I've always loved their pastel colours, and with the early morning sun shining on them, they look especially pretty.

For all I know, he could be drawing anything, though… and it's none of my business.

In fact, it might be better if we crossed the road to avoid any chance of a confrontation. I step away from the wall, pulling Jasper, who seems reluctant.

"Come on," I whisper, and he looks up, although his eyes dart down the road, and for some unknown reason, he tugs on his lead just as I'm stepping off the kerb. I'm caught off guard and accidentally let go. "Jasper!"

He barks, and although he doesn't dart out into the road, thank God, he dashes wildly along the pavement, his ears flapping. I have no choice, and I set off in pursuit, calling after him. Not only am I worried for my dog's safety if a car should come along and startle him, but I'm almost certain he's going to knock that man flying, and I don't even want to think how badly that will end.

"Jasper!" I call again, and this time, the man looks up.

My dog is almost upon him, and fearing the worst, I slow down, cringing against the inevitable. It doesn't happen, though. The man somehow grabs Jasper by his collar before he can pass by, and holds him steady, raising his head and looking at me, a frown set firmly on his face.

Oh, great…

Chapter Six

Seb

It's the sound of a woman's voice that makes me look up.

Oh, God. It's her. Again.

What is this? A conspiracy or something?

And what on earth is going on?

She's running right at me, and…

Oh, I see. Her dog's got loose. The daft thing is charging down the pavement in my direction, and while it would be easy to let him carry straight on, that wouldn't be a very gentlemanly thing to do.

I lower my sketchpad to the floor, quickly pocket my pencil and reach out just in time to grab the dog's collar as he darts past… or tries to.

"Woah," I mutter as he stops and looks up at me. "Where do you think you're going?"

He doesn't try to get away, but stops, panting hard, and looks up at me, just as the woman approaches. She's no longer running at full pelt, but is jogging now… or is doing her best, in that tight skirt she's wearing. It's hugging her hips. Her breasts are heaving too, beneath her blouse, and I take a moment to stop staring, remind myself I'm supposed to be a gentleman, and focus instead on her face… although the sight of her flushed cheeks doesn't really help my predicament. In my confusion, I nudge the dog forward, still holding his collar, and say, "Yours, I think."

Even I'd have to acknowledge that my words sound sarcastic, and my voice dismissive, but it's too late to take them back… and besides, I'm feeling even more distracted today than I was yesterday, or last night

It's been years since I've thought of a woman in terms of hips and breasts and flushed cheeks, and even if I am surprised by my reaction, I can't deny the attraction.

She picks up his lead from the ground, wrapping it around her hand. "I'm sorry if Jasper disturbed you," she says, narrowing her eyes at me.

"It's fine. He didn't…"

"Thank you for stopping him." Her words cut off my attempted apology, but before I can say anything else, she turns and walks away, crossing the road, her dog trotting obediently at her heel now.

Does she have to be so abrasive?

Part of me wants to call after her, although whether I'd be asking what her problem is, or trying to complete my apology, I'm not sure. Maybe I'd just settle for quizzing her about what happened to make her like this. That's what I'd like to know. Something obviously did. A man, I'm guessing. Why else is she so dismissive?

I shake my head. She wasn't dismissive of her boyfriend, was she?

So perhaps it's just me she doesn't like.

I pick up my sketchpad, turning around just as a man walks up to her on the other side of the street. They seem to know each other, judging by the smile on his face, and as I watch, they hug, and she kisses him on the cheek. He pulls back, nodding his head as he looks down at her, which makes me think she must have said something, and then he puts his hand on her shoulder.

There's something affectionate about that gesture, especially when it's accompanied by the concerned expression on his face.

Good Lord. What's wrong with her? Does she have a different man for every day of the week?

Obviously nothing women do would ever surprise me, but this one is so open about it, she takes the biscuit.

I huff out a sigh and, giving up on my sketch, I fold my chair and make my way back to the car, relieved that I didn't embarrass myself by pursuing that apology.

I feel out of sorts, yet again. It's becoming a habit with that woman, and I try to rid my mind of her before I get home. I need to concentrate today if I'm going to stick to the deadline. After all, I've got to make up for yesterday's appalling performance.

I did it.

I had a much better day.

That's to say, I completed the outline of the illustration. I even made a start on painting the background, and I'm feeling reasonably confident that, despite my hiccup, I'll still get finished on time.

I thought it would be easy to stop thinking about that woman. Let's face it, she means nothing to me. I don't even know her name, or where she lives, or what she does for a living. But it transpired that ridding my mind of her altogether was impossible. She kept creeping back in, the image of her flushed cheeks vying with that disappointed expression on her face. Chasing her dog caused her pinked cheeks, but I was entirely responsible for that disenchanted look in her eyes.

If I'm being honest, I feel a little guilty about that. I didn't have to bite her head off, and I regret it now. I could have been more friendly, if nothing else.

Still, it's too late to do anything about it, and I'm sure she hasn't given me a second thought all day.

"No, she's got too many other men to think about," I muse out loud, sighing, although I'm not sure why.

I glance down at the illustration, feeling pleased with my day's efforts. I could carry on, but I'd be working in electric light, which plays havoc with the colours, and my back is killing me. It's time to call it a day.

Besides, I need something to eat.

I didn't work through lunch today, but I only grabbed a quick cheese sandwich and brought it up here, so I didn't lose the momentum I'd gained through the morning. It's paid off, but now the thought of heating something in the microwave really doesn't appeal.

It's not like me to dine at the pub two nights in a row, but who's judging?

And besides, I've earned it today…

Except I think I'll drive there tonight. The weatherman said it might rain, which is a shame, and I hope the forecast is wrong. I'd like to get out early tomorrow to finish my sketch of the houses on the harbour. It was going well this morning until I was interrupted.

Still, I refuse to think about that, or the woman who interrupted me.

Instead, I'll go to the pub so I can enjoy a nice meal in my own company.

I grab my keys and wallet, pulling on my coat as I head out of the door. I have to turn my car around, but it's easy enough, and I drive down the track and onto the main road.

It takes no time at all to reach the village and I park with no trouble at all. Despite my best efforts, my mind is still full of the woman, and as I walk around to the front door, waiting for a family to exit the pub, I can't help wondering if she'll be here again tonight. Is that wishful thinking? It could be, I suppose. After all, I've thought about her all day, on and off.

Except that doesn't make sense. Why would I want to see her again? Not only does she mess with my head and make it difficult for me to concentrate, but she's already got two men in tow. For all I know, she could be here tonight with a third.

Nothing would surprise me.

She's a woman, isn't she?

I step inside, my eyes immediately alighting on her. She's sitting alone at the bar, her dog lying on the floor beside her, and I let out a sigh. Is that disappointment or relief? I can't be sure.

For a second, I wonder about turning around and walking straight back out again, but why should I change my plans? She's probably waiting for one of her many boyfriends, and there's no reason for either of us to acknowledge the other.

With my head down, I stroll up to the bar, keeping my distance, although it's not that easy. There are a lot of people in here tonight. Still, there's a gap of at least six feet between us, which should be more than enough, and once I've ordered, I'll find a seat. It'll be fine…

"What can I get you?" The young lady behind the bar comes up to me with a smile on her face.

"I'll have a glass of red wine. Something full bodied."

She nods her head and turns, grabbing a glass from above her head, just as I feel something nuzzling against my ankle. I look down to see the woman's dog, who's wandered over, having clearly recognised me from this morning.

"Hello." I bend and stroke his head, which he seems to like, tipping it one way and then the other. He's very cute, I must say, with a soft black coat, and long fluffy ears, and he looks up at me with big brown eyes, like he wants me to do something… although I'm not sure what.

"Jasper, come here," the woman says, and I look up to see she's blushing, staring at her dog, and looking embarrassed.

"It's okay." I make a conscious effort to sound friendly. "I don't mind." She shrugs in the most dismissive way imaginable, and I look back down at her dog, who seems to enjoy my company, even if his mistress doesn't. "I mean it," I add. "I know you think I'm rude, or obnoxious, or something, but…"

"I don't think anything of the sort." She sounds most indignant, which makes me smile.

"Yes, you do."

She opens her mouth, but then closes it again, clearly having decided not to give another false denial of the obvious truth.

At that moment, the young lady behind the bar comes back with my drink and I ask her to set up a tab for me. She smiles her acknowledgement and goes away again, and rather than leaving things in a rather awkward limbo, I pick up my glass and move just a little closer to the woman, her dog following me.

"Are you waiting for someone?" I ask. I'm pretty sure she is. She doesn't seem the type to come into a pub by herself.

She takes a sip of her white wine and turns to me, tilting her head.

"I am, as a matter of fact. My brother's supposed to me meeting me here. Only he's late, as usual." She rolls her eyes. "I don't know why he makes plans, when he knows he won't keep them."

I lean back slightly, surprised by the amount of information she just gave me. I'd expected a straight 'yes', or 'no' answer to that question, but her reply is quite revealing, in its own way.

"Are you always this judgemental?"

"Judgemental?" She frowns up at me.

"Yes. Don't you ever make allowances for other people… for the fact that something might have come up, that they might be busy, or just have forgotten they're supposed to be doing something?"

She twists on her seat, taking a deep breath. "Excuse me, but what gives you the right to talk to me like that? You don't even know me. And for your information, I'm not judgemental at all."

"Really? Your brother's late, but rather than giving him the benefit of the doubt, you automatically blame some kind of character flaw, and right him off as Mr Unreliable."

"I didn't say that, but in any case, it's not that far from the truth. My brother's renowned for doing things like this."

"So you don't think it's possible he's just forgotten?"

"No. Even Stephen doesn't have that bad a memory. I think even he can be relied upon to remember an arrangement he only made this morning. And in case you don't believe me, I imagine you saw us."

"Saw you?"

"Yes. I bumped into him on the harbour, right after you stopped Jasper from running away from me."

"You mean he's the man you kissed?"

"Yes. Why?" I realise the error of my ways, and can't help smiling at my own ability to leap to conclusions and make judgements, based on faulty evidence. "What's funny?" she asks, sounding both confused and angry.

"Promise not to hit me?"

"Why?"

"Because I assumed the man you kissed this morning was your boyfriend."

She pulls a face, as though she's considering that prospect. "Stephen? My boyfriend?"

"You can't blame me for getting it wrong. You seemed quite affectionate, and it's not as though you look alike."

"No, because he's my half-brother."

"You're still close, though?"

"Yes, we are. We share the same father, but not the same mother."

She looks up into my eyes and for once, there's nothing negative reflected back at me. I'm not entirely sure what it is I'm seeing, but there's no animosity, or disappointment, or uncertainty, and feeling a little buoyed by that, I move nearer, just by a foot or so, Jasper standing between us now.

"How did that come about?" I ask.

"My mother died when I was very young and my father remarried and had Stephen with his second wife a few years later."

"So you're older than him?" She certainly didn't look it.

"Yes. But before I tell you my entire life story, can I ask you a question?"

"Of course."

"Why would you assume I'd want to hit you for thinking Stephen was my boyfriend? I'll admit it's a weird thought, but it's not something that would make me resort to physical violence."

"Maybe not, but to be honest, I noticed you in here last night, with another man, and then saw you this morning, and…"

She tilts her head, frowning. "And you assumed I had men tucked away in every corner of the village, did you?"

"Something like that."

She shakes her head, looking perplexed, and takes another sip of wine before she says, "I don't know whether to feel insulted or flattered by that. And just so you know, the man I was with last night was my boss, not my boyfriend. We'd had a difficult day at work, and he brought me for a drink before leaving to see his girlfriend. Or, to be more precise, he went to propose to her. He didn't mean to. He told me he wanted to wait and buy the ring first. Not that it's any business of yours…"

"I know it's not. But in case it escaped your notice, I didn't ask."

She falls silent, breathing hard after her outburst, and dips her head. "Sorry," she mumbles.

"That's okay."

"I—I didn't mean to…"

I hold up my hand, and she stops talking. "You don't need to elaborate. I get that you're sorry. Although I think our conversations might go a lot more smoothly if you'd stop seeing everything I say as a criticism."

"I don't."

"Yes, you do. I made a mistake. I'm the one who should apologise, not you… especially as I've just called you judgemental, and gone on to prove I'm exactly that myself." She's dumbfounded by my admission and just stares at me. "I'm sorry for casting you in the role of a scarlet woman," I say, and she surprises me with a smile.

"It's certainly a first."

I smile back. "Is my apology accepted?"

"As you've made it so graciously, yes it is."

"Good." I gaze at her for a moment, captivated by the sparkle in her eyes and the slight blush on her cheeks. I don't know what's put that there, but it has nothing to do with chasing after her dog this time, that's for sure. "What are you going to do about your brother?" I ask.

"Give up on him," she says, shaking her head. "He's a hopeless cause."

"You could do that," I say, taking my courage in both hands as I step into unfamiliar territory. At least, it's not somewhere I've been for quite a while. "Or you could call him and find out where he is."

"Would that be so I can leave if he's not coming, and you won't have to stand here and talk to me anymore?"

She really is brutal. "I don't have to talk to you now. This place is big enough that we could ignore each other if we felt like it. We managed last night, didn't we?" She gazes up at me, but doesn't reply, and I wonder if that was too harsh. It might well have been, and I take a deep breath, moving a little closer to her. I'm still on unfamiliar ground, but I'm getting more used to it. "What I was going to say was, if he can't make it, we could have dinner together."

Her eyes widen, confusion etched on her face. I suppose I can't blame her for that, but it's been years since I've done this, and I'd forgotten this awful feeling of being kept waiting… being hung out to dry. A few agonising seconds pass before she licks her lips, bites on the bottom one, and then says, "You want to have dinner with me?"

"Yes."

"Why?"

Good question. I'm wondering about that myself. I know I'm attracted to her. Who wouldn't be? But there's something more to it than that. The problem is, I don't know what that 'something' is, and she's waiting for an answer.

"Because I'd like to get to know you. I'd like to find out why you hate men so much."

Should I have said that? The first part was okay. The second part was an afterthought that I probably should have kept to myself, the frown on her face confirming that.

"I don't hate men."

In for a penny… "So it's just me you're not keen on."

"I didn't say that, did I?"

"No, but in that case, I have to assume it's not personal, and your grudge – whatever that might be – is something you have against my sex as a whole."

"Maybe. But you're not fond of women, either, are you?"

"I won't deny that's true. Although I've got a good reason."

"So have I," she says, sitting up straight and squaring her shoulders.

"Fine. Why don't we compare reasons over dinner?"

She pauses again, her eyes never leaving mine, and then, without a word, she pulls her phone from her handbag and presses on the screen a few times.

"Stephen? It's me…"

I turn my head, looking the other way, while she talks to her brother, her silent agreement to my suggestion making me smile, even if it surprises me. I didn't think she'd accept. But I never thought I'd ask, either.

Don't get me wrong, I'm not about to change my mind, or retract my invitation. I'm looking forward to spending an evening with her. Despite our differences, I like her, and I can't deny the relief I felt when she explained that she's not romantically attached to either of the men I've seen her with. Does that mean I want that kind of attachment myself, though?

I'm not sure.

I want something… I think.

To get to know her? Yes. I wasn't lying about that.

To share our stories? My skin turns a little icy at the prospect. I don't mind hearing whatever she's got to say, but as for revealing my own secrets? What was I thinking?

I can hardly back out though, can I? Not now I've just suggested it.

But the thing is, there are only a handful of people who know what happened, and only three of us know all of it. It's personal. Really personal. And I'm not sure I'm ready to share it.

Chapter Seven

Anna

"I'm so sorry. I've been trying to get hold of you all afternoon." Stephen sounds frazzled, and although I want to feel sorry for him, I can't.

"And what's been stopping you?" I keep my voice quiet, so the man beside me won't be able to hear. I don't want him to criticise me again… even if he apologised for doing so before.

"People," Stephen says.

"Guests, or staff?"

"Both. Although it's all been made worse because, on top of everything else, the new deputy manager who usually works the evening shift called in sick earlier this afternoon. That means I've got to stay on and cover for him. I can't ask Laura. Not when she's already doing so much. She's been here since seven this morning, and she worked late yesterday."

"Why? What went wrong yesterday?"

"We had a minor crisis to do with the catering for Ed and Nicki's wedding."

"I see. So, what you're trying to tell me is, you're not going to make it to the pub."

"That about sums it up, although it's no excuse. No matter what was going on, I should have found the time to call… or at least send a message. I'm sorry. I'll make it up to you, I promise." There's just a moment's pause, and then he says, "Are you okay?" his voice filled with concern.

I know he's thinking about our conversation this morning, when we met on the harbour, and I can't blame him for worrying. I was upset at the time, and doing a very poor job of hiding it. Stephen noticed, and when I explained what had happened, he offered to speak to the man. I begged him not to, and that's when we agreed to meet up tonight. I think he sensed I needed a bit of bucking up. Heaven knows what he'd say if he knew that same man was sitting beside me, and had just invited me to have dinner with him.

I'm unsure what to say myself.

It's a pretty confusing state of affairs.

He was so unpleasant again this morning, when there really wasn't any need. He'd made me feel inadequate, but I suppose that wasn't his fault. It was mine. It was my interpretation of his words, rather than the words themselves that was the problem… and I think that's why I'm sitting here talking to my brother, rather than walking home by myself.

I don't think it's got anything to do with the man's azure coloured eyes, or the way he keeps smiling at me.

Of course it hasn't.

"I—I'm fine," I say, remembering to speak at last.

"I'll call you tomorrow."

"I'll believe it when it happens."

Stephen's chuckle makes me smile, and we end our call. I take a moment to put away my phone and then turn to the man, who raises an eyebrow.

"Well?" he says.

"He's definitely not going to make it. He's been held up at work."

I half expect him to say 'I told you so', but he doesn't. Instead, he looks around, and then turns to me again.

"Where would you like to sit?" he asks.

There's a table by the window, close to where he sat last night, and I nod towards it.

"Over there?"

"Fine." He holds out his hand and I stare down at it, then raise my eyes to his. "You're going to tell me you're perfectly capable of getting down from that stool all by yourself, aren't you?" he says, although he doesn't pull his hand away.

"No. Sorry. I didn't realise that was what you were offering."

"I see." He nods his head towards his hand, so I take it, using it for support as I jump down.

"Thank you," I murmur.

"You're welcome."

He takes my glass, along with his own, and waits for me to lead the way to the table. Jasper seems to know exactly where we're going and doesn't deviate at all, sitting beneath the table the moment I stop.

The man puts down the drinks before moving behind me, and I turn and look up at him.

"Is something wrong?"

"No. I was wondering if I could help you."

"What with?"

"Your coat."

"Oh. Sorry."

He shakes his head. "Why are you apologising again?"

"Because I'm not used to men behaving like gentlemen."

He smiles. "I'll try to be the exception, shall I?"

I don't know what to say, but I don't need to worry. He fills the moment by removing my coat, while I juggle with Jasper's lead, unwilling to let him go, just in case he runs off, like he did this morning.

The man puts my coat over the back of one of the chairs, then holds it, waiting for me to sit. Even I've worked that out this time, and could kick myself for being so blind to his earlier kindnesses. Before I sit, though, there's something I need to do.

"Sorry," I say again, and he tilts his head.

"What for?"

"I just need to trap Jasper's lead under the chair."

He nods his head, taking the lead from me and raising the front of the chair, placing the lead around the leg.

"There. Okay now?"

"Yes, thank you."

He holds the chair once more, and I sit.

"Won't be a minute," he says, then dashes away, returning just moments later with two menus. I feel guilty now. I could have grabbed those on our way past the bar.

"Sorry. I could have done that," I say, and he stares down at me, removing his coat, which he places over the back of his chair before sitting, facing me. He's wearing jeans and a turquoise polo shirt, and for a moment, I'm struck by his athletic build. I hadn't been expecting that, and while he's not like one of those muscle men you see in magazines, with ludicrously bulging biceps, he's definitely toned… and very handsome.

"You seriously need to stop apologising." He shakes his head at me, handing over one of the menus, and although I take it, I glance out of the window to my left, feeling a little embarrassed. That's as much because of his comments as it is because I've just been admiring him. To be more precise, I've been ogling him, even though I don't know his name, or the first thing about him. "What's making you blush?" he asks, and I turn to face him again.

"I'm not blushing. It's warm in here, that's all."

"Oh." He smiles. "Is that what it is?" He puts down his menu, resting his elbows on the table, and gazes across at me. "I was just thinking how strange it is to be sitting opposite a beautiful woman, wondering what to have for dinner, when I don't even know what to call you."

Now I'm definitely blushing, although he doesn't remark on it this time. I don't give him a chance.

"I was thinking the same thing." Suddenly, I realise what I've just said, my blush deepening. "I—I didn't mean about me being beautiful. I meant…"

"I know what you meant. Shall I rectify the situation and start the introductions?" I nod my head and he leans a little closer. "I'm Sebastian Baxter, although just about everyone I know calls me Seb."

"I'm Anna Goddard. No-one's ever shortened my name, I'm afraid."

He smiles. "It's nice to meet you, Anna."

"You, too… although I don't know why we've never met before. It always strikes me that everyone in Porthgarrion knows everyone else."

"Except I don't live in the village," he says. "I live in the house on the top of the cliff."

I know the one he's talking about, and it's enormous. "Are you saying you're a recluse?"

"Not really. I'm just busy."

"Doing what?"

"Illustrating children's books."

"Is that how you can afford such a lovely house?"

He smiles. "It's not mine… more's the pity. I've been renting it since last spring."

"So, you're new here? You're not a native of Porthgarrion?"

"No. Can't you tell?"

"I suppose the accent is a give-away."

"At least the lack of a Cornish accent, anyway," he says, and I nod my head. "What about you?" he asks. "Where do you live?"

"In one of the houses in the terrace opposite the police station. Except mine isn't a house, it's a flat."

"And can I take it from your lack of Cornish accent that you're not from these parts, either?"

"You can. I've been here for a little longer than you, but not much."

"How do you like it?" he asks.

"Very much. I'd love to be able to settle here one day."

"You're not settled now?" He tilts his head, like he's thinking, or mulling over my comment, anyway.

"Not really. I rent my flat…"

"And you don't like it?" he says.

"I'm very happy there. It's a lovely little flat, but I think I'd prefer to live in a house, with at least a small patch of garden, or a space where I could grow herbs and flowers in pots." I've never said that to anyone before. Not even Stephen. Although I think that's out of fear he might say something to Laura, and she'd be offended.

"You like gardening?"

"To be honest, I wouldn't know. I've never really tried. But I'd like to, I think. I imagine it's quite therapeutic."

"I'm just discovering that for myself," he says, and we both take a sip of wine. "What made you decide to rent, rather than buy? Was it the shortage of properties?"

"No. I—I didn't have much choice at the time. I moved here in a hurry, and my brother let me sleep on his sofa for a while."

"Your brother was already living here?" he asks.

"Yes. He's the manager at the hotel. My landlady works with him, and when he found out she was putting her flat up for rent, it seemed like too good a chance to turn down."

"Because his sofa wasn't very comfortable?" he says with a smile.

"Because I needed to start again, let's put it that way."

"I can understand that." He twists his wineglass in his hand. "What do you do for a living?"

"I'm a secretary."

"With a boss who's just got engaged. But who is he?"

"He's Ben Atkins."

I briefly recall my conversation with Ben when I got into work. He seemed especially pleased, and wasted no time in telling me he'd thrown caution to the wind, decided rings weren't essential, and had proposed to Gabriella last night. Needless to say, she'd accepted, and he was thrilled. So thrilled that he bought us cakes to have with our morning coffee.

Sebastian frowns for a second, like he's trying to remember something, then nods his head. "Of course. He's the solicitor, isn't he? The one on the harbour?"

"Yes."

"I thought so. I've seen the sign on the door by the estate agents."

"That's the one. He's been here for years."

He smiles. "I'd keep that quiet, if I were you. You make it sound like he's as old as the hills."

I chuckle. "He's not. He told me he's going to be fifty next year."

"And you don't think that's old?"

"Not at all."

"So a forty-five-year-old must seem like a youngster to you?"

"Now who's the one trying to make someone feel old?"

He tilts his head, and then blushes, which is quite difficult with a tan like his. There are definitely two red dots on his cheeks, though. "I wasn't implying you're older than that. I mean…"

"It's okay. I understood what you meant."

"And thought you'd make fun of me?"

"Maybe." He grins, then picks up his menu. The action seems a little dismissive and I lean forward. "Have I said the wrong thing?"

He looks up. "Of course not. I just thought we ought to decide what we're going to eat."

"Oh, I see."

"Don't look so worried." I wasn't aware I was. "I definitely prefer being made fun of to hearing you apologise for every little thing you say and do."

It's my turn to blush – again – and a smile touches at his lips. "You said that on purpose, didn't you? To embarrass me."

He nods his head, trying not to laugh, and I can't help giggling. I'm surprised by how much I'm enjoying myself, and how easy-going he is. I think I might have been wrong about him… in more ways than one. He's not only a gentleman – or trying to be one – but he's fun, too. He stares for a moment, and then chuckles. "Come on… let's choose what we're going to have."

I lower my gaze to the menu, my eyes settling on the salads. It's ironic really. That's the last thing I feel like eating, but it's probably more becoming to eat like a bird, even if I'm ravenous. It's what Fergus would have expected, although he's not here, and I smile, thinking about the fact that I didn't worry about his opinions when I was having lunch with Stephen the other day… which feels like progress. Still, I should probably be good tonight, and I return my attention to the menu. There's a hot smoked salmon salad that's served with roasted beetroot, shallots and a horseradish dressing. That doesn't sound too bad, and I'm about to close my menu when I notice the crispy pork belly. My stomach actually groans at the thought, and I forget all about salmon and beetroot, reading of crushed potatoes, and apple and mustard sauce, my mouth watering at the prospect.

"I'm having the pork belly," Seb says, catching me by surprise. "What about you?"

"The same," I reply, and he smiles.

"Great minds think alike."

He takes my menu, before I can pretend to have less of an appetite, and change my mind back to the salad, and he walks up to the bar.

I know I shouldn't, but I can't help studying him as he waits his turn. I wasn't wrong about his build, and now more of it is visible, I let my eyes roam over his broad shoulders and narrow waist, wondering how he can eat things like pork belly and still look like that.

Life's so unfair sometimes…

I watch him give our order, and hear him laugh as Ed says something to him, and then he turns, and I look away, so he doesn't think I've been watching the whole time.

"How old is Jasper?" he asks, sitting back down again.

"He's four, although I've only had him for a few months. He's a rescue dog, you see."

"He's adorable."

He reaches beneath the table to stroke Jasper's head and scratch under his chin, and I have to smile at the loving expression on my dog's face.

"He'll take any amount of that," I say and Seb smiles, continuing with his attentions for a moment or two longer before he stops, sips at his drink and tilts his head at me.

"If I remember rightly, you were going to tell me why you hate men so much."

I was rather hoping he'd forgotten about that. Faced with the prospect of revealing my past, I feel a lot less confident about it than I did when he first threw down that challenge. That's how I saw it, I think. But now, I'd rather just carry on talking than tell him about Fergus and what he did to me.

"I think you were going to tell me about your dislike of women," I say, to throw him off guard. "And as this was your idea, and you're trying to be a gentleman, I think you should go first."

He sighs, shaking his head. "I should have kept my big mouth shut," he mutters, and I wonder if he feels the same way I do.

"Can I assume that whatever it is, is something you don't enjoy talking about?"

"You can."

"In that case…"

He holds up his hand, and I stop talking. "No. You're right. This was my idea." He pauses, looking down at the table. "Although I'll have to ask you to remember, this is very personal."

"Hey…" He looks up again. "You don't have to tell me if you don't want to."

"No. I said I would." He takes another sip of wine, putting down the glass, and then looks out of the window. "My wife had an affair."

His words are stark, but not entirely unexpected. I think I'd guessed he was going to say something like that, and I nod my head.

"Can I assume she's your ex-wife now?"

He looks back at me. "Yes. I should have said that. We got divorced."

"I'm sorry." He frowns. "Had you been married long?"

"Just over five years, but we'd been together for three years before that."

"And was this recent? The divorce, I mean?"

He sighs again, shifting in his seat. "I suppose that depends on your idea of recent. It happened seven years ago, so I guess some people would say it's ancient history."

"But not you?"

"No."

"You must have loved her very much."

"I did," he says, nodding his head, although he stops abruptly. "That's to say, I thought I did."

"But you didn't?"

"I can't have done, can I? I didn't even know her. The woman I married would never have done what she did. She was kind, and loyal, and trusting… and a complete fabrication."

"And now you don't think any woman can be kind, and loyal, and trusting because she cheated on you?"

"It was a little more than cheating. That's why I said she had an affair."

"You think there's a difference?"

"Yes. To me, cheating means something else entirely."

"So, like a drunken one-night stand or a fling you regret the morning after?"

"Something like that."

"And an affair?"

"That's so much more. It involves time, commitment, and so many lies."

"Could you have forgiven your wife if she'd cheated… if she'd had a one-night stand?"

"No. That's not what I'm saying. I'm just trying to get across how much more pain there is in an affair… especially when that affair is with your best friend."

Oh, God.

I hadn't seen that coming, but I can understand his reticence to talk now.

"Your best friend?"

He nods his head. "He was the best man at our wedding, too."

"Which of them do you find it harder to forgive?"

"I don't know," he says, looking out of the window again. It's spitting with rain, but I'm more focused on Seb than the weather. "I've asked myself that question quite a lot over the last seven years," he says. "Most of the time, I want to blame Pippa, because she was the one who made vows, and promised not to break them. But Dominic and I had known each other since our first day at junior school. I can't understand how he could have done that to me."

"I know this is going to sound like a really stupid question, but if he was your best friend, and she was your wife, you must have lived fairly close-knit lives. Didn't you have any idea what was going on? Were there no signs or clues?"

"It's not a stupid question at all," he says flatly and turns to face me again. "It's another one I've asked myself over and over, wondering what I must have missed."

"And what did you come up with?"

"Nothing. But I think that's because Pippa was always so independent. That was one of the things I most admired about her. She was often out in the evenings, or away at weekends, and I didn't mind that, because I was usually working. I didn't expect her to sit around, waiting for me to finish what I was doing. I liked the fact that she wasn't one of those clingy women who can't move, or breathe, or raise a finger without a man by their side. Women like that have never interested me in the slightest, and I was relieved to find someone who felt the same way. We both valued our independence and got on with what we wanted to do. That's how it had always been, and it worked for us… or I thought it did."

"And it didn't occur to you that, when you're in a relationship, you're not supposed to want to lead entirely separate lives?"

"We weren't entirely separate. We did things together, too. But she respected my space, and I respected hers... until my agent cancelled a late afternoon meeting at the last minute. I knew Pippa was going out for the evening, straight from work. She'd made a point of reminding me that morning. So, I thought I'd surprise Dominic, and maybe take him out for a drink, or get a takeaway... only to find Pippa's car outside his house, and the two of them inside, scrabbling to put their clothes back on."

I open my mouth just as the waitress appears at our side, carrying two plates of hot food. In a way, I'm grateful for the interruption. Things were getting quite intense then, and even though seven years have passed since that scene he was describing, I can still feel the hurt pouring off of him.

Chapter Eight

Seb

That's the first time I've said any of that out loud. The last time I talked about it was when it actually happened, and I'd been dreading having to open up to Anna, even though it was my idea in the first place.

The thing is, now it's out there, I'm surprised by how much of a relief it is.

My hands might have been sweating, and my pulse racing, but she was so kind about it all. She even tried to give me a way out, which I couldn't possibly take, not when I'd goaded her into this dinner with the prospect of comparing notes on our pasts.

I'd expected to feel that same lancing pain I've always felt whenever I've even thought about Pippa and Dom, but there was nothing, and in reality, telling Anna has just helped put it all into perspective.

It's in the past. It's over with.

It's time to move on.

I stare down at the plate of delicious food in front of me, the smells wafting up and making my tummy rumble, but I ignore it for a moment and stare across the table at the beautiful woman before me.

"I'm sorry," she says before I can utter a word.

She apologises a lot, even when there's no need, and I don't like how that makes me feel. It suggests someone in her past has convinced her that everything is her fault.

On this occasion, I feel even worse. Her apology bothers me more than all the others, and I shake my head.

"It's okay. I think it's more about wounded pride than anything. At least it is now."

"And then?"

"It hurt. Of course it did. I felt betrayed and belittled, humiliated and annoyed with myself for not seeing it coming… for not seeing those signs which I don't think were there, but which I still imagine I must have missed." I let out a sigh, glancing out of the window again. That's something I've done from time to time during our conversation, so I didn't have to see the sadness in Anna's eyes. Now, I just need the distraction from how lovely she looks, so I can finish what I'm trying to say. "I moped around for a while, drinking too much, discovering it doesn't pay, and only makes you feel worse in the long run. But I'm over her now."

"You are?"

I look back at her. "Yes."

She smiles. "What happened to Pippa and Dominic? Do you know?"

"They got married within a few weeks of our divorce coming through, and they've got three kids now."

She tilts her head, then looks down at her food. "Shall we eat while it's still hot?"

"Definitely."

She helps herself to pepper, passing it to me, and then we both start eating. The pork is exceptional, but as for the mustard sauce…

"I love the sauce, don't you?" Anna says and I nod my head.

"I was just thinking that. It's got exactly the right amount of mustard."

She takes a sip of wine before she forks some potatoes into her mouth and looks up at me again.

"How did you meet your wife?" she asks.

I'd been hoping she'd talk about herself now, but in a way I'm pleased she wants to know more about my past.

I don't mind talking about it so much now, and I think a part of me is hoping her interest might mean she wants to get to know me better.

It's a nice thought, because I feel the same way about her, and as we continue to eat, I lean a little closer.

"A friend introduced us at a party," I say, adding a little more pepper to my dish. "It wasn't Dominic, I hasten to add. He wasn't even in the country at the time, so…" I shake my head, recalling those days, when I'd envied his job in New York, and all the trappings that came with it.

"Did you like her straight away, or was it the same as it was with us, where you hated the sight of her?"

I look up at her. "I've never hated the sight of you. Far from it."

She blushes. "Sorry. It was a turn of phrase. I didn't mean…"

"Don't apologise." I say, interrupting before her guilt runs away with her. "I know we didn't get off to the best start, but that was mostly my fault."

"No, it wasn't."

"Yes, it was. And on the bright side, at least you're prepared to admit to there being an 'us' in all this… or the chance of one."

Her blush deepens, but when I smile, she smiles back, which feels promising.

Oddly enough, I don't think I was looking for anything promising, or for an 'us', when I starting talking to Anna at the bar. I think I was just hoping to stop her from seeing me as her enemy. Now, the idea of there being an 'us' is starting to appeal. In fact, I can't think of anything I want more…

"So which was it?" she asks, getting back to her food and our conversation. "Instant attraction? Or something that needed a little more work?"

"It wasn't like that. Our first meeting was more work-related, if I'm being honest."

"Why? Did you do the same thing?"

"No. Pippa worked in publishing, and at the time, I was just starting out in illustration."

"Just starting out?"

"Yes. I haven't always done this."

"What did you do before, then?"

"I was a graphic designer. By the time I met Pippa, I'd had enough of it. The industry was changing, and I wasn't in the mood to change with it. Besides, I'd just turned thirty and felt like trying something new."

"I see." She frowns, finishing the last of her potatoes.

"You sound confused."

"I'm not. I just don't understand why Pippa being in publishing was significant to your first meeting."

I smile at her. "Because the timing couldn't have been better. I'd just handed in my notice at the graphic design company I'd been working for, and I'd already decided I wanted to illustrate children's books. The problem was, how to get into it."

"You mean you had no work and no prospects, but you'd handed in your notice, anyway?"

"Yes. I have occasionally been known to do crazy things like that."

She smiles and I smile back. "Can I assume Pippa worked for a children's book publisher and fortuitously arrived on the scene with a contract in her hand?"

"No. Far from it. Her employers were academic publishers. They were based in Oxford, not too far from where I lived."

"You're from Oxford?"

"Not originally. I went to university there, and liked it so much, I stayed on."

"I see."

"Do you?"

"Not really." We both laugh. "I can understand your fascination with Oxford, but I still don't see the connection between her being in academic publishing and you wanting to illustrate children's books."

"She had contacts," I say. "And she was willing to share them."

"In return for what?" she asks, her lips twisting upward at the corners.

"Nothing." She seems surprised by that. "It really was purely business when we first met. There wasn't anything else between us, other than my hunger to rob her of any names she was prepared to part with."

"What did you do with them once you'd got them?"

"Made a nuisance of myself."

She chuckles, and pushes her plate to one side, her meal completed. I copy her, leaving just a few potatoes, too full to eat another mouthful.

"Did it lead anywhere?" she asks, sipping at her wine. "I'm assuming it must have done."

"It certainly did. It was a little circuitous, but through one of the people Pippa had put me in touch with, I met an agent called Rodney. I hadn't been looking for an agent, but it turned out he's worth his weight in gold… although I'd never say that to his face. He'd want even more of a percentage than I'm already paying him."

She smiles. "Was he helpful?"

"Very. Once he'd seen my work, he signed me up, and within a couple of weeks, I had my first paying job. That one led to another, and another, and before I knew it, I was snowed under."

"And all because of Pippa."

I tilt my head. "I like to think my talent and hard work might have had something to do with it."

"Of course," she says, holding up her free hand… the one that isn't cradling her wine glass. "You must have met her again, though."

"I did. A few months later, I bumped into the guy who'd held the party. I was telling him how well things were going, and realised I really ought to thank Pippa for the introductions. I asked our mutual friend for her number and called her that weekend. We talked for ages, and while we were talking, I remembered she'd been pretty, and slim, and tall, and… well, you get the picture."

"I do," she says, sighing as she gazes down at the table.

I wonder if I've just said the wrong thing. I almost certainly have, but I hope Anna doesn't think I'm making comparisons. How can I ask, though? We don't know each other well enough. Not yet…

"I suppose I was being shallow, but I asked her to have a drink with me the following day."

"While thinking about how tall, pretty and slim she was?" Anna asks, without a hint of disapproval.

"Naturally." She grins, which makes me feel better about my faux pas. "Drinks led to dinner…"

"That same night?"

"Yes. It transpired she'd been thinking about contacting me, but hadn't been able to think of an excuse. We got on well, and… let's just say things progressed from there."

I'm not about to tell her we had sex on our first date, but judging from her expression, I think she might have guessed. Still, it doesn't need to be put into words.

"And yet it was three years before you got married?"

I have to smile. Not only does that question show she was paying attention earlier, but it proves Anna knows exactly what happened on my first date with Pippa. Okay, maybe not *exactly*, but she knows enough. She knows we didn't hang around.

"She moved into my place after about six months, and I proposed about a year later. The wedding took some planning, though. Pippa wanted all the bells and whistles... and a magician."

"I'm sorry... did you just say you had a magician at your wedding?"

"No. I said Pippa wanted one. I had to draw the line somewhere."

"Was there anything else you said 'no' to?"

"Not an outright 'no'. I've never really liked magicians, so there was no way I was ever going to agree to that, but I also had to curtail her idea for me to hand illustrate every single place setting."

"Excuse me?"

I nod my head, remembering the arguments. "Pippa wanted the place cards for all the guests at the reception dinner to be individually hand drawn, with something that represented each of them. It was a nice idea, but there were eighty people coming to the wedding. There was no way I could get that done and earn a living at the same time. In the end, Dominic came up with the compromise of me illustrating the table centrepieces instead. There were only eight of those... thank goodness."

Anna tilts her head to one side, looking thoughtful. "I suppose, as your best man, Dominic must have been heavily involved in the planning."

"He was. He'd been working in New York when I first met Pippa, and didn't come back until after I'd proposed to her. I couldn't wait to introduce them, and ask him to be my best man… more fool me."

"I'm sure it didn't feel like that at the time."

"No. When we were organising the wedding, it felt like he was the calming influence."

"Did you need one?"

"Sometimes. There were days when it felt as if Pippa was more concerned about the wedding than the marriage, and it was a relief to sit down with Dom and have a glass of wine. He was someone I could talk to… or so I thought."

"When did their affair start?" she asks. "Do you know?" It's an inevitable question, and one I've asked myself more times than I can remember.

"Not really. They both promised they didn't sleep with each other before the wedding."

"Did you believe them?"

"I don't know. I think the thing that made me wonder was the fact that I hadn't asked the question. They'd both blurted it out, as a kind of justification, like they felt it needed to be said. Naturally, that piqued my interest, and I asked if they'd been attracted to each other before Pippa became my wife."

"And?"

"Dom said he had."

"That was honest."

"I wasn't in the mood for giving out prizes for honesty."

"No. I don't expect you were. What did Pippa say?"

"She didn't. I took her silence to mean the feeling was mutual, so I asked if they'd kissed or done anything else before the wedding. Pippa blushed then, and Dom said the most pathetic thing…"

"Why? What did he say?" she asks, and I think back for a moment, remembering the scene… the two of them standing there, Pippa still half dressed, Dom looking embarrassed in a pair of jeans he'd obviously just pulled on, but hadn't fully fastened.

"He said they'd fought the attraction for as long as they could." I hear Anna's sigh as she shakes her head. "As well as being crass, that wasn't even a direct answer, and I struggled not to hit him."

"I can imagine."

"After that, I didn't see the point in asking anything else. Pippa still hadn't got all her clothes on. Dom was standing there, bare chested and blushing, and to say the atmosphere between us was awkward is the understatement of the century."

"It must have been terrible." She leans closer, frowning. "If you don't mind me asking, why did she go through with the wedding, if she and Dominic were so attracted to each other?"

"I honestly don't know. I never got to the bottom of that. Like I say, I didn't feel like talking anymore, so I left them to it and went home."

"What happened after that?"

"I didn't expect her to, but Pippa followed me. She arrived about ten minutes after me and seemed really surprised to find me packing her things."

"You were packing *her* things?" Anna leans back again, looking at me like I just kicked her dog.

"I know it might sound harsh, but the house was mine. She'd moved into it before we even got engaged, and we never got around to putting it in our joint names. She was the one who had the affair, not me, so I didn't really see why I should be the one to leave."

"I suppose I can see your point."

"Pippa couldn't, just like she couldn't understand when I said I wanted a divorce."

"What did she expect?"

"I don't know. I was too busy packing her things to give it much thought. Once I was done, I threw her cases down the stairs and told her to go back to him."

"Which she obviously did."

"Yes."

"And what did you do?"

"For a long time, I moped around, trying to work out where it had gone wrong. I kept thinking it had to be my fault... assuming that, because I'd been so wrapped up in work, she must have felt neglected."

"Had you been? Wrapped up in work, I mean?"

"Yes. At the beginning, I was making a name for myself, building a reputation in the business. Then, once I became more successful, it was all about deadlines. Things could get chaotic from time to time, and I'll admit I spent a lot of hours at my drawing board, and not so many with Pippa."

"Did you ask her if that was a contributing factor?"

"Not at the time. I was too hurt to speak to her for quite a while, but when the divorce was going through, we needed to have a conversation about some of the furniture, and I swallowed my pride and asked her why. I needed to know where I'd gone wrong."

"What did she say?"

"She didn't give me a definitive explanation, but she said I hadn't done anything wrong. She'd understood how important my work was to me when she moved in, and she didn't have a problem with it. I remember her saying one of the things she liked most about our relationship was that we didn't lean too heavily on each other. We'd both agreed on that, it seemed. She said she was happy for me to do my thing, and she liked that I was happy for her to do hers. Naturally, I wanted to point out that it hadn't gone too well in the end... because her 'thing' had involved screwing my best friend. I held my tongue, though. We were trying to be civil to each other."

"How did that work?"

I tilt my head one way and then the other. "Moderately well. I couldn't forgive either of them, or forget what they'd done, but I wasn't vindictive about any of it."

She frowns. "You threw her out, Seb."

"Can you blame me?"

"No, but…"

"I didn't leave her with nothing," I say, feeling the need to defend myself. "The house might have been mine, but I was ready to acknowledge that if we'd ever moved, we'd have bought a place together, in our joint names. The fact that we'd never done that wasn't anyone's fault. So, I paid her a lump sum. I had to re-mortgage to do it, but it seemed like the right thing to do."

"Sorry. I didn't mean to sound like I was judging you."

"It's okay."

"So she never explained why she'd started the affair with Dominic?"

I shake my head. "We only talked about it once more. She'd come to the house to pick up some things she'd left in the attic, which had somehow been forgotten, and as she was leaving, she looked at me and said she still loved me."

"She really said that?"

"Yes, but then she added that she loved Dom more."

Anna raises her eyebrows and puffs out her cheeks, shaking her head. "That must have hurt."

"I don't know. I think I was beyond being hurt by then. It was certainly the closest I came to getting an answer, even if it wasn't one I wanted to hear. Hearing her say that made me feel inadequate, but I wondered afterwards if that was what she wanted."

Anna stares at me for a moment, and I see something in her eyes. It looks like a kind of understanding, although I can't see how that can be. She can't have any idea how it felt to be in that position... can she?

I hope not.

"I assume you didn't have any children?" she says, bringing me back to my senses.

"No. We'd talked about it before we got married, and agreed it was something we both wanted, but after the wedding, Pippa always put me off. She used to say things about her career, needing a bigger house, and waiting for the time to be right, but I realised afterwards, it was because of Dominic." I shake my head. "A child would have changed everything... for all of us."

"It certainly would."

I finish my wine, my story complete, and put down the glass before I sit back in my seat and look across the table at her.

"How did I do?" I ask, and she frowns.

"What does that mean?"

"Does my story give me grounds?"

Her face clears. "Not to be fond of women, you mean?"

"Yes." Although I'm not sure we can even apply that description anymore. I'm becoming more and more fond of the woman opposite me as the evening progresses.

"I suppose so."

"You only suppose so? Why? Is yours so much better?"

She shrugs her shoulders. "That depends on your perspective."

"Tell me, then."

"My story, or my perspective?"

"Both. I've bared my soul. Now it's your turn."

She sighs and I can sense her reluctance. I open my mouth, about to give her the same way out that she gave me earlier, when she leans forward. "I was going to say I was cheated on, but now you've redefined it, I'm not sure I can anymore."

That's a complicated start. "What did the guy do? Did he have an affair?"

"No. At least… no, not really."

He either did, or he didn't. "Then he cheated in some other way?"

"Yes… and no. It's hard to explain. The circumstances were… different."

"In what way?"

"He was married. Not to me, obviously. To someone else."

For a split second, I wonder if I can have heard her right. She definitely said the word 'married' then. I know she did, and it takes just a moment longer for my blood to turn to ice, and then ignite, like a volcano. The sensation is jarring, and I push my chair back, shaking my head at her as I stand and lean over the table.

"What's wrong with you?" I raise my voice, unable to help myself, even though the shock makes Anna jump. "You're no better than Pippa. Do you expect my sympathy or something? Because you're not going to get it. You're the kind of woman I despise… the type who doesn't care what she does, or who she hurts, just as long as she's getting what she wants, when she wants it."

There are tears in Anna's eyes and the sight of them makes me stop, breathing hard.

She's staring up at me, her bottom lip trembling, but I can't bear to look at her anymore.

With a shake of my head, I grab my coat from the back of my chair and stride straight out of the pub.

Chapter Nine

Anna

I stare after his retreating figure, even as he blurs, and then disappears through the door, letting it slam behind him.

So much for being a gentleman.

I don't bother to look around. The silence that's descended across the entire pub is enough of a clue that I've become the centre of attention. Jasper's standing now, circling around my feet, clearly as disturbed as everyone else. I can feel people staring at me, and then the beginnings of a few murmured words, and I struggle not to cry, knowing what they will have heard. *The kind of woman who hurts people to get what she wants.* That was what he said, and to make it worse, he didn't even give me the chance to tell my story. He heard that Fergus had been married and blew up at me... just like that.

I sat and listened to everything he said about Pippa. Even when he revealed how he'd been so attracted to her, because she was tall and pretty and slim... in other words, the polar opposite of me. I got his not-so-subtle hint that they'd made love on their first date, too.

Why would he have said all that when he'd just been talking about 'us'? Or about the chance of an 'us'? Didn't he realise how insensitive he was being?

I tried to make light of it… to make allowances for the fact that he was in the middle of a difficult story, and perhaps not thinking straight, but even so…

I didn't need that much detail.

And I certainly didn't need that explosion of temper.

Just because his ex-wife cheated – or had an affair – he had no right to humiliate me in public.

I can't stay here any longer, though. It's bad enough that Sebastian so clearly despises me. I don't need the people of Porthgarrion gossiping behind my back as well.

I swallow down my tears and stand, picking up my coat from the back of my chair. I take two attempts to free Jasper's lead from the leg, and then I glance down at the empty plates and wine glasses, realising someone's going to have to pay for what we've eaten and drunk this evening… and that the 'someone' in question will have to be me.

I'm not even to be allowed a dignified exit.

As if I had any dignity left.

I take a deep breath, walking up to the bar. There are a few people sitting there, but they all turn away, or suddenly pretend to make conversation. I feel shunned, even though I've done nothing wrong, and I wish I could just leave, even though I can't.

"Are you okay?"

I look up to find Ed staring down at me, concern written all over his face.

I nod my head, unable to speak for a second, and then swallow hard, because I know I have to say something. "What do I owe you?"

He shakes his head. "Don't worry about it."

Oh, God… does he have to be so kind? It only makes things worse.

"No. I want to pay." And get the hell out of here.

He sighs, hesitates for a second, and then nods, turning around and going over to the till. He's back within moments, bringing the card machine with him, along with a till receipt, which he hands to me. I don't even look at it, but just give him my credit card, which he puts into the machine for me, offering it back so I can input my pin number. My hand is shaking, but I manage to get the number right, and he takes the machine back, staring at it for an interminable time, until it spews forth a receipt.

"Do you want me to see you home?" he says, handing the piece of paper to me.

"No, thank you. I'll be fine."

"You're sure?"

I wonder how shocked or upset I must look for him to be so solicitous, when he's busy, and no doubt has much better things to do than take care of me.

"I'm positive. But thank you."

I'm about to turn away, but he coughs, grabbing my attention. "Seb was out of order just then."

"I know he was."

"Most people understand there are two sides to every story."

I glance around, wondering if anyone else shares that point of view. "Hmm… the problem is, I didn't get to tell mine."

I can't hold back my tears any longer and as they fall, I turn around and leave as quickly as I can.

Jasper needs a walk, and although I'd rather go home and cry, I can't. Instead, we make our way along the harbour, both of us relieved it's stopped raining now, and I cry there instead, the lights misting and people blurring. One or two of them slow their steps, like they want to say something to the sobbing woman with the dog, but they clearly think better of it, and pass on their way... thank God.

By the time we get home, I'm exhausted, but I still need to feed Jasper. He sits obediently beside me while I prepare his food, and when I put it on the floor, rather than wolfing it down, like he usually does, he nuzzles up to me, as though he knows something's wrong.

"It's okay, boy," I say, stroking his head. I think he knows I'm lying, but hunger obviously gets the better of him, and after just a moment's pause, he turns his attention to his food.

I clear up and heat myself a mug of hot chocolate in the microwave while Jasper finishes, and once he's done, I settle him in his basket, switch off the lights, and go to bed.

The hot chocolate is supposed to help soothe my nerves and get me off to sleep, but it's not working. My mind is so full of what's happened this evening, there's no chance of sleep claiming me anytime soon.

It's not just Sebastian's outburst that's causing me so much confusion, or that he painted his wife in such glowing terms. It's the whole evening, including the fact that he invited me to dine with him in the first place. He said he wanted to get to know me, and I believed him. Why wouldn't I, when he kept looking at me all the time with those electric blue eyes? There was something about the way he called me 'beautiful' and 'lovely', as though he really meant it. It felt as though he wanted more than dinner and conversation, and despite the odd hiccup, I'm not ashamed to say, I'd been thinking the same thing myself. There was a definite attraction. I could feel it... right until he was so utterly vile to me.

Finishing my hot chocolate, I turn onto my side, hugging my arms around myself. I haven't felt this bad since Fergus and I split up, which is ludicrous, really. Why should I feel bad about Sebastian and his opinions? It's not as though he means anything to me.

A tear falls onto the pillow, but I don't wipe it away. Or the next one, or the next. I hate myself for letting him get to me, but he's opened up that chasm of feelings… the ones that hurt the most, that cut the deepest.

What's worse is, I let him.

I wake feeling dreadful, but I suppose I should be grateful for small mercies. At least I woke up. I don't mean anything melodramatic by that… simply that at least waking means I must have slept. It can't have been for very long, though. I know I was still awake at three-thirty, but who needs more than a couple of hours' sleep, anyway?

My shower isn't even remotely invigorating, and although I wish I could sit at home feeling sorry for myself, that's not an option. I have to get to work… after I've walked Jasper, that is.

"Come on, boy," I say, picking up his lead from the dining table, where I left it last night. He leaps up, obviously more excited by the prospect of the outside world than I am, and once I've secured his lead to his collar, he waits patiently for me to pull on my coat, and then springs out of the door the moment it's opened.

Out of habit, he turns to the right, but I pull him back.

"Not that way. Not today." He looks up at me and tilts his head in the most adorable way. "We're going a different way today," I say, and start up the hill.

He falls into step beside me, but because this isn't our usual route, he stops at every single lamppost, just to check them out.

I don't mind. We've got time, and he seems quite happy.

At the top of the road, I turn left. The footpath ends abruptly, and I recall the reason I hate walking this way – especially with Jasper. It's downright dangerous. But I console myself that at least there isn't too much traffic… and there are no obnoxious artists either. That said, I'm pretty sure the entrance to his house is somewhere up here, although we won't be walking that far.

Jasper looks up at me, a definite spring in his step. Despite my misgivings, he seems to be enjoying the new scenery and stops every few paces to sniff at twigs and snuffle in the hedgerows. I suppose it makes a change from lampposts, although I keep a watchful eye on him, to make sure he doesn't run off.

I'm still upset by what happened last night, and I'm livid with Sebastian for not even listening to my story. That chasm he reopened has made me feel like everything that happened between Fergus and me was my fault… like I was the 'mistress', and entirely to blame for everything that took place. I felt like that at the time, and for a long while afterwards, until Stephen convinced me I was wrong, and that my ex was actually just a devious bastard.

As usual, it's Jasper who decides when he's had enough, and the campsite is still quite a long way in the distance when he stops to sniff at something beside the road, and then turns around and heads for home.

"I see. That's it for this morning, is it?" He doesn't look up at me, but keeps his nose down, his tail wagging as usual. He's happy, if nothing else.

My phone rings, making me jump. It's early for anyone to call, and I pull it from my coat pocket, checking the screen. It says 'Stephen', and I frown, connecting the call.

"Is everything okay?" I ask, not bothering with the niceties of a 'hello'.

"Yes." He sounds surprised by my question.

"I don't normally hear from you this early."

"I know. I'm just getting ready for work, and I thought I'd give you a ring to apologise again for last night."

"That's okay."

"It isn't, though. I feel terrible about letting you down, especially as I know how much you hate sitting in pubs by yourself."

"I wasn't…"

I stop talking, wishing I was awake enough to think before speaking.

"Yes, you were. I could hear the noises in the background."

He's misunderstood, but I'm not sure that helps. I can hardly lie to him, or accuse him of hearing things, in which case, I may as well bite the bullet.

"I meant I wasn't alone."

"Oh? Who were you with?"

"Um… a man."

"A man?" he says, and I can hear him smiling, and probably sitting down with a cup of coffee, crossing his legs and settling in to hear all the details. "Do tell."

"There's nothing to tell."

"Why not?"

"Because the man in question was the rudest, most obnoxious individual I've ever had the misfortune to waste an evening on… that's why not."

"Oh." I picture him uncrossing his legs and sitting forward, frowning now. "Who was he?"

"That man I told you about… the one on the harbour."

"And you're surprised he was rude? I thought he was renowned for it."

"So did I, but he convinced me otherwise, and talked me into having dinner with him."

"And then proved you should have trusted your instincts?"

"Something like that. We were having a nice time to start with. He told me about his ex-wife and how she'd had an affair, and I was just going to tell him about Fergus, and what he did, when he flew off the handle at me. The moment I mentioned Fergus was married, he assumed I must be some kind of home-wrecker, and yelled at me in front of an entire pub full of people."

"That's it," he says, and I imagine him standing and puffing out his chest. "I'm going to find this guy and have a word with him."

"No, you're not. If anyone's going to put him straight, it'll be me." *If I can be bothered.*

"But it took you so long to get over what Fergus did, and even now, after all this time, you're not really living your life, are you? You still apologise for everything that happens, whether or not it's your fault. You're a shadow of who you used to be, Anna."

"Thanks."

"You know I'm not criticising. You've come a long way from where you were, but you're not there yet, and for this… this idiot to judge you when he has no idea what happened, it's…"

I can tell how angry he is now. He's probably pacing, pushing his fingers back through his hair, his blood pressure at boiling point.

"You need to calm down, Stephen. It's not your battle. It's mine."

"I know, but you hate confrontation and this guy needs to be told."

"You're not wrong, but in this instance, I'd rather do the telling myself."

I probably won't. Stephen's right, I hate confrontation, and why would I want to talk to a man who has such a low opinion of me? Besides, if I was interested in talking to Sebastian, I wouldn't be avoiding him, would I?

I've done an excellent job, even if I say so myself.
I've made it to Friday, and I haven't seen Sebastian once.

He's clearly a man of habit, so just staying away from the harbour first thing in the morning seems to have done the trick. I thought it might. Let's face it, I'd never met him before last Monday… and I'll be happy if I never see him again.

Admittedly, I haven't enjoyed walking up the winding road towards the campsite every morning, but beggars can't be choosers.

Still, that looks like it'll all be over after today.

Tomorrow is Saturday, so I'll be able to have a bit of a lie-in and take Jasper out along the harbour, like I usually do at weekends. I've never seen Sebastian on any of my Saturday or Sunday walks, but weekends are always much busier, and I imagine he prefers to sketch when there are fewer people about.

On top of that, Ben mentioned last night before we left the office that we should be able to return to our normal hours on Monday.

I can't say I wasn't relieved by that. It's been hard work this week. At least we've achieved a few things, though. The case of the warring neighbours came to an abrupt end yesterday, when the couple on the other side backed down. That was a surprise to both Ben and me, and we still don't know what was behind their capitulation. It could have been that they ran out of money for fighting their case, or simply that they'd had enough of arguing. Who knows? The point is, it's over, and apart from a few loose ends that need tying up, and a fairly significant invoice to be paid to Ben, we can file that one under 'W' for waste of time.

As for Mr and Mrs Green, Ben couldn't find anything obvious in the company's bank accounts, so he's put in a request to Mr Green's solicitors, asking for full disclosure on their client's business expenditure since he and Mrs Green separated. We're still awaiting a response, and while we're waiting, there isn't really very much to do.

The good thing is, with work having calmed down a little, as well as getting an extra hour in bed, I'll be able to get back to my normal routine. I can take my morning walks along the harbour at a later hour, like I used to, without fear of running into Sebastian. Like I say, he seems to be an early bird, and as he was never there before, I can't see why he would be now.

As for today, though, I'm still going in early to help with those property completions, so I'll continue to stick to my alternative route, avoiding the harbour, and walking out towards the campsite. It might be overcast, with rain threatening, but it feels safer to keep away from Sebastian's haunts, even if I doubt he'll be there… not in this weather.

"Are we going?" I say to Jasper, who looks up at me from his basket. I think even he's sensed the drop in temperature and increase in cloud, and isn't too sure about braving the outdoors today. Obedient as ever, though, he trots over and waits for me to attach his lead to his collar. I do up my coat and wrap my scarf around my neck to keep out the wind. It feels necessary today, and once that's done, I open the door, checking I've got my keys and phone in my pocket, before glancing up, my breath catching in my throat when I see Sebastian leaning against the wall opposite, by the door to the police station. It's closed, which isn't surprising at this time of the morning, but he's staring right at me, and pushes himself off of the wall, striding across the road. He's wearing jeans and a cream sweater, thick-soled boots, and that olive green utility-style jacket he always seems to have on. As he gets closer, he puts his hands in his pockets, his eyes never leaving mine.

I have a split second to make a decision. Stay where I am, or duck back inside the house and slam the door in his face. I feel nervous about the former, but the latter seems childish. It's the sort of thing he'd do, and I won't lower myself to that level.

I'll stand my ground. That's what I'll do. And I won't let him get to me.

I stare up at him as he stops right in front of me, although I keep my mouth firmly closed. As far as I'm concerned, he can do the talking, because I've got nothing to say.

He gazes at me for long enough that it becomes uncomfortable, making me wonder if he expects me to speak first. For a second or two, I even ask myself if he's waiting for an apology. If he is, he's in for a long wait, because hell will have to freeze over before I apologise to this man.

Eventually, he lets out a sigh, lowers his eyes to my lips, closes them for a second, and shakes his head. "I'm sorry," he whispers.

"What for?" I'm surprised by how strong my voice is, but decide that even if I don't have anything to say, I'm allowed to ask questions. In fact, I'm damn well entitled.

He frowns. "You know what for."

"I do, but I want you to say it." *You owe me that much, at least.*

"You're going to make me suffer, are you?"

"After you publicly humiliated me? What do you think?"

"Fair enough." He looks down at the space between us, like he's gathering his thoughts, and then raises his head again, his eyes boring into mine. "I'm sorry I jumped to conclusions and judged you without listening to what you had to say."

That's a fairly decent and accurate apology, but it doesn't change a thing as far as I'm concerned.

I step out of the house, forcing him to move back towards the edge of the kerb, and he watches as I pull the door closed.

"I should hope so, too," I say and turn, walking up the hill.

"Is that it?" he calls after me and I spin around, walking backwards still.

"What did you want, Sebastian? Was I supposed to fall at your feet, just because you apologised?"

"No, but…"

He looks so contrite, and so lost, but I don't feel sorry for him, and I don't wait to hear what else he might have to say. Instead, I turn around and continue on my way. I don't quite do a fist pump, although I do smile to myself… but only because he can't see my face.

It feels like a minor moment of triumph, and I don't see why I shouldn't enjoy it.

The wind has picked up, and as Jasper and I reach the top of the hill to turn left, it grabs my scarf, tugging at it.

"Gosh," I mutter and Jasper looks up at me, as though he thinks continuing on our way is a pretty silly idea. "Come on. A bit of wind never hurt anyone."

He lowers his head in resignation, and follows me as I turn left, trying not to think about Sebastian, or how long he might have been waiting outside my flat… or his apology.

There's no point putting the man on a pedestal, just because he showed some human decency for once. I imagine he's regretting it now, though. I didn't bow and scrape to him as he no doubt expected… and it serves him right.

I feel a drip of rain on my cheek, which is quickly followed by another.

"Oh, heck."

My coat doesn't have a hood, and I didn't bring an umbrella, not that I think it would have been much use in this wind.

Within seconds, though, the rain is lashing down, and Jasper decides for me, turning around, and tugging on his lead, making it clear he's going home, even if I'm not.

"Good idea, boy," I say, and follow him, picking up the pace.

I try to make a kind of hood out of my scarf, but give up, my feet squelching in my shoes. As far as I recall, the forecast was for showers, not torrential downpours, and we're practically running by the time we get halfway down Church Lane, relieved that it's not much further until we get home. I'll have to dry my hair and change my clothes before I can go to work, but I should have time. It's not as though Jasper's had a long walk, and I delve into my pocket for my keys, looking up and stopping in my tracks, Jasper letting out a slight yelp as I pull him back, staring at the outline of a man standing opposite my house. He's leaning against the wall, just like Sebastian was earlier, but it can't be him, can it?

Surely not.

Jasper tugs my arm and I start walking again, getting to my front door and opening it before I let Jasper off of his lead, so he can run indoors. I'm about to step over the threshold myself, when I hear my name being called, and turn to find Sebastian is crossing the road again.

He's soaked to the skin, but doesn't break his stride, and steps up on to the pavement, standing by my open door, as I duck inside out of the rain.

"I'm sorry, Anna."

He sounds so desolate, it's hard not to be moved.

"You already said that. I heard you the first time." I might be moved, but I'm still angry.

"Did you?" he asks. "Did you really hear me?"

"I think so. I get that you feel bad about what you did."

The rain is pouring down and part of me wonders if I should invite him in, although I'm reluctant. It feels like a sign of forgiveness, and I'm nowhere near ready for that yet.

"I feel worse than bad," he says, tilting his head, raindrops dripping from his nose. "Have you been avoiding me?"

"I've been walking Jasper a different way for the last few days, if that's what you mean." It's the same thing, but I don't want to admit how much he hurt me, or the steps I've taken to prevent it happening again.

He nods his head. "I see. So you probably wouldn't want to have dinner with me again, would you?"

He's got to be kidding. "Do I look like I need my head examining?"

He flinches slightly, but I fail to see why I should feel guilty for being abrupt with him, after everything he said and did.

"No. You don't. You look beautiful."

"Stop it."

"Stop what?"

"Stop flirting. It won't work."

"Does that mean there's no way you'd reconsider? No way you'd think about giving me a second chance?"

"A second chance at what?"

"Getting to know you… at maybe trying to create that 'us' we were talking about the other night."

"Why would I want to do that? So you can jump down my throat again?"

"I won't jump down your throat, Anna. I promise. But I'd like to listen to your story… if you'll let me."

Chapter Ten

Seb

I don't think I've ever felt as bad as I have over the last couple of days. Even when Pippa and I split up, it didn't feel like this. Perhaps that's because what happened with Pippa wasn't my fault, and there's no-one but me to blame for what I did to Anna.

At the time, I felt justified. I heard her say her ex was married, and I saw red. I flew off the handle, seeing her as another Pippa... or another Dominic. Either way, another home-wrecker. The moment I closed my front door, though, I realised how unfair I'd been. I hadn't listened. I'd just reacted... or over-reacted.

I'd seen tears in Anna's eyes, too. But rather than sitting down and apologising, talking it through, and behaving like an adult, I'd stormed off, like the child I'd momentarily become.

That was no excuse, though. There were no excuses. Which was why I got straight back into my car and returned to the pub. I wanted to say sorry, to make it up to her, if that was possible. I'd enjoyed our evening, and I thought she had too... until that awful ending. It seemed important to ensure that wasn't our ending, and I strode through the door, my heart and feet both turning to lead when I saw the table we'd been sitting at was empty.

The plates were still there, though, along with our glasses and screwed up paper serviettes. It was all exactly as I'd left it. Except Anna wasn't there anymore.

I glanced over at the bar, wondering if she'd decided to get another drink. But there was no sign of her there, either. I pushed my fingers back through my hair, unable to decide what to do. She'd told me she lived in one of the terraced houses opposite the police station, but the problem was, I didn't know which one. I could hardly go knocking on every door, could I? I felt lost, but as I turned to go, Ed caught my eye. There was something about his expression that made me walk up to the bar, and he stood, watching me, his frown set firm.

That's not like Ed. He's always greeted me with a smile. But he didn't that night, so something was clearly wrong.

"You're back then." His voice was unusually gruff. It matched the frown.

"Yes. I take it Anna's gone?"

"She has."

I lowered my head. "I feel like such a loser."

"You won't find any arguments here."

He was being harsh, but I deserved it, and I looked up again. "It was all my fault. What happened between us… Anna wasn't to blame." It felt important that he didn't think she'd done anything wrong.

"I know. It didn't take a genius to work that out."

"Was she okay?" I asked. "When she left, I mean?"

"What do you think?"

"I don't know. That's why I'm asking."

"She was crying, if you must know." I was surprised by how hard it was to breathe when I heard those words. "You hurt her."

"I know," I said, stepping away from the bar. "I know."

I left then. Further conversation seemed unnecessary, and as I went home, I drove slowly past the terraced houses, checking out the ones that had lights on, hoping for a sign of Anna. If I'd seen her, I'd have stopped, but she was nowhere to be found, and I continued on my way, feeling dreadful by the time I parked outside my house.

I sat there for a while, unable to process what I'd done, but having seen the tears in her eyes, I had more than enough imagination to picture Anna crying. I knew I'd hurt her, and it wasn't a good feeling.

I got up earlier than usual the next morning. It was easily done. I hadn't slept, so getting up was a relief. During my wakeful night, I'd decided to go down to the harbour, hoping Anna would walk her dog, and I might be able to persuade her to talk... once I'd apologised, of course.

I sat by the wall, not bothering with the pretence of a sketchpad, but just watching for her. Except she didn't show.

She didn't come yesterday morning either, even though I got there slightly earlier, just in case.

That was when I realised she was avoiding me.

It was also when I realised I had to find a way to see her. Not just because I felt guilty for the way I'd spoken to her, nor because I owed her an apology. I had to see her, simply because I missed her. We might have only shared a single meal together, but I couldn't let that be all there was between us.

I could hardly call at her office, though. Nor could I wait outside it, just in case her boss saw me there, and wondered what I was doing. I felt as though I was in enough trouble already, without the local solicitor questioning me. Besides, taking our personal problems to her work environment would only embarrass her, and I didn't think that would help my cause.

I wracked my brain for a while, trying to figure it out, and in the meantime, I got on with work.

I was surprised I was able to, but the deadline wasn't just beckoning, it was screaming at me. So I finished the stegosaurus, then packaged up all the illustrations and sent them to the publisher, relieved that, not only had I made it by the skin of my teeth, but that I didn't have anything else to do... not immediately, anyway. I hadn't forgotten the new project Rodney had mentioned, but I knew his breakfast meeting with the client wasn't due to happen until today, and there was little chance I'd hear from him until later this morning at the earliest.

With that in mind, I got up at the crack of dawn again, and drove down to the village, taking my place just along from the police station. That might seem almost as foolhardy as standing outside a solicitor's office, but I hoped that Anna would have to come out sooner or later to walk Jasper, and eventually, she did...

Had I expected her to fall at my feet, like she suggested?

Of course not.

Had I expected her to stay and talk?

I'd hoped she might, but when she didn't, and she walked off up Church Lane instead, I decided to wait for her to come back.

I didn't feel as though I'd said everything that needed saying, and besides, I wasn't in the mood for giving in so easily. The least I should do was try harder to make things right with Anna before admitting defeat.

So, I crossed the road and went back to where I'd been standing, leaning against the wall, while I waited.

It started to rain within a few minutes, and not long after that, the rain turned into a downpour. My coat may be practical, but it's not waterproof, and it wasn't long before I was soaked through.

It would have been easy to give in then, and head for home. Anna wouldn't have been any the wiser. But the thing is, I'm stubborn.

Or I can be.

I knew she'd be back, and sure enough, she was.

She looked as wet as I felt, and Jasper didn't seem too pleased about the conditions, either. He took the first opportunity to scamper inside the house the moment Anna opened the door, but she waited while I crossed the road, and although I tried not to read too much into that, I knew she was at least giving me a chance. Either that, or she was just curious about why I was still there.

I explained that. I said 'sorry' again and then told her I wanted her to have dinner with me. That threw her, but I can't blame her for the way she responded. I'd insulted her in public the last time we'd been together. It must have been confusing that I'd want to try again.

That was when I told her she looked beautiful, and she accused me of flirting with her. I didn't deny it, but I seized the opportunity to explain why I wanted to see her again.

It meant swallowing my pride, admitting that I wanted more, and asking for a second chance. But I reasoned to myself that pride is of no use whatsoever when you're miserable… and I was miserable.

She narrowed her eyes at me then, like she didn't trust me, or believe a word I was saying.

"Why would I want to do that?" she said. "So you can jump down my throat again?"

I hated the doubt in her voice, but I deserved every word she was saying, and I knew I'd have to work hard to regain her trust.

"I won't jump down your throat, Anna. I promise. But I'd like to listen to your story… if you'll let me."

"You've remembered that my ex was a married man?" she said.

"Of course." It wasn't something I was likely to forget.

"And you honestly think you can hear my story and not judge me?"

"I can."

She shook her head, her disbelief quite obvious and understandable.

I patted my pockets then, searching for the business cards I always carry with me. I fully expected them to be pulp, but fortunately, I'd put them in an inside pocket, so they were only damp at the edges, and I pulled one out, handing it to her.

"My mobile number's on there," I said, nodding at it as she held it in her hand. "If you want to score a few points by telling me what really happened, give me a call, or text me. I won't judge you, I won't hurt you, and I won't make you cry, either… whatever you tell me."

She looked up at me, tears welling in her eyes, and I wondered if I was about to break my word, but she swallowed hard, blinking a few times, before she took a half step back.

I was being dismissed, and I knew it.

"I'm really sorry, Anna."

She sucked in a breath and nodded her head, closing the door on me.

I stared at it for a few seconds and then walked away.

Soaked to the skin, I've driven home and parked the car, leaving a patch of rainwater on the seat, and have let myself into the house. I'd like to take the time to think over what just happened, but I'm dripping on the floor, and quickly remove my coat as I dash through the living room on my way to the kitchen. I hang it over the back of one of the chairs by the island unit, and then move the seat, so it's close to the radiator. It seems like the most sensible place to dry off the soaking garment.

My jumper's wet, and so are my jeans. I figure I might as well change, and I make my way back through the living room and up the stairs, stripping out of my clothes, then going into the bathroom to dry off with a towel. With a head full of images of

Anna, none of which feel too promising, I put on fresh jeans and a thick shirt.

Despite my problems, it's quite comforting to feel warm and dry, having been so wet, and although I could head straight for my studio, a hot cup of tea would help, so I go back downstairs and put the kettle on, just as my phone beeps.

I glance around, remembering I stupidly left it in my coat pocket. It must be soaked, although the beeping suggests it's still working, and I walk across, pulling it from the pocket, and giving it a wipe on a tea towel before I turn it over, to see I've got a text message.

When I open it, the number is unknown to me. It's not someone on my contacts list, and the message is just one word long. It simply says 'okay'.

"Okay what?" I muse, shaking my head as I type…

— *Who is this?*

It seems like a logical question… one I would have been saved the trouble of asking if the person had just put their name. Somehow I doubt the message is for me anyway, and I put down the phone on the island unit, picking it up a second later when it beeps again.

The response is another single word, but this time, it makes me smile. It says 'Anna', and I sit down on one of the seats, leaning on the island unit.

— *Hi. Sorry. I didn't realise it was you. Are you saying okay to dinner?*

I don't put my phone down this time, but hold on to it, hoping she won't take long to reply.

She doesn't.

— *I'm saying okay to scoring points over dinner.*

I nod my head, a smile forming on my lips.

— *That's fine. I'll meet you in the pub at six-thirty. I'll be the one in sackcloth and ashes.*

She comes back almost immediately.

— ***I hope it's not too uncomfortable for you.***

I respond with a smiling face emoji, to which I don't expect an answer… and I don't get one.

I could sit here all day and just stare at my phone… at those few words which offer so much hope. At least, it feels that way to me. And even if I am reading too much into a simple gesture, I don't care. I want to have hope. For the first time in a very long time, it feels like there's a chance for something better.

Just as long as Anna can forgive me.

Staring at my phone all day wasn't an option.

That was because, not long after I sent that last message to Anna, I got an e-mail from Rodney. He'd had his meeting with Louis, and was sending me the briefing notes for the new project. They were considerable, and I didn't particularly want to read them on my phone, so I made myself a cup of tea and went up to my studio, feeling significantly better than I had for days.

I was impatient to see Anna, but I had work to do, and I opened my laptop so I could read the brief more easily.

To be honest, it wasn't anything too complicated. It was just long-winded, and once I'd finished reading it through, I sat back, working out the best course of action.

The deadline was the biggest surprise of all. It was tighter than I'd have liked. Not silly, but tight. The upside being that the illustrations themselves are simple and the style the client wants is similar to one I've used before.

Despite that, there was one serious fly in the ointment. The client had requested a sample. They wanted to see how I'm going to interpret the author's ideas and put an individual stamp on this book, which will mark it out from its competitors.

And they wanted the sample by Monday.

When I read that, I let out a groan.

Monday?

It felt like a joke, except I knew it wasn't. I knew that, because Rodney had gone so far as to apologise in his e-mail, and explain that he'd tried to get some extra time, but that Louis couldn't accommodate it. Or rather, the author couldn't. He's evidently going on holiday on Wednesday and between them, he and Louis want everything agreed before he leaves.

I didn't particularly need another deadline hanging over me so soon after the previous one. Nor did I want to work all weekend. But it looked like I wouldn't have any choice, and once I'd resigned myself to that fact, I settled down and got on with the sample.

The thrust of this book is to educate children about endangered animals living – or trying to live – in the world's rainforests. Each page will feature a different animal, and for the purposes of the sample, they'd given me free rein to select which of the animals I wanted to illustrate. After some consideration, I went with a harpy eagle. Mostly, that was because, when I looked on the Internet for some inspiration, I found a picture of one, with very ruffled feathers, and a particularly grumpy expression. It gave me an idea for the illustration, and I've been working on it ever since.

I've had to stop, because it's a quarter to six, and I need to get ready to go out, but looking down at my day's achievements, I'm feeling quite pleased with it. There's still a lot more to do, but it's getting there.

I'm hungry now, having worked through lunch, but that doesn't matter. I'll be having dinner soon… with Anna.

I smile, making my way into the bedroom, and then on into the shower, where I strip off. This room is another example of Sean Clayton's obsession with black and white, and derivatives thereof. The tiles are pale grey, the fittings are white, and although it's not entirely to my taste, I love the huge shower, which is separated from the rest of the room by a glass screen.

It's quite luxurious, but I don't take too long. The very last thing I want is to be late, and once I've washed and shampooed my hair, I get out, drying off quickly.

I select yet another pair of jeans and a white shirt, putting them both on, and adding a casual jacket, before going downstairs again.

It's not even ten past six yet, but I'm going to leave now. I'd rather be waiting for Anna when she gets there than make her have to wait for me, and I gather up my wallet and phone from the kitchen and head out of the door.

The drive takes no time at all, and after finding a parking space not too far from the entrance to the pub, I go inside, relieved to find that Ed doesn't seem to be working behind the bar tonight. I'd have faced him if I'd had to, but his disapproval of the other evening is still a little fresh in my mind.

"What can I get you?" the young lady behind the bar asks once she's finished serving a couple further toward the back of the pub.

"A dry white wine, please."

I'm not in the mood for anything heavy this evening, and she nods her head, turning away to get my drink. I stay near the door, so Anna can't miss me, and once the young lady returns with my drink, I ask her to set up a tab.

"You're dining here?" she asks.

"I am, but I'm waiting for someone."

"Okay." She turns away, and I take a sip of wine, surprised by how nervous I feel.

I suppose that's because I know I can't afford to get this wrong. Anna might have been willing to give me a second chance, but if I screw this up, she won't give me a third. Even I know that.

The door opens and I turn, my stomach flipping over, when I see Anna walk it. Her eyes lock on mine within an instant, and although there's nothing affectionate in her gaze, I take heart from the fact that she's here.

She looks amazing, too. She's wearing jeans and a sweater, and is carrying a coat, having clearly gone home to change, and I get up from my stool to greet her.

"Hello," I say, and although she nods her head, she doesn't say a word. "What can I get you to drink?"

"A dry white wine, please."

I raise my hand, and this time it's a young man who comes to serve me, taking my order and returning with the drink in no time at all.

"Shall we find a table?" I ask. It's already getting busy in here, and I glance around, spying a table at the back of the pub. "How about over there?" I ask, pointing it out. It's not the same one we sat at the other night and she glances at it and nods her head.

I pick up her drink and she follows me, dodging between other customers, until we reach the table, where I put down the drinks and turn to her.

"Shall I take your coat?"

She hands it to me and I put it over the back of her chair, which I hold out for her, waiting until she's sat down before I remove my jacket and take a seat opposite her.

There's an awkwardness between us that I don't like, but I won't be defeated by it, and I lean my elbows on the table.

"You didn't bring Jasper with you."

"No. I left work a little earlier than usual and took him for a long walk. It struck me he could fall asleep at home just as easily as he could here."

"I see."

"As long as I'm not out too late, he'll be fine."

I'm not sure if I should take that as a hint that she won't be here for long, or if she's just letting me know that's how things work when you've got a dog.

"Okay," I say, determined not to be downhearted. Or not to show it, anyway. "I guess we should probably look at some menus."

I get up again, fetching them from the bar and I bring them back, handing one to Anna, who opens it, glances down, and takes no time at all before she closes it again and looks up at me.

"You've decided already?" I say and she nods her head.

"I'll have the crab and chilli linguine."

I check the menu, trying not to smile.

"Is that because it's the second most expensive item on here?"

"Yes," she says with complete candour. "I'm not in the mood for a steak. If I was, I'd have asked for that and made you pay the extra six pounds."

I laugh, unable to help myself, and taking her menu, I get up and return to the bar.

The young man comes over, and I place our order, handing back the menus, before I return to Anna, who's just taking a sip of wine.

She looks even more beautiful than usual tonight, and I take a breath, letting it out slowly.

"I'm sorry," I say and she frowns at me.

"I thought we'd already covered your apologies."

"I don't feel as though we did so in enough depth."

"Why not?"

"Because you still haven't said you forgive me. I behaved appallingly. No matter what happened in your past, I didn't have the right to do what I did, or say the things I said, and I'm sorry."

"You apologise very well," she says, surprising me.

"Thank you."

"Is it something you've had a lot of practice at?"

"Not especially."

She leans in, shaking her head. "Do you know what I find hardest?"

"What?"

"That you didn't even wait around to find out the truth. You assumed I had to be in the wrong."

"I know, but as I said this morning, I'd like to hear about it now, if you still want to tell me."

"I thought that was why we were here."

"It is. Partly. Although, if you remember, I also said I'd like a second chance."

I thought her acceptance of my invitation had been her way of saying she was prepared to grant that, but now I'm not so sure and I hold my breath as she tilts her head, her eyes fixed on mine.

"I know you did. But I haven't decided how I feel about that yet."

I guess that told me. "Okay. But just so you know, my aim is to turn one dinner into two… and then into something more."

"That might be your aim, Sebastian, but we've got a long way to go before I'll consider that."

'*We've* got a long way to go'? I like the sound of that and even if she's not falling at my feet, I can't help smiling.

"As a first step, do you think you try calling me Seb again?"

"I'll think about it."

Chapter Eleven

Anna

I know I'm laying it on a little thick, but the humiliation that went along with what he did to me the other night is still too recent a memory for me not to have it at the forefront of my mind. Especially as we're back at the scene of the crime, and I can so easily picture the expression on his face, right before he stormed out.

He was quick to judge.

And to make assumptions.

And no matter what he says, or how many times he repeats the word 'sorry', I'm still not ready to forgive him.

I appreciate my distrust is partly down to Fergus and what he did, and that I shouldn't allow my past to cloud my present. Doing that makes me no better than Sebastian. But at the moment, all he's doing is proving that my negative opinion of men is perfectly justified.

I take a sip of wine to calm my nerves, wondering why I said 'okay' to this. It was probably because I was so busy thinking about scoring points, I forgot that part of the deal was explaining my past. I don't find that easy, no matter how much I want to put him straight, and I gulp down yet more wine, in the hope it'll help.

"Would it make it easier for you to start your story if I asked questions?" Sebastian says and I look up at him. "You seem nervous."

"I am."

"I won't bite your head off again. I promise."

"I know. It's just, this is hard for me." He opens his mouth, but I hold up my hand. "Before you remind me that it can't have been easy for his wife either, try to remember, we don't want to end up back where we were the other night."

"I'm aware of that. I wasn't going to mention his wife. All I was going to say was, I know how you feel. I found it hard to tell you my story, too."

"Oh. Sorry." I feel guilty now for always assuming the worst of him… especially as that's something I keep accusing him of. I sip at my wine again, trying to stop my hand from shaking, as he leans in.

"You don't have to apologise."

I think I probably do, but we can't keep saying 'sorry' all night. It won't get us anywhere.

"I don't know where to start," I say instead, and he smiles.

"I was going to ask where you met him, but I suppose the first thing to cross off the list is whether you knew he was married."

"Of course I didn't."

He frowns at me, shaking his head. "Okay. I get the message. I was just trying to establish whether it was one of those situations where a man convinces a woman that his marriage is over, then persuades her to become his mistress, telling her he'll leave his wife, even though he knows he won't."

"I wasn't his mistress."

"If he was married, and you were——"

"It wasn't like that." I raise my voice a little and he sits back. "I'm sorry."

"Stop apologising, for God's sake."

He holds up his hands. "Please, Anna. I'm just trying to understand."

"Okay." I take a breath, trying to calm down. "Ask me some questions, then."

He nods his head. "What was his name?"

"Fergus."

"And how did you meet?"

"At a bar. I'd gone with some colleagues from work to celebrate someone's birthday, and Fergus was there with his brother and some of their workmates. It was a Friday, so I think they were just there because it was the end of the week. I don't think it was a special occasion for them."

"What did you do back then… for a living, I mean?"

"I was a legal secretary still, but much more junior."

"And where was this?"

"In Gloucester."

He smiles. "You're from Gloucester?" I nod my head. "I know it well," he says and when I tilt my head, looking for an explanation, he adds, "Pippa's family are from Cheltenham."

"Does that mean you have unhappy memories of the place?"

He shrugs his shoulders. "We never lived there ourselves, but I always liked it when we went to visit, and I got on okay with her relations. It wasn't their fault she cheated, and although it made things awkward for a while, I still talk to her brother from time to time."

"Is that how you know about the marriage and the three kids?"

"Yes. Were you wondering about that?"

"It hasn't been keeping me awake at night." After his outburst, it was the least of my worries, but I'll confess to feeling confused by his current knowledge of his ex. That said, I'm not going to admit any such thing to him.

He looks down for a moment, and when he looks up again, I regret my harshness. His eyes are so sad, but before I can apologise, he sighs and says, "So, you lived in Gloucester?"

"I did."

"With your parents, or on your own?"

"With my parents. I'd only just finished university, and I couldn't afford to get a place of my own."

"Did you like your job?"

I smile, which has the same effect on him. "Yes. I loved it. I worked my way up, got promoted a couple of times, gained a few more qualifications, and eventually, by the time I was in my early thirties, I was a paralegal."

"You never wanted to become a solicitor?"

"No. It was hard enough becoming a paralegal. The thought of doing any more training was too daunting for me."

"Don't put yourself down."

"I'm not. I liked what I was doing."

He nods his head, sipping his wine. "And then you met Fergus?"

"Oh, no. I'd already met him by then. Sorry, I skipped forward a bit. I met Fergus when I was twenty-five, and to be honest, he was my first serious boyfriend." I stop talking. Why did I say that out loud? Especially to Sebastian, of all people. I can feel myself blushing, and look down at my glass, wishing the ground would swallow me up.

"Hey..." I hear Sebastian's voice, and wait a second before looking up at him, hoping my blush will have faded. His eyes are filled with sympathy, mixed with confusion. "Why are you embarrassed? I didn't have a serious girlfriend until I was in my mid-twenties."

"Maybe not. But I'll bet you had a few that weren't serious before then."

"I might have done," he says, a cheeky smile appearing on his lips. It's an expression I haven't seen on him before, and it makes him look ten years younger.

"Well, I didn't."

"You didn't what?"

"Have a boyfriend that wasn't serious."

"You mean he was literally your first proper boyfriend?"

"I'd dated," I say quickly, in the hope he won't think I'm a complete loser. "But nothing had ever come of it before."

"More fool the men of Gloucester," he replies, leaning in a little.

His reply makes me smile and for a second or two, we just stare at each other.

"Are you flirting with me again?" I say, to break the moment.

"I didn't admit to flirting with you earlier. Not that I'm dismissing the idea, but I think I need to work a lot harder than that to win you over."

His eyes lock on mine again, and I feel something different. It's like he's pulling me in to him, even though neither of us is moving. I can't let him do that, though. I haven't forgiven him yet.

At that moment, the waitress brings our food. She doesn't ask who wants which one, simply depositing a shallow bowl in front of each of us, and it's then that I notice our dishes are identical.

"You ordered the linguine too?" I say, looking from Seb's bowl to my own.

"Yes. It sounded really nice, and I didn't feel like having steak, either."

"Can I get you anything else?" the waitress asks, and we both shake our heads, although neither of us looks up. We're too busy staring at each other.

She leaves and we both snap out of our trance, picking up cutlery and placing serviettes across our laps, while breathing a little harder than I think we were before.

"So," Seb says, as he wraps some pasta around his fork. "We've established you met Fergus in a pub, when you were twenty-five years old."

"Yes. He introduced himself, and asked me to join him when all my other friends had left."

"Are you saying you hung back in the hope something might happen?"

"Maybe." I'm fairly sure I'm blushing again, but we both ignore it. "He seemed friendly, and very good-looking… and I was clearly shallow."

"Don't say that. There's nothing wrong with having your head turned."

"Maybe not." It feels wrong now, though… with the benefit of hindsight.

"What did Fergus do for a living?" he asks, adding a little pepper to his food.

"He and his brother owned a building firm. I only found out later how big it was, and how many people they employed. That first night, when he told me he was a builder, I imagined him carrying bricks and hammering nails. He certainly had the body for it…" I let my voice fade, my cheeks on fire this time, although Seb's smiling.

"It's good to know you can be as superficial as the rest of us."

"Thanks."

"It wasn't meant as an insult. It was just an observation, that's all. My initial attraction to Pippa was based entirely on how she looked."

I shake my head, enjoying my pasta while we talk. "I don't think either of us should be proud of that, do you?"

"Not especially. I'm just saying you've got nothing to feel embarrassed about."

"I don't."

"Then stop blushing."

I put down my fork and take a sip of wine, although I'm not sure it'll help with my rosy complexion, and then I look up to find Seb's staring at me.

"What's wrong?" I say.

"Nothing."

"Then why are you looking at me like that?"

"If I tell you, you'll only bite my head off."

"Why?"

"Because I was just thinking how beautiful you are. And before you accuse me of being superficial, in this case, nothing could be further from the truth."

I don't know what to say to that… other than, "Thank you."

His smile becomes a grin, and after just a moment, we both get back to our pasta.

"I'm going to assume you and Fergus started dating?" he says.

"Yes. He asked me to have dinner with him the following evening."

"Was he married at the time?"

"He was. But I didn't know that."

"He didn't wear a ring?"

"No."

He nods his head. "If it's not a stupid question, how did you date? How did he fit in seeing you on a regular basis while living any kind of life with his wife?"

"To start with, it wasn't too difficult, I shouldn't think. We were only meeting up a couple of times a week, and I imagine he explained that to his wife by saying he was working late, or seeing friends, or something." His face darkens, and I wonder if his ex-wife ever said things like that to him. "Seb?" I say, and he looks up, his eyes filled with undisguised anger. "I'm sorry if Pippa used excuses like that with you, but if she did, it's not my fault, so don't get cross with me."

"I'm not," he says, his face clearing. "Honestly. I was just remembering what it felt like when I realised how much she'd lied to me. I was working long hours myself, but it never even occurred to me that when she said she was going out for drinks with someone from work, or away for the weekend with an old schoolfriend, that she was really going to see Dom."

"I get that, but try to remember, I'm not the one who lied to you."

He puts down his fork and reaches over, taking my hand in his as he shakes his head. "I'm sorry. I shouldn't be imposing my memories onto your story."

"No, you shouldn't. Our situations are very different, although I realise you can't help remembering things."

"No, I can't. I can be grateful, though."

"What for?"

"Aside from the fact that you're being very understanding, you've started calling me Seb again."

"Yes… well… it felt appropriate."

"Good." His smile widens, as though he knows there's a distinct thaw happening inside me – so much so, I feel like I'm burning up – and then he releases my hand and picks up his fork again. "What happened further down the line?" he asks. "You can't have carried on dating like that indefinitely. Surely you thought about moving in together at some stage."

"We did."

"And what happened?"

"We moved in together."

He drops his fork, sitting back in his seat. "How? I mean, the guy had a wife already. How could you move in with him?"

"Easily. At least, it felt that way at the time." I take a mouthful of pasta and chew on it, while deciding where to start with my explanation, because while I've said it was easy, talking about it isn't. "I suppose we'd been together for about two or three years, when I got the chance to buy a fabulous apartment in a small village about twenty minutes north of Gloucester. It was one of eight in a huge converted Victorian mansion house, and it belonged to the mother of someone I knew at the office, who was going into a nursing home, and although it needed a lot of work, it was so pretty, I just fell in love with it."

"So you bought it?"

"Not exactly. I suppose you could say I felt like my relationship with Fergus was stagnating. We saw each other regularly, but we'd never… we'd never spent the night together."

"Even after a couple of years?" he says, sounding surprised.

"No. I was still living with my parents, and he… he told me he was sharing a flat with his brother. It was difficult." 'Difficult' doesn't really describe what it was like at the time. It was awkward and contrived, and I never felt like I could relax with him, no matter where we found ourselves, whether that was in his car, or a hotel room, or even at my parents' house, when they were on holiday – just the once. It never felt right, and I hoped that if we moved in together, things would improve. They did… a little, but I'm not about to share that information with Seb.

He nods his head. "I can see that."

"I wanted to know if he was serious about us… if we had a future together, so I told him about the apartment, and suggested we could buy it."

"What did he say?"

"He jumped at the idea."

"You're kidding."

"No. He agreed to it, and even came to look around it with me, but when it came to signing the forms and getting the mortgage, he did everything in his company's name."

"To hide it from his wife?"

"At the time, he said it was for tax purposes, and I believed him. I wasn't sure about the prospect of his brother effectively owning part of our home, but Fergus assured me it was just paperwork, and I had nothing to worry about… so I didn't."

Seb nods his head, like he's thinking. "Okay, so you bought a flat together, and you moved in with the guy. But how did that work in practical terms when he was married to someone else?"

"To me, it worked the same way it always had. We only ever saw each other on set days, so nothing changed, except that Fergus actually stayed the night."

"How could he? Didn't his wife notice his sudden absence from home?"

I shake my head and he stares at me, bewildered. "He wasn't absent from home. Either of them. At least no more than he always had been."

"But…"

"Do you remember me saying that his company was a lot bigger than I'd expected?"

"Yes."

"Well… it transpired they had construction sites all over the country, and once we'd started seeing each other regularly, Fergus told me that part of his job was to visit them and check up on things. He explained that he had to spend at least half his working week doing that."

"I see. I'm guessing the reality was that, when he said he was away, he was really with his wife?"

"Yes."

"And you didn't mind spending so much time by yourself?"

"Not really. It was how it had always been for us, and I think you just accept things as 'normal', if you've never known any different. Besides, I was busy myself, what with work, and studying, and fixing up the apartment, to make it how we wanted it."

"Surely one of you – either you or his wife – must have missed out on weekends?"

"No. He split them between us. His week was incredibly regimented. It had to be for him to keep up, I guess."

"How did he manage it?"

"He'd leave me on a Saturday evening, always saying that his first port of call was somewhere miles away, like Edinburgh, or Newcastle, and that he was driving up overnight, so he could rest the next day and get a head-start. I'd be by myself then until Wednesday evening, when he'd always be back home by the time I got in from work."

"And he'd stay until Saturday again?"

"Yes."

Seb shakes his head. "He had it planned out like clockwork, didn't he?"

"He had to."

"What changed?" he asks. "Something must have done."

"I suppose it was turning thirty that did it." I finish the last of my pasta and push the plate to one side before continuing, "I still hadn't qualified as a paralegal, but hitting a big birthday like that, it put things into perspective."

"Because…?"

"Because I wanted to have children."

He pauses with the last forkful of pasta halfway to his mouth, and tips his head. "You didn't want to get married?"

"Yes, I did."

"Did you tell him that?" he asks, eating the pasta, and placing his fork on the plate.

"There was no point. It was something that had already come up before we even started living together, when he told me he wasn't interested in marriage."

"Of course he wasn't." I let out a sigh, which he must be able to hear, because he reaches across the table again, taking my hand. "Sorry. That wasn't meant as a criticism of you."

It felt like it was, but I'm aware of how my interpretations can skew my responses.

"Was it meant as a criticism of him?"

"Yes." I smile at his honesty, and he smiles back, nudging his plate aside, and resting our joined hands on the table. "How did you find out he wasn't interested in marriage? He can't just have dropped it into the conversation while you were wandering around the supermarket."

"No, he didn't. We went to a wedding."

"Seriously? As a couple?"

"Yes. We did a lot of things as a couple, including going to the supermarket… and going on holiday."

"You went on holiday with him? How?"

"His wife would go away once a year with a group of friends. She'd always done it, and after he met me, he'd tie our holidays in with hers. It was quite straightforward, really. We were never away for more than a week, and he always chose the destination, making it like a surprise for me. It seemed very romantic, but with hindsight, I know it was because he couldn't risk me choosing the same resort as his wife."

"I guess not." Seb takes a sip of wine. "We've got sidetracked. You were telling me about a wedding?"

"Yes. It was my immediate boss who was getting married, so I really had no choice in whether I went, and I asked Fergus to come too. The wedding was in Hampshire, close to where her husband's family lived. It was being held on a Saturday, and although he prevaricated a little, he eventually agreed. He even said he'd stay over at the hotel with me, which I hadn't expected."

"He must have had to make an excuse to his wife for not coming home to her at the usual time."

"He must have done, although I don't know what he told her. It was a lovely wedding, and to be honest, it made me wish Fergus would propose to me."

"Did you say something to him?"

"Not in so many words. I just…"

"Dropped a few hints?" he says with a smile.

"Something like that."

"Can I assume he didn't take the bait?"

"He did the exact opposite. He told me in no uncertain terms that he didn't believe in marriage."

"On what grounds?"

"He'd seen too many divorces. That was what he said."

"What did you say?"

"I laughed. The firm I worked for dealt with a lot of family law… handling divorces and all the fallout that comes with them. If he thought he'd seen a lot of sparring couples, he hadn't seen anything compared to me, and I hadn't been put off." I take a sip of wine. "I could see it was pointless trying to change his mind, though, and to be honest, it didn't feel like the end of the world. Lots of people live together and don't get married."

"That's what you told yourself, was it?" I narrow my eyes at him and he holds up his free hand. "Don't get angry with me."

"I'm not. I just hate that you can see through me so easily."

He stares at me for a moment, then sits back. "I was going to get another drink. Do you want one?"

"Yes, please."

He smiles, releasing my hand, and stands, picking up our empty glasses before he goes to the bar. His departure felt quite abrupt, but I don't want to read too much into anything tonight. Not after what happened last time. Maybe he's just thirsty. Or perhaps he needed a break. I know it's not unwelcome as far as I'm concerned, and I sit back, looking out of the window. From here, I can see the sea, rather than the harbour, and even though it's getting dark, it looks as though the wind must have picked up. The waves seem more choppy than they did earlier.

"Here you are." I turn at the sound of Seb's voice as he sits back down, placing a glass of white wine in front of me. He's got what appears to be water in a tall glass with lots of ice.

"You're not having more wine?" I say, and he smiles.

"I'm driving, so I'd better not." I nod my head and pick up my glass, clinking it against his, before we both take a drink and set them down. "So, where were we?" he says.

"I think I was explaining that, even though I knew Fergus didn't want to get married, I still wanted to have children."

"Did you talk to him about it?"

"Of course. My thirtieth birthday had been the previous Friday, and Fergus had taken me out for dinner. It was after he'd gone on the Saturday that I realised time was moving on. I wasn't getting any younger… and so when he came back on the Wednesday, I sat him down and asked how he felt about it."

"It wasn't something you'd discussed before? You'd been together for five years by then."

"I know, but I guess it just never came up." I sit forward slightly and put my hand halfway across the table, hoping he'll take it, which he does, holding it in his. "Maybe if we'd talked about it sooner, I might have realised…" I let my voice fade, trying not to think about all the signs I missed, and whether this was another one.

"Hey… I wasn't suggesting it was your fault. Having the 'children' talk isn't easy. Lots of people avoid it."

"You didn't though, did you?"

"No. And look where that got me." I sigh and he squeezes my hand. "What did Fergus say? When you asked how he felt?"

"He seemed keen. Although he maintained there was no rush."

He shakes his head. "So, you agreed to wait?"

"We did. Everything he said made sense, when he said it. Thirty might have been a milestone for me, but he pointed out that it would be more logical for me to complete all my studies first, and maybe get a year or two of experience under my belt before taking time out to have a family. It was sensible, and I knew that. Just because my body clock was ticking didn't mean we had to listen to it. So, I qualified as a paralegal, my boss even threw me a party at the office, and then I settled down to work. I waited a while, and then, when the clock started ticking a bit louder, I spoke to Fergus again."

"And?"

"He told me he'd been thinking about it, too, but he wasn't sure the apartment was suitable."

"Was it? Or was he making excuses?"

"Looking back, I know he was making excuses, and that if I'd been paying more attention, I'd have been aware of that. But at the time, I didn't see it. And to be fair, he had a point. I loved that place, but it wasn't practical."

"How many bedrooms did it have?"

"Two, but the second one had been converted into an office for Fergus, which he said he really needed. It wasn't bedrooms that were the biggest problem, though. It was the garden, and the management committee."

He shakes his head. "You've lost me."

"The property had a communal garden, and a management committee that looked after it, along with the rest of the common parts of the building. We paid a maintenance fee every year for repairs and upkeep, and they laid down rules about what could and couldn't be done."

"And those rules included not having children?"

"Not exactly. I don't think they could have banned us from doing so, but we'd looked into getting a dog or a cat not long after we'd moved in, and been told in no uncertain terms that there was a very strict 'no pets' policy. Even if there wasn't a 'no children' one, I didn't like the idea of a child not being able to run around outside."

"No. I'm inclined to agree with you there. So, what did you do?"

"Fergus and I talked it through and agreed we needed to find a house. The problem was, we both wanted to stay in the village, and that wasn't easy. Houses didn't come onto the market that often. But I kept trying, and in the meantime, we carried on as we were, like people do. Years passed, and because we weren't unhappy, we let them."

"Things must have come to a head, though."

"They did. Fergus had been juggling the lies for so long, it was only a matter of time before it all collapsed around him."

"How?"

"The first thing was that his mother-in-law died. Obviously, I didn't know he had a mother-in-law back then, but her death meant he had to spend more time with his wife, and not with me."

"How did he manage that?"

"He called me out of the blue one Tuesday and said he wouldn't be able to get home the next day. He said there was a problem at one of the sites, and he didn't know when he'd be back, and then he disappeared on me."

"He disappeared?"

"Yes. I called him every day, but he never had time to talk. Sometimes he wouldn't even answer, and I'd leave a message."

"Did he call you back?"

"Yes, but he'd always have an excuse not to stay on the line for too long."

"And you didn't get suspicious?"

"I thought it was odd, but after a couple of weeks, things went back to normal… which I guess was after the funeral. Then, about two months later, his father became seriously ill. He'd never talked about his parents and, to be honest, I'd assumed they must be dead. It came as an enormous shock to discover they were both alive, and complete strangers to me, even though I'd been living with Fergus for nearly ten years."

"I can imagine."

I nod my head. "Of course, Fergus's father going into hospital caused all sorts of problems for him. He got the call from his mother when he was with me and, in his shock, he accidentally blurted out what had happened. Naturally, I wanted to help. The hospital wasn't far away, and I offered to go with him. He did his best to sound grateful, but of course, I was the last person he wanted to get involved. How would he explain me to his parents?"

"Exactly. And his wife would have been there, too, wouldn't she?"

"Yes. That's why he refused to let me do anything. He said his relationship with his father was strained and he didn't want me to be a part of it. Except that didn't make sense… not even to me. I couldn't understand why he was away so much visiting his father, if they didn't get on with each other. It didn't add up."

"Did you confront him about it?"

"Not exactly. I—I jumped to the conclusion that he'd made the whole thing up, that he must be having an affair, and I confronted him about that."

"What did he say?"

"He denied it and told me I was being silly."

"I think that's what a lot of them say, isn't it? People who are having affairs, I mean. It's a good way to hide their secrets and lies, by making the other person feel like they're being paranoid."

"I don't know. It's what Fergus said, and he sounded very convincing. I know I felt I was being silly."

"Because he wanted you to."

"Maybe, but at the time, I blamed myself for doubting him. I felt guilty because his dad was sick, and I was accusing him of cheating. It wasn't a good time."

"And none of it was your fault."

"I know. At least, I know that now. Back then, I was just relieved when his dad got better, and we could go back to normal."

"And did you?"

"Yes. Then, not long afterwards, I found a house. It was during my lunch break and I was so excited about it, I called Fergus, even though it was a Wednesday and I was due to see him that evening. He said he was in a meeting, but we'd talk about it later. I was supposed to be working, but I spent most of that afternoon looking at this beautiful house on the estate agent's website, imagining us living there, even though I'd never seen it in the flesh. It was everything we'd talked about, with three lovely bedrooms, and a beautiful garden, and I couldn't wait to get home to him, so we could call the agents and make an appointment. I even left work a bit early. I remember driving home and wondering how long it would take to sell our little apartment, and how quickly we could move into the new place." Seb frowns, tilting his head. "I was thirty-seven by then. I hadn't expected to have to wait so long to start a family… not that it was anyone's fault. Life had just got in the way, or so I believed." I take a gulp of wine. "Until I got home."

"Was he there?"

"Yes. I pulled out my phone to show him the house, but he said he didn't want to talk about it. He sat me on the sofa and said he had something to tell me. I honestly wasn't sure what he was going to say, but the last thing I expected was that he'd say he was married… and had been for over twenty years."

"Twenty years?" I can hear the disbelief in Seb's voice. "He was older than you, then?"

"Yes. By ten years. In the course of his confession, as well as telling me most of the ins and outs of how he'd gone about living a double life, he admitted that he and his wife had known each other since they were at school together. Her name was Heather, and he spoke of her with great affection."

"Even though he'd been seeing you for twelve years?"

"Yes."

"Did they have any kids?"

"They had a son."

Seb's eyes widen in surprise. "A son?"

"Yes. His name was Rupert. He was eighteen, and about to go to university, and that was what had brought everything to a head."

"How?"

"Because Heather had decided she wanted to move out of Gloucester to somewhere quieter… namely to the village where Fergus and I lived. She'd set her heart on it and had found them a house."

"Not the house you'd been looking at?"

"The exact same one. She and Fergus had been there, looking over it, when I'd called him."

"Oh, my God."

"I know. She wanted them to put in an offer straight away, but he'd persuaded her he needed to go over his finances, and it could wait twenty-four hours."

"While he revealed his secret to you?"

"Yes. He had no choice… not if they were going to be living just down the road."

"What did you do? What did you say?"

"I don't remember saying anything. Once his explanations were over, Fergus sat down, with his head in his hands and said his world was crumbling around him, like he wanted me to feel sorry for him. Which I didn't."

"Good."

I smile, although it's an effort. "After a short while, he seemed to come to, and moved closer to me. I can still remember the look on his face when he said that he and Heather moving to the village didn't have to change our relationship."

"Excuse me?"

"He said we'd just have to be more careful, and that obviously we wouldn't be able to go out in public together anymore. He'd still pay his share of the mortgage and the bills, but there wouldn't be any more dinners, or walks, or drinks at the pub… and certainly no more holidays."

"What kind of relationship was he planning, exactly?"

"Certainly not the one I'd grown used to. He kept saying it would be okay, and he'd come round to the house whenever he could."

"Jesus." Seb's gritting his teeth, but I know how he feels. It's how I felt back then. It's how I'm feeling now, reliving it all.

"I couldn't believe what I was hearing. He wanted to treat me like his mistress… no, like a prostitute, really. I was supposed to become someone he visited for sex, who he'd pay to keep, even though I'd always believed I was the only woman in his life… even though I'd been dreaming of us becoming a family."

"Tell me you threw him out."

"You bet I did. He kept arguing his innocence, but I'd stopped listening to him by then. I think I'd stopped feeling too. I was numb with shock. It was only after he'd gone that I realised I'd have to move. If he and his wife were going to be living in the village, I couldn't stay, could I?"

"So you sold the apartment?" he says, looking sad.

"Eventually. It was complicated."

"Because of Fergus?"

I nod my head. "He and his wife got into a bidding war with another family over the house they wanted to buy. It dragged on for a while, and I think Fergus was concerned that if we put our place on the market, Heather might find it. They didn't need much space, with it just being the two of them, and she might have been tempted to go for the easy option."

"What did you do?"

"I moved out and came down here to stay with my brother. That was Stephen's suggestion, and he called Fergus and told him he could take care of the mortgage payments."

"Did he?"

"Yes. He and Heather won the bidding war, and once that was settled, and they'd exchanged contracts on the new house, he put our place up for sale. By then, I was settled here. I'd got a job and found somewhere to live, although I couldn't afford to buy when all my money was tied up in the apartment I'd owned with Fergus."

"You were never tempted to go back to Gloucester?"

"Why?"

"Well… if nothing else, the job prospects have got to be better there."

"Maybe. But I'm happy here."

"Even though you're a qualified paralegal, working as a secretary?"

"Yes. I wouldn't want to go back now, anyway. I felt so used, and so stupid… and so guilty. Without meaning to, I'd been the other woman in someone else's marriage for twelve years, and I hadn't even realised what was going on under my nose."

"That wasn't your fault. You weren't stupid, and you had nothing to feel guilty about."

"Yes, I did. You remember what it felt like to be lied to for years and years, don't you?"

"Yes, I do… but what's your point?"

"It's not to upset you. All I'm saying is, can you try to imagine what it feels like, knowing you're only half the story? I'd been lied to and deceived, just like you, but in my case, there was more to it. There was someone else who had an even greater claim to having been betrayed… by me. Believe me, it's not a good feeling, Seb."

I'm struggling not to cry now, and I lower my head, unable to look at him anymore.

Chapter Twelve

Seb

I'm shocked. Who wouldn't be having heard Anna's story? But it's more than that. I hate the fact that she blames herself so much for everything that happened.

I suppose it makes sense of why she apologises so much, though.

She thinks it's all her fault.

She's trying hard not to cry, and although I'd love to get up, pull her into my arms, and tell her it's over now, I can't. Not because it isn't over, but because it's too soon for things like that.

She hasn't said she's forgiven me yet, and I'm having difficulties forgiving myself now I know what she's been through. I felt bad for judging her before, but having heard what her ex did to her…

I give her a minute, then grip her hand a little tighter until she looks up.

"Are you okay?" I ask.

"Yes." I can tell she isn't, and I need to do something about that, however small.

"You didn't betray anyone, Anna."

"That's not how it felt at the time. He was hers, not mine."

I take a deep breath, unable to deny what she's just said. It was how I felt when I found out about Pippa and Dom. He'd taken what was mine… or that was how I interpreted it, when stupid male pride was all that mattered.

"How does it feel now?" I ask, because I know the benefit of hindsight is a wonderful thing.

"Like something that happened to someone else. At least I'd like to pretend it did… even if I can't."

I can understand that. I often think I'd rather my entire marriage had happened to someone else… but we can't alter history just to suit ourselves. All we can do is learn from it, and I'm trying. I really am.

"I've read about things like that, but I always thought they were made up," I say, wondering if she'd rather talk about her situation in more general terms, to make it less personal.

"No." She shakes her head. "It really happens. It happened to me, although I felt so stupid for not seeing it."

I guess she's not interested in a more generic conversation, then.

"Why do you keep calling yourself stupid?"

"Because it's the truth. Obviously, once Fergus told me what was going on, his behaviour made more sense, but I kept asking myself why I didn't pay more attention… why I didn't see it coming."

"And what did you answer?"

She shrugs her shoulders. "I didn't. I couldn't work it out."

"Exactly. Because you weren't stupid, or blind, or easily led, or any of those things."

"What was I then?" She tilts her head at me. "Why did I let it happen?"

"Because you loved him, like I loved Pippa… and when you love someone, you believe in them. You trust them. And there's nothing wrong with that. It's how love is supposed to be, and if you want my opinion, Fergus played on that."

"Did Pippa?" she asks.

"Probably. She also played on the fact that I'd preoccupied myself with work. That didn't apply in your case, but the point I'm trying to make is that it wasn't you who was stupid, it was Fergus."

She shakes her head. "No, he wasn't. He can't have been. Just the planning and organisation of what he was doing took a great deal of intelligence."

"No, it didn't. He just needed to remember where he was supposed to be, and when… and with whom. He didn't need to be clever for that. Trust me, in the relationship you had with him, he was definitely the stupid one."

"And how do you work that out?"

"Because of the way he treated you. Any man would be a fool to do that to a woman like you."

I know I've probably overstepped the mark, but I don't care. This is about more than stories and comparing notes… at least, it is for me.

She stares at me for a moment, then frowns, which isn't promising, and then she pulls her hand from mine, which is positively scary.

"So would you say a man was a fool if he invited me to have dinner with him, and then yelled at me in public, and stormed off, leaving me to foot the bill?"

"Yes, I would. I'm a fool, and I don't mind admitting it. I'm also really sorry for what I did, although I'm surprised Ed didn't say anything about you paying for dinner."

She glances towards the bar, her frown deepening. "Ed's not here tonight."

"I know. I'm talking about the other night."

"What other night?"

"The night I invited you to have dinner with me, then yelled at you, and stormed off. That night."

"I don't understand. You didn't speak to Ed. You left. In a hurry."

"And then I came back."

"You did?" She's surprised, and it shows. Her frown has faded, and her eyes are wide, with just the slightest hint of a sparkle.

"Yes."

"Why?"

"Because I got home and felt terrible about what I'd done, so I came back to apologise. I wanted to make it up to you, only Ed said you'd already left. What he didn't mention was that you'd paid for dinner."

"And you didn't think it was odd that he didn't ask you to settle the bill?"

"No. I was too busy thinking about the fact that he'd told me you were in tears… and then I was preoccupied with feeling like an even bigger loser than I did already."

She blushes, bites on her bottom lip, and takes a deep breath. "Yes… well…" she says, and although I know she came here to score points, I think I can chalk that one up on my side.

I need all the help I can get.

She glances down at her watch, finishing her drink. I'm not sure if that's a silent reminder that she can't stay for too long, but I'm aware she needs to get back to Jasper. My heart feels a little leaden at the prospect of our evening ending so soon. It might have been difficult, but I've enjoyed her company.

Hearing her story was hard, although I'm sure it was much harder to tell, and while I'll happily acknowledge that her past is far more complicated than mine, that's not the most prominent thought in my mind right now.

What I'm thinking at this very minute is that I don't want her to leave. I'd rather sit here and gaze into her espresso-coloured eyes and count the amber flecks within them. I'd like to make her smile… or maybe even laugh. And I definitely want to see her again.

And again.

And again…

I never thought I'd feel this way after what happened with Pippa. I'd consigned myself to a single life. But no matter how bad it was in the past, I can't think of a single reason not to try for a better future with Anna.

Not anymore.

"I—I should probably leave," she says, and although that's the last thing I want to hear, I can't help smiling at her slight hesitation. Can it mean she wants to stay too, and that she would, if she could?

"I wish you didn't have to." I might as well be honest. Absolutely honest. She smiles, but says nothing. Not that I really expected her to. "I'll just go and pay." I stand, but don't move away. "You won't leave while I've got my back turned, will you?"

"No," she says, shaking her head, although that smile doesn't leave her lips.

"Good."

I wander to the bar, attracting the attention of the young lad who served us earlier. He fetches the bill, and I hand over my debit card, paying as quickly as I can. He thanks me, offering the receipt, and I return to Anna, who's already putting on her coat.

"Can I walk you home?" I ask, pushing my chair under the table.

She looks up, her brow furrowing. "I thought you said you were driving."

"I am. But it won't kill me to walk home with you and then come back here for my car."

"Oh... okay." Her face clears as she's speaking, her lips twitching upward, and I step aside, grabbing my jacket before I let her lead the way out of the pub and onto the harbour.

It's dark and I move to the outside, so she's closer to the buildings as we walk slowly away from the sea and up Church Lane. I know our time is limited. Her house isn't far away at all, but I want to make the most of these last few minutes.

"I hope tonight hasn't been too onerous," I say, looking down at her.

She tips her head back, her eyes fixing on mine. "It could have been worse," she says. "Telling you was a lot easier than telling my brother. It was all still a bit raw then."

"It would have been." A thought suddenly occurs and I stop. Anna stops with me, her confusion obvious.

"Is something wrong?"

"No. I was just thinking. You said Fergus had a brother, too, didn't you?"

"Yes. Clive. What about him?"

"Didn't he realise what was going on? They shared a flat, didn't they? They worked together. Surely he knew what was happening."

"Of course. He knew all about it."

"I'm sorry?"

She shakes her head, looking down at the space between us. "I didn't realise until we came to sell the apartment, but Clive knew exactly what his brother was doing."

"And he didn't think to say something? He must have known Fergus's wife, and you, for that matter."

"He did."

"Then I don't understand. How could he share a flat with Fergus, knowing what he was doing, and keep quiet about it?"

"Because they didn't share a flat. Fergus was married to Heather. He didn't need to live with Clive."

"So that was another of his lies? There was no flat."

"Yes, there was. It's just that they didn't share it."

"Oh, so Clive lived there by himself?"

"No. He used it for…" She stops talking and blushes.

"For what?"

She looks up at me. "What do you think? Clive was married, too… but he saw other women on the side."

"Women? Plural?"

"Yes. They'd meet at the flat."

"How did you find out about this?"

"I didn't. Fergus told me. That was why he said we could never go there when we first started seeing each other… because Clive was always entertaining someone or other."

"Is that what you meant when you said it was difficult?"

"Partly," she says, blushing. "The most ironic part about that was how outraged Fergus sounded whenever he talked about Clive's lifestyle. He used to say how sorry he felt for his sister-in-law, knowing what Clive was doing, when all the time…"

Her voice fades and I move a little closer. "They were two of a kind… good for keeping each other's secrets, but not much else."

She smiles. "That about sums it up."

We turn, taking the last few steps to Anna's house, and she pulls her keys from her handbag. She's about to open the door when I reach out and grab her hand, which makes her gasp, and she spins around, looking up at me. As she opens her mouth to speak, I step closer… so close I can hear her breath hitch.

"Can I come in?" I ask, taking my courage in both hands. "It's still early and I don't want our evening to end yet."

She lets out a long breath, pulling her hand from mine. That's becoming a habit with her, and it's one I don't want us to get into.

"I don't think that's a very good idea," she says.

"Why? Are you worried about what might happen?"

She frowns, her eyes darkening as she takes a step back, straight into the wall behind her. "God, you can be arrogant sometimes."

"I'm not being arrogant. I was just going to say that you've got nothing to worry about. We don't have to do anything… not if you don't want to."

"Says the man who slept with his wife on their first date."

I move closer, and although I don't touch her, I put a hand on the wall above her head, leaning in slightly. "Pippa's not my wife. She's my ex-wife. And this isn't our first date. It's our second."

She narrows her eyes at me. "What does that prove?"

"That I can wait, when I want to."

Her lips twitch, although she tries hard not to smile. "You're incorrigible."

"At least I'm not arrogant anymore."

"I didn't say that."

"No, but you were thinking it." She shakes her head, although she doesn't say a word. "Are you sure you don't want to invite me in?"

"Positive."

"Is that because you've scored your points now, and you don't want to see me again?"

"No."

"Good. So, can I assume you're willing to give me another chance?"

"Not yet."

I move a little closer… close enough that if we both breathed in at the same time, her breasts and my chest would collide in perfect harmony.

"I'm on probation, am I?"

"Yes." She smiles, and I copy her, relieved that at least I'm not out in the cold.

"What about one dinner becoming two?"

"We've already had two dinners, remember?"

"Okay. What about it becoming more?"

She tilts her head. "What did you have in mind?"

That feels like she's flirting, and I take a chance, closing the gap so my body is touching hers. I'm not crushing her. I'm not pinning her to the wall, but we're touching, and every nerve ending in my body is screaming out for more.

"Why don't you come to my place tomorrow night?"

"What for?"

I have a hundred and one ideas rushing through my brain, all of which are incredibly appealing. But I don't want her to think I'm being arrogant… or even incorrigible.

"Dinner," I say and she finally gives in to that smile.

"You mean you can cook?"

"Of course I can cook."

"Okay."

"Okay what? Okay, you'll come for dinner, or okay, you believe I can cook."

"Okay, I'll come for dinner," she says.

I'm so relieved, I can hardly speak, but I have to. "You know how to get to my place?"

"Not really."

"You take the turning on the left after the campsite and follow the track. You can't miss it."

She nods her head. "What time do you want me?"

All the time. "Seven?"

We stare at each other for a moment, and I wonder about kissing her, although I'm not sure I should. Not yet. It might spoil everything, and I don't think I could handle that. We've come so far this evening, but we've still got a way to go yet. First and foremost, I need her to forgive me, and saying 'yes' to dinner isn't the same as saying I'm forgiven.

"I'll see you tomorrow," I say, stepping back, because one of us has to, and she's got a wall behind her.

"Do you need me to bring anything?"

"I don't think so."

"In that case, I'll see you at seven."

She puts the key in the lock, turning it, and although I'd dearly love for her to change her mind about inviting me inside, I know she won't. I move away and wait for her to enter the house, closing the door behind her.

I walk back to the pub, and although I ought to feel relieved and happy, I just feel like a fool. That's got nothing to do with the fact that I'm acting so out of character, practically falling over myself for Anna. Although I have to say, I've never done that with any woman before… not even Pippa. It's also not about Anna scoring almost all the points, either. I don't mind that in the slightest. She deserves it, after what I've done to her. The problem is, I've just realised that, as she didn't bring Jasper with her this evening, she's bound to have to take him for another walk, and if I'd been thinking straight, rather than flirting, and contemplating what might happen next, I could have offered to go with her. It would have given us more time to talk and perhaps offered another opportunity for me to steal a goodnight kiss…

Like I say, I've been a fool.

That's nothing, though, compared to my other mistake of the evening.

I stop, looking up at the inky night sky and wonder what on earth possessed me to say I could cook. The answer is obvious. It was male pride getting in the way of sanity… again. But honestly…

What's wrong with me?

I get back to my car, climbing inside, and clutch the steering wheel, wondering what I'm going to do. There's no way I'm serving Anna cheese on toast, or a ready-meal. I'll have to come up with something... although heaven knows what.

I'm about to start the engine when my phone beeps and I pull it from my pocket, a smile forming on my lips when I see Anna's sent me a message, and I click on it, and read...

— *Sorry. I forgot to thank you for dinner. It was lovely.*

I hit the reply button, and type out...

— *There's nothing to apologise for. Although I'm intrigued... was there a reason you forgot to thank me?*

I know I could just say 'you're welcome', or something equally bland, but I enjoy flirting with her. It may not be something I'm used to, but I'd like to do more of it.

She doesn't come back and I wait, wondering if I've gone too far again, when my phone beeps for a second time.

— *There was a man on my doorstep, distracting me.*

Distracting her? That sounds hopeful. I smile and reply...

— *Maybe you should have invited him in.*

She comes back straight away.

— *Maybe I will next time.*

— *I'm looking forward to it.*

I press send and put my phone down on the passenger seat. The natural response to my message would be something along the lines of 'me too', but I don't think Anna's there yet, and I'm not expecting her to reply.

I turn on the engine, almost jumping out of my skin when my phone beeps, and I clutch it up, reading...

— *Don't get too sure of yourself. I only said 'maybe', and besides, I've yet to taste your cooking.*

She's definitely flirting, and I love it. If only she hadn't reminded me that I can't cook. Even so, I can't leave her message unanswered.

— I'm never sure of myself with you. But I'd like to turn that 'maybe' into a 'yes'.

She comes back straight away this time.

— We'll see. Thank you again for tonight.
— You're welcome.

Maybe I should have said that in the first place. Except I've enjoyed the last few minutes… despite the reminder of my culinary inadequacies.

Okay, so I can keep myself from starving, but heating ready meals isn't cooking… not in the way Anna will expect. Why didn't I just say I'd take her out again?

Because I'm trying to impress her?

Probably.

Because I'm hoping for something a little more intimate than the pub?

Almost certainly.

It's backfired now, though, hasn't it?

What hope is there for intimacy, or even forgiveness, if I give her food poisoning first?

Before I came to bed last night, I set my alarm for six, because even though today is Saturday, I knew I had a lot to do.

And I'm not just talking about dinner with Anna.

I'm talking about Monday's deadline.

That hasn't gone away, and I was only too well aware when I climbed into bed that if I was going to get this sample illustration completed in time, I'd have to spend at least part of today working.

That 'part' has comprised every minute until three o'clock in the afternoon. I'd intended stopping sooner, but I got carried away with the eagle's feathers, and lost track of time. I also forgot to have lunch, but I made a quick cup of tea, and sat at the island unit scouring the Internet in search of something easy to cook for dinner tonight. Refusing to be defeated by my own ineptitude, I found a recipe for citrus Dijon chicken, which seemed simple enough. It came with step-by-step instructions that even an idiot like me couldn't get wrong, and once I'd made a shopping list and finished my tea, I went to the supermarket to buy all the ingredients.

Fortunately, the recipe being simple meant the list wasn't too long, and I got back in plenty of time to marinate the chicken and tidy the house a little, before taking a shower.

I've still got twenty minutes until Anna's due, and as I come downstairs again, I'm feeling pretty pleased with myself.

I follow the instructions, putting the chicken into the oven, and the potatoes on to boil, and double check the wine is chilling in the fridge, just as I hear Anna's car pulling up outside.

Who said cooking was complicated?

I smile to myself, going through to the hall, and pull the door open, as she climbs out of her Volkswagen and turns, looking up at me.

"What a lovely house."

"I know." I smile down at her. She's wearing black trousers and a pale pink sweater, and because she's driven here, she hasn't bothered with a coat, which gives me a chance to look at her properly, and marvel at how stunning she is, although I need to remember to speak… "I can't claim any credit. As I said to you, it's not mine. I just rent it."

"It's still beautiful."

She moves forward, coming up the steps that lead to the front door, and waiting while I stand aside to let her in.

She pauses as I close the door, and I notice her looking around, as she lowers her handbag from her shoulder, letting it fall gently to the floor by the wall.

"The decor isn't exactly to my taste," I explain, and she looks up at me, smiling.

"It's a bit stark, isn't it?"

"It is, but you get used to it."

Her eyes alight on the paintings, and she moves closer to them. "These are nice."

"Thanks."

She turns again, tilting her head. "Did you paint them?"

"Yes. Why? Are you wishing you hadn't said you liked them now?"

"No. It's just I've only ever seen you sketching before. I didn't realise you could paint."

"I can do all sorts of things."

I can even cook… evidently.

"I'm sure you can," she murmurs, fighting her smile, just like she did last night, and while it would be easy to take advantage of her good humour, step closer, and kiss her, I don't want to push my luck. Besides, we've got an entire evening ahead of us, so I should probably pace myself.

"Do you want to come into the kitchen?"

She nods her head, and I lead the way through the living room to our destination. "Oh my. This is lovely," she says as we cross the threshold. She looks around, taking in the white units and grey work surfaces. "Your landlord doesn't have much imagination when it comes to colour, though, does he?"

"No."

"Is the whole house like this?"

"Mostly, although the studio is completely different."

"There's a studio?"

"Yes. At least, I use it as a studio. It was an office before."

"An office? Did your landlord used to work here?"

"He used the room for writing, I believe."

"Writing what?"

I move to the fridge to get out the wine and salad. "Sorry… I haven't explained, have I? The house is owned by Sean Clayton. The novelist."

"Oh, goodness. I didn't realise."

"Have you read any of his books?" I ask, fetching glasses from the cupboard.

"No. But I know who he is. I had no idea he lived here, though."

"I thought everyone in Porthgarrion knew about him."

"Ahh, but I'm not from Porthgarrion," she says, giving me a smile as I open the wine and pour it out.

"Good point." I hand her a glass and we clink them together before taking a sip. Then I put mine down. "I've just got to tip some salad into a bowl, and dinner's ready."

"That sounds like my kind of salad," she says, sitting up on one of the seats by the island unit.

I've bought a pre-prepared salad, because I didn't want to have to test my chopping skills, and find them wanting, and once I've poured it into a bowl, I bring it over.

"I had to work today, so I've cheated a little," I say. It feels like a better excuse than telling Anna I'm incapable of using a kitchen knife.

"I cheat on salads all the time," she replies with a smile, delving into the bowl and retrieving a slice of pepper, which she munches on, looking up at me. "That's when I can face eating them, of course."

"You don't like salad?" Oh, God… have I messed up here?

"No. I quite like it. But I usually only have it when I'm feeling guilty for eating too many bad things, so it has an association of punishment about it."

"Bad things?" I say, tilting my head at her.

"Yes. You know… anything with calories in it."

I smile. "CI can't imagine you've ever needed to worry about your weight."

"No… Fergus did enough worrying for both of us," she murmurs, although she immediately looks up, a blush settling on her cheeks.

"Did he used to criticise?" I ask, our conversation suddenly serious, and after just a second's hesitation, she nods her head. "Then he was even more of an idiot that I thought." I take a slice of cucumber for myself, munching on it. "How do you cheat, exactly? With the salad, I mean?"

"I buy individual ones, rather than wasting time and money getting all the ingredients I'd need to make a salad interesting. It works out cheaper in the end, when you're on your own… especially as the thought of eating salad for more than one meal is a foreign to me."

I laugh at her response. "In that case, we'll have something different next time… something with calories in it."

She smiles and I turn around, opening the oven door and grabbing a tea towel to remove the chicken. I place it on the island unit and Anna leans over.

"That looks a bit pale. Are you sure it's cooked?"

"Positive. It's had five minutes more than the recipe said."

She looks up, frowning. "Do you have a sharp knife?"

"Yes." All the knives are in the block, because I haven't needed to use any of them, and I reach over and grab the smallest of them, giving it to her. She stands, coming around to my side of the unit, and prods the chicken, watching as blood streams out.

"It's nowhere near ready," she says.

Oh, shit.

"Why not? I don't understand."

She spins around and looks at the dials on the oven. "This is set to one hundred degrees," she says, reminding me I left the oven on. "That won't cook anything… not even a meringue."

I'm not sure what meringues have got to do with our dinner, but I join her at the oven, and double check. She's right. The dial is set to one hundred.

"I'm such an idiot. Why didn't I notice? I could have sworn I set it to one-eighty." I look back at the practically raw chicken. "What are we going to do? The potatoes are cooked, and…"

"Don't panic," she says, resting her hand on my arm just for a moment, before she removes it again, and turns the dial up to one hundred and eighty. "Put the chicken back in. It won't take long."

"And the potatoes?"

She ponders for a moment. "Have you got some mayonnaise?"

"Yes."

"In that case, we'll be fine."

I'm glad she thinks so, but I don't say a word and do as she says, returning the chicken to the oven before I wander over to the fridge, surprised to find Anna right behind me.

"Oh, good," she says, reaching around me. "You've got some chives, too."

"I needed them for the marinade."

I don't tell her I used scissors to chop them, because using a knife was too complicated.

"Is it okay if I use the rest of them?" she asks, looking up at me, the bright green chives already in her hand.

"Of course."

I don't know what else I'd have done with them, and as I hand her the mayonnaise and close the fridge, she wanders back to the island unit.

"I'll need a chopping board, a knife, and a bowl that's large enough to hold the potatoes," she says, and I nod my head, fetching everything for her. Then I stand, feeling a little superfluous as I watch her chop the chives with expert precision, before she drains the potatoes. She puts them and the chives into the bowl, adding a good dollop of mayonnaise and mixing everything together.

"Potato salad," I say under my breath, realising at last what she's doing, and she looks up at me, frowning.

"Of course. What else would it be?"

It could have been anything as far as I was concerned, and as I watch her mixing the potatoes, I can't help smiling… and admiring her.

"It's time I confessed," I say, and she drops the spoon, looking up at me, her brow furrowed, and a worried expression on her face.

"Don't say that."

"Why not?"

"It's what Fergus said right before he told me he was married. If you're going to…"

"My confession is a lot less serious than that," I say, interrupting her and she takes a breath, nodding her head, like she's giving me permission to continue. "All I was going to tell you is, I can't cook."

She smiles. "Believe it or not, I'd noticed. Although I'm inclined to ask why you invited me to dinner, if you knew you couldn't cook it, and why you said you could. I'm also intrigued by what you live on."

"The answer to your second question is I eat out a lot, and when I'm here I live on ready meals and things I can put on toast, like cheese and baked beans."

She nods her head. "And the answer to my first question?"

"To be honest, I like you. A lot." 'Like' doesn't really cover it, but if I told her the truth, I don't think she'd believe me. Not yet. She'd probably say I was crazy. She might leave, too. So I'm staying quiet for now.

"You like me?"

"Yes. I hoped that if we could keep seeing each other, you might thaw a little towards me."

"You didn't have to bring me here and poison me to achieve that. We could have met at the pub again, or I could have cooked at my place."

"You didn't seem in the mood for inviting me in… if you remember?"

She blushes and focuses on the potatoes for a moment. "Okay. You win that one."

I move closer to her. "That's not my aim. This isn't about scoring points anymore. I'm just saying I'd like to spend some more time with you."

"You've said that before."

"And I'll say it again. I want to get to know you."

"What about your innate distrust of women?"

"I'm having second thoughts about it… at least where you're concerned." I move closer still. "Is your innate distrust of men going to be an issue?"

"I don't think so," she says, looking up at me again. There's something in her eyes… something other than that slight sparkle. I don't know what it is, but it makes me hope.

"Does that mean you've forgiven me?"

"I might have done."

There's a mischievous note to her voice, and she's trying hard not to smile. "Have you been deliberately making me suffer?" I ask, narrowing my eyes at her.

"Maybe." I smile, shaking my head. "You deserved it, Seb."

"I know."

For a moment or two, we just gaze at each other. This means something. I know it does, but before I can say or do anything, she sniffs, and then grabs the tea towel, dashing for the oven.

"Chicken!" she yelps as she pulls out the tray and examines its contents.

"Is it okay?" I ask, joining her.

She nods her head. "I think so." She puts it down, prodding it with the knife again.

"Is it safe to eat?"

"It is," she says. "Why don't you sit down?"

"Because you're supposed to be my guest."

"Hmm... but I'm the one who can cook." She nods towards the seats. "You sit. I'll serve."

I do as I'm told, sitting on the other side of the island unit, while she dishes up the chicken and potato salad onto the plates I'd already put out. Somehow, she makes it look even better than it did in the pictures on the Internet, and once she's done, she joins me.

"Thank you for this," I say, offering her the salad bowl.

"You're welcome."

We both start eating, and after she's taken a mouthful of chicken, she turns to me. "Is something wrong?" I ask.

She shakes her head. "No. On the contrary. I was just going to say the marinade is excellent."

"At least I got something right."

She chuckles and gets back to her food. "You said you had to work today," she says. "Why was that?"

"I've got a new project that's just come in, and the clients want to approve the style I'm going to be using before I make a start. The problem is, they want the sample by Monday, which means I've got to work the weekend."

"I see." She puts down her knife and fork, taking a sip of wine. "Is that something you do often?"

"Not if I can help it. I think I explained, it was something I did when I was married, and I know it was a mistake."

"I don't think you can blame yourself for what happened, even if you were working weekends from time to time."

"It was a bit more often than that, but I don't blame myself in that way. All I'm saying is, if I'd been more focused on my marriage, and put less emphasis on my work, I might have realised things weren't what they seemed." I turn in my seat, so I'm facing her as she puts down her glass. "But you can't talk.

You blame yourself for what Fergus did, even though you're not responsible for any of it."

"I wouldn't say I blame myself, but you're right, I do feel responsible. However you look at it, and however much I might try to deny it, I was his mistress."

"Because that was what he made you. It's not as though you were aware of the situation."

"I know… I know. That's what Stephen kept telling me."

"Then stop assuming guilt. And stop apologising. Too many of your sentences start with the word 'sorry'."

She stares at me for a moment, like she's going to argue, then lets out a breath. "Do we really want to talk about our exes?"

"No. I know I don't."

"What do you want to talk about, then?"

"Us."

"Is there an us?"

"You know I want there to be." I reach over and turn her seat, so she's facing me, our knees touching.

"Even though experience has taught us both that it doesn't always end well?"

I take her hands in mine, holding them between us. "Why are you talking about the end? We haven't even got to the beginning yet. Not properly."

"What marks the beginning, then? We've had two and a half dinners together. How many do we need before we reach the starting point?"

"Dinners don't count," I say, shifting to the edge of my seat. "We can eat until the cows come home. For me, the starting point in any romantic relationship is the first kiss. That's how you know if you're right for each other."

I lean in, releasing her left hand, so I can move my right hand up to cup her face, tilting her head back as my lips meet hers

Chapter Thirteen

Anna

The moment our lips meet, it's as though everything around us stills, even though there are sparks flying. There are. I can feel them… everywhere.

His tongue flicks against my lips and I moan into him, letting him in, wanting more… needing more. He delves with surprising tenderness. Even his beard isn't as sharp or abrasive as I'd thought it might be, and I let my hand drop to his thigh, moving it up, higher and higher. What would be the point in pretending we don't both want this, when it's obvious we do? I think that became apparent last night, when Seb suggested something might happen if I let him into the house. I may have accused him of arrogance, but I won't deny I was tempted to find out what that 'something' might be, and the only reason I didn't act on the temptation was because I wanted to make him suffer a little longer.

I edge closer, just as he pulls back, and I stare up into his eyes, my body on fire, my skin tingling.

"So?" My voice is a breathless whisper.

"So what?" he says, sucking air into his lungs.

"Are we right for each other?"

"I damn well hope so," he growls, and puts his hand behind my head, pulling me close, his lips crushed to mine.

I put both hands on his thighs now, just to stop myself from falling into him… although I don't know why I'm bothering. I wouldn't have a problem with us being that close, and I don't think he'd mind, either.

His tongue isn't delving now; it's darting… discovering, and he stands, leaning over me. I part my legs, relieved I wore trousers and not a dress, as I move my hands to the outside of his thighs and brush them up to his hips. He groans and tilts his head the other way, consuming me. I could do this all night. To be honest, I could do a lot more than this, but before I get too comfortable, Seb pulls back, stuttering out a breath, his eyes wandering over my face, like he can't quite believe what he's seeing.

"Sorry. I got a bit carried away there." He smiles down at me, letting me know he's not sorry at all.

"Don't apologise. I enjoyed it."

His smile twists into a boyish grin as he sits back down again. "I suppose we ought to finish eating, after you went to so much trouble to cook everything."

"I only made a potato salad. You did the rest."

"I almost gave us food poisoning," he says, picking up his fork.

"True." He looks at me and chuckles, and we both get back to our lukewarm chicken. My lips are still tingling and I feel like I'm floating… like nothing is the same as it was when I arrived. It's a lovely sensation, but I have to admit, there's a part of me that can't quite believe it. There's another part of me that's absolutely terrified, and after a couple of mouthfuls, fear gets the better of excitement and anticipation, and I put down my fork again. "Can I say something?"

Seb turns to me. "Of course."

I take a breath, wondering how to phrase this… or if I should just make up something else, rather than revealing what's really on my mind. It doesn't feel right to hold back, but we've only shared two kisses. He'll think I'm mad…

"I'm scared," I say, and he drops his fork, twisting right around so he's facing me again before he takes my hands in his.

"What of?"

"Getting hurt again."

"And you think I'm not? It's hard for both of us. Learning to trust again is going to be difficult."

I suck in a breath, looking down at our joined hands for a second before I raise my head again, our eyes meeting. "I can't play games this time."

"I'm not playing at anything."

"What I'm trying to say is, we have to be honest with each other… about everything."

"I agree." He purses his lips, then opens his mouth, like he wants to say something else, but I pull my hand from his and rest it on his thigh, which seems to stop him, mid-thought.

"With that in mind, would it… would it be too much – or too soon – for me to tell you I think I'm falling for you?"

He stares at me for a second, then grabs my hand back, raising them both, and letting his lips brush over my fingers.

"It's not too much, or too soon," he whispers, without taking his eyes from mine. "To be honest, I was going to say something like that earlier, when I told you I liked you, but I thought you'd probably say I was crazy."

I laugh at the irony of how in tune we are, despite our differences. "I was thinking exactly the same thing. Considering how contrary I've been with you over the last few days, I wasn't sure you'd believe me, but I can't help how I feel… and I don't want to keep it to myself."

"Neither do I." He smiles and leans closer, resting his forehead against mine. "You weren't being contrary. You were being completely justified. I deserved everything you said and did."

"Maybe. But I think I'd rather just forget about that now."

"Me too."

He releases one of my hands, bringing his up to cup my face, and then tilts his head slightly so our noses are touching. He doesn't kiss me, but this feels just as intimate. We're breathing in harmony, and there's an air of anticipation in this which I've never felt before. It's electric and enticing.

Seb leans back before I do, but I don't mind. It still feels like we're connected, and I like that.

"We really should eat," he says, and I nod my head.

This time, we hold hands while eating, as though neither of us is completely ready to let go, and even though the chicken's gone cold, it still tastes good.

Seb clears the plates, once we've both finished, and puts them straight into the dishwasher, before coming back to me.

"Would you like some more wine?" he says, retrieving the bottle from the fridge and holding it up. "We could sit in the sunroom, if you want."

"That sounds very tempting, but I've just realised the time." He turns, glancing at the clock on the microwave.

"What happened to those two hours?" he says, looking back at me.

"I don't know. I suppose we must have been busy enjoying ourselves."

"We must have been." He smiles.

"The downside is, I have to leave."

"Already?" He's crestfallen, and it's obvious. He puts down the wine bottle and steps up beside me. "You can't stay a little longer?"

"I wish I could, but I've got to get back to Jasper."

"Of course." He nods his head, letting out a sigh, and moves closer still. "Can I see you tomorrow?"

"Don't you have to work, so you can get your job finished for Monday?"

"I do, but only during the day."

"Okay. In that case, why don't you come to my place for dinner?"

He smiles. "I'd love to. I'm intrigued to see where you live, and at least you won't have to run out on me to get back for Jasper."

"That's one good reason."

"I can think of another," he says, cupping my face with his hand.

"Hmm… the fact that I can cook."

He chuckles. "That wasn't what I was thinking, but I can see it might have its advantages."

I'm pretty sure I can work out what he was thinking. There's something in his eyes that gives it away… even if he hadn't already mentioned wanting to turn dinner into something more.

He leans in, his lips dusting over mine just gently before he pulls me forward on the seat and lifts me into his arms. I feel I ought to protest, or at least ask if I'm too heavy, but he doesn't seem to have a problem, and as I raise my legs to wrap them around him, he turns, sitting me on the work surface.

I leave my legs where they are, so he's trapped within them, and he raises his hands, capturing my face as he deepens the kiss. I arch my back, my breasts heaving into his chest, and he groans into my mouth, making it clear he wants more. He's not alone. I want more, too.

Except I don't have time… not tonight.

I pull back, leaning away from him, and he gazes down at me.

"Before you say you need to go home, can I just point out that I can't help you down from there? I can't even move… not with your legs wrapped around me like this."

"I know. The only thing is, I've got a problem."

"Oh?" He tilts his head, his lips twitching, like he's trying not to laugh. "Have your legs stopped working? Are they going to be like this permanently? Because if they are, you won't hear any complaints from me."

I giggle, unable to help myself. "No. That's not the problem."

"Then what's wrong?"

"I don't want to leave."

"Okay, then stay."

"I can't."

He scratches his head, as though he's thinking, although I'm not sure he is. There's a twinkle in his eyes that makes me doubt it. "It seems we have a bit of a conundrum."

"Hmm… part of me knows I have to go, but the other part…"

"Yes?"

"The other part would like to stay here and kiss you… forever."

He closes the gap between us, one hand behind my head, the other moving around, just above my backside, pulling me closer to him as his lips touch mine. I raise my hands to his shoulders, letting them rest there, my stomach turning somersaults, my skin tingling with excitement.

He pulls back eventually, and this time, I lower my legs and let my arms fall to my sides.

"I—I wish I didn't have to go, but I do."

"I know," he says, putting his hands on my waist and lifting me down to the floor. "I wouldn't have stopped otherwise."

I smile up at him as he takes my hand, leading me to the front door, where I left my handbag. He bends to pick it up, handing it to me.

"What time shall I come over tomorrow?" he asks, turning to me and putting his hands on my hips.

"Whenever you're ready."

"Okay. I have to get this illustration finished, but if I'm going to be later than seven, I'll call you."

"It's fine. You don't have to worry."

"Yes, I do. It's called being considerate. I'm trying it out for size."

I smile and take a step closer, looking up into his eyes. "I think it'll fit you perfectly."

"I hope so," he says and dips his head, kissing me yet again. I love the way his lips feel on mine, and the way my body reacts to his. It's not like anything else I've ever felt before, and I really don't want to go. If it wasn't for Jasper, I wouldn't…

As I pull back, I let out a long breath. "That's five kisses now."

"And?"

"I thought it only took one to start something… and to find out if we're right for each other."

"It did. The next three were pure pleasure, and that last one was meant to be a goodnight kiss."

"Oh. I see."

"Sorry. Didn't I make that clear?"

"Not really."

"In that case…" He swallows my giggle with yet another kiss and I lean against him as his arms come around me.

"I have to let you go," he whispers as we part with mutual reluctance.

"I wish you wouldn't."

"Don't tempt me."

I step away, hoping to make it easier for both of us. "I never thought leaving would be so hard."

"I never thought letting you go would feel like such a wrench."

"I'll see you tomorrow."

"I can't wait."

"Neither can I."

I back away towards the door, and open it. Seb doesn't move an inch until I'm at the top step. I wonder if he's hoping I'll change my mind and come back inside, even though he knows I have to go. I stop and wait, and after just a second's pause, he comes forward and joins me, walking me to my car, and opening the door for me.

"Drive safely," he says as I get behind the wheel.

"I will." I look up at him, wondering if he'll lean in and kiss me. He doesn't, and in a way I'm relieved. If he did, I think I'd have to stay… and I can't.

I have to concentrate on the narrow lane that leads back to the main road. It's dark, and although the headlights help, I'm not the most confident of drivers. Even so, I take a glance in my rear-view mirror, and see Seb's still standing outside his front door, watching me. He stays there for as long as I can see him.

I might not like driving very much, but at least the journey is short, and in any case, I've got a lot on my mind.

Had I expected things to turn out the way they did tonight? Not in the slightest.

Even if Seb dropped a hint outside my door last night about what might happen if we were alone together, I couldn't have foreseen that being alone with him would feel like it did, and now I'm just bursting with anticipation. So much so, I can't seem to stop smiling.

I'm relieved it's dark when I get home, and that no-one can see me parking my car quite badly, and walking around to the front of the terrace of houses with a daft grin on my face.

It never felt like this when I was with Fergus. I was never this giddy, or silly… or alive.

Jasper leaps up from his basket the moment I open the door and I crouch down to stroke his head.

"Did you miss me? I'm sorry I'm so late, but if you only knew what I've given up to come home, I'm sure you wouldn't mind."

He stares up at me, tilting his head, like he's contemplating that statement, trying to decide how he feels about it, and then he looks up at his lead, hanging from the hook, which is his way of saying apologies are all well and good, but he needs to go out.

I smile, and put down my handbag before attaching the lead to his collar, and then grab my coat. It's too cold to leave the house without one now, and once we're ready, we go straight back out again.

There are still a few people walking along the harbour. They're mostly couples, hand in hand, or arm in arm, looking out to sea, staring at each other and enjoying the romance of this place.

It is romantic, too… although I've never really noticed it before. Probably because I've never had a reason.

Until now.

Jasper seems to be having fun, trotting along, getting attention from a few passers-by, and sniffing at just about every lamppost. But after half an hour, he's had enough, and turns around abruptly, heading for home.

"I see," I say to him. "You want your bed now, do you?"

He looks up at me with such a pitying expression in his eyes, as though he thinks my question is superfluous, and I have to chuckle. To be fair, I should probably go to bed myself. I've got a busy day tomorrow… although how well I'll sleep is anyone's guess.

My mind is too full of Seb to contemplate closing my eyes.

We get back to the flat in no time at all, and I've barely shut the door when I hear my phone beeping.

I could kick myself for leaving it behind, but I quickly release Jasper's lead and rummage through my bag, finding my phone, and turning it over to find I've got three new messages… and they're all from Seb.

I shrug off my coat, hooking it back up, as I click on the first one.

— *Hi. I know you've only been gone for ten minutes, but I miss you already. Pathetic, isn't it? Let me know you got home safely. x*

I smile, sitting on the sofa, and putting my feet up even though Jasper jumps up with me and tries to hog the rest of the couch.

"Seriously?" I look down at him, and he tilts his head, clearly thinking he's as entitled to sit up here as the next person.

I move my feet to make room, and click on the second message.

— *It's been twenty minutes now. I'm getting worried. Let me know you're okay? x*

Oh, God… I should have taken my phone with me.

The third message has only just come in.

— *I'm pacing the kitchen floor now. I've got everything crossed that you took Jasper for a walk and either forgot your phone, or have it on silent. If I don't hear from you in the next ten minutes, I'm coming down there to check you're okay. x*

I shake my head and tap on the reply button.

— *Sorry. You're right. I forgot my phone when I took Jasper out. I didn't mean to make you worry, but I'm absolutely fine. Thank you for caring. You can stand down now ;) x*

He must have his phone in his hand, because his reply is immediate.

— *Thank God for that. And please don't apologise. It's not your fault. You weren't to know I was going to text you… and then panic. You don't have to thank me for caring, either. It's like falling for you. I can't help it. x*

I stare at his words for a second or two, my heart expanding, filling with love for him. Love… already? Who'd have thought?

Should I tell him I'm not falling anymore?

No. Not by text.

And I don't want to call him, either. I'm enjoying this, and besides, who says, "I love you," for the first time over the phone? No-one of my age, that's for sure.

— *Thank you for this evening. I had a lovely time. x*

I press send, wondering if that sounds a bit neutral. It's too late now, though, and he replies quickly yet again.

— *Which part did you enjoy most? The bit where I almost poisoned you, or kissing? x*

I chuckle, deciding to have some fun.

— *You didn't almost poison me. x*

— *Only because you saved the day, and that's not an answer. x*

— *Yes, it is. x*

My phone rings, making me jump. Seb's name is at the top of the screen, and I answer straight away.

"No, it's not," he says.

"What do you want me to say?"

"Tell me you liked my kisses."

"I loved your kisses."

Oh, heck…. the 'L' word slipped out. You see? That's what happens when you're talking, not texting.

I hear him sigh. "That's a relief."

"Were you really worried?"

"Of course I was."

"Why?"

He pauses for a second. "Because I've screwed up in the past. I've made mistakes, not just with Pippa, but with you, and I don't want to get it wrong anymore."

Oh, my goodness. I hadn't expected him to say anything like that.

"You're not getting it wrong, Seb. I loved everything we did tonight. I—I've never enjoyed being kissed as much as I did by you."

"Really?"

"Yes. We promised to be honest with each other, and that's the truth. Your kisses are… intoxicating."

There's a moment's silence and then he says, "I'm so tempted to drive down there and pick up where we left off."

My body tingles at the thought, and I won't say I'm not tempted too, because I am.

"I'd love to say 'yes' to that, but you've got a lot of work to do tomorrow."

"And?"

"And I think I'd rather you weren't distracted by deadlines."

I hear him suck in a deep breath. "I suppose I can see your point. It'll be better to get this illustration done, so I can give you my undivided attention."

"That was what I meant, I suppose. I don't want to sound selfish, but I don't want you to be thinking about anything else other than us when we're together."

"I won't be."

"In which case, I'll see you tomorrow evening, when you've finished your job."

"Okay. Sleep well." I wish we were saying all this face to face, not over the phone, but I'm not going to mention it. He'll only start talking about coming down here again, and I meant everything I just said. I'd rather wait than know he's thinking about something else.

"You too."

I wake to the sound of my phone beeping, and although I'm still feeling drowsy, I turn over and reach for it from the bedside table. I brought it in with me last night when I came to bed, and

I flip it over to find a message from Seb, which I click on, wiping the sleep from my eyes and sitting up a little before I read it.

— **_Good morning. I hope you slept well. I got up a couple of hours ago and made a start on work, so there's no chance of me being late tonight, but I wanted to send you a message to say hello, and let you know I'm thinking about you. x_**

He's absolutely adorable, and I re-read his message, wondering how any of our misunderstandings ever came about. Still, I refuse to dwell on that now, and I let out a satisfied sigh, unable to wipe the smile from my face as I type out my reply.

— **_That's so lovely, Seb. I'm thinking about you too. I hope you got plenty of sleep, despite your early start, and you're not working too hard. x_**

I turn over, snuggling down under the duvet, feeling very pleased with life as my phone beeps again.

— **_What's this? Are you worried I won't have any energy left by tonight? If you are, then don't be. I might be old, but I'm not that old ;) x_**

That wasn't what I'd meant at all, and while I could correct him, it's more fun to play along.

— **_Glad to hear it. x_**

— **_I'd dearly love to prove that to you right this minute, and I would if it wasn't for the fact that I need to get this illustration finished, so I can devote myself entirely to you. x_**

— **_I like the sound of that. x_**

— **_Until tonight... x_**

I send him back a row of three kisses, because I can't think what to say, and I lie back, resting my head on the pillows, staring up at the ceiling, my body humming.

I've always prided myself on being quite sensible, but I feel anything but that at the moment. I feel drunk on love, even though it's only eight o'clock in the morning.

Speaking of which, Seb isn't the only one with a busy day ahead of him, and I throw back the covers and jump out of bed.

Showering takes no time at all, and once I'm dressed in jeans and a jumper, I take Jasper for a walk, and then come back, feeding him before I feed myself on a couple of slices of toast, and a very necessary cup of tea.

With that out of the way, I make the bed and tidy the flat, wondering what Seb will make of it. Compared to his house, it's tiny, but I hope he doesn't feel out of place here. I want us to both feel like we can belong, and fit in, wherever we are.

As the day progresses, I get more and more excited about our evening. I'm not nervous. I'm tingling with anticipation. Let's face it, we both know where our kisses are leading… and I think it's what we both want.

I know I do.

The recipe I've chosen for tonight is something I've made before, because I don't need any last-minute kitchen dramas, and once the preparation is done, I lay the table, and then take a shower.

I decide on a dress, choosing one that's denim coloured, with short sleeves and white embroidery on the bodice. On most women, it would probably be quite short, but on me, it finishes just above my knees, which feels like it's sensible, but not too sensible.

I check my hair looks okay, and put on a little make-up, without going overboard, and then come back out into the kitchen, putting the dinner into the oven and setting the timer, just as the doorbell rings.

It's a little after six-thirty, and I really hope this is Seb, and not someone else, about to ruin our evening together.

I rush to the front of the house, pulling open the door, and smile when I tilt my head up to see him standing there. He looks divine, in dark jeans and a white shirt, with his green coat over the top, and I step back to let him enter. I close the door, and the moment I turn around, he captures me and pulls me into his arms, bending his head as I look up and let our lips clash. His tongue flicks against mine as he holds me tight against him, letting out a soft groan.

He pulls back, gazing into my eyes.

"Sorry. I couldn't wait another second. I've missed you so much."

I smile. "I've missed you, too."

He studies my face, which ought to feel uncomfortable, but doesn't, and then leans away slightly, finally standing back for me to take his coat. "You'll be relieved to know I finished the sample illustration, so I'm all yours," he says, while I hook it up alongside my own.

"Good. At least I'll know your mind isn't otherwise occupied."

"When I'm with you? I don't think that's possible."

He smiles and I smile back. "Would you like some wine?"

"Okay."

He captures my hand before I can walk away, and I lead him through to the kitchen at the back of the house. "Dinner's going to be about thirty minutes," I say, looking at him over my shoulder.

"Do you think we'll be able to find something to do?" he says, grinning.

"Probably."

I open the fridge and he finally releases my hand, letting me pour the wine, and offer him one of the glasses.

"I like your flat," he says, looking towards the living area at the front.

"It's small, but..."

"Perfectly formed," he says, moving closer and looking down at me. "Just like you."

"That's very corny, Seb."

"Really? I've been working on that line all day."

I giggle, leading him to the sofa, where we both sit, and he turns to me, taking my wine and putting it with his on the coffee table in front of us, pulling me closer.

"I'm sorry… I've just got to…" He stops talking, his lips meeting mine in a bruising kiss, which captures my breath. My heart follows and my senses go into overdrive as his hand wanders north from my waist, grazing over the swell of my breast, up to my shoulder, then neck, and finally cheek, cupping it. He tips my head back, leaning over me, and changes the angle of his head, moaning softly as he deepens the kiss. His hand roams back down again, lingering over my breast this time, kneading it gently. Sparks fly through my body, and I edge downwards in my seat. Seb copies me until we're both lying out, side by side. I wrap my leg around him and he moves his hand behind me, resting it on my backside and pulling me on to him. It's impossible not to feel his arousal, and I let out a long sigh, circling my hips. He mirrors my action, then somehow manoeuvres me onto my back, lying on top of me, and taking my hands in his, holding them above my head, on the arm of the sofa. I'm beyond the point of stopping, and I think he is too, just as the alarm sounds on the cooker, making us both jump.

"Can I take it our time's up?" he says, releasing my hands and raising himself above me.

"I'm afraid so."

He huffs out a sigh, and rolls off of me, onto his side, so I can stand. My dress is twisted, and one of us has pulled Seb's shirt from his jeans… probably me, I imagine. His hands seemed to be otherwise occupied, and that thought makes me blush.

"What's wrong?" he asks, sitting up and taking my hand.

"Nothing."

"Then why are you blushing?"

"Let's just say it's been a while since I've done that."

"I know the feeling."

"Was… was it okay?" I ask, suddenly nervous that he might be disappointed.

He stands, looking down at me, and captures my face between his hands. "It was perfect."

I can't help smiling. "It was, wasn't it?" He grins and we stare at each other, breathing hard, until I finally come to my senses. "Dinner!"

He chuckles and lets me go, picking up our wine glasses and following me to the kitchen. "Is there anything I can do?"

"No, I don't think so. If you want to sit at the table, I'll bring everything over."

He turns, taking the wine with him, and makes his way to the dining table, which is between the kitchen and living area, and although he's walked past it a couple of times now, he stops in his tracks, as though he's only seeing it for the first time.

"This is pretty."

I study my handiwork, and realise that while he's not wrong, the scene isn't complete, and I rush over with a box of matches, quickly lighting the candles, and straightening the flowers.

"That's better."

He smiles and puts down the wine, taking a seat, while I go back to the kitchen to dish up our dinner. It doesn't take long, and I carry the plates over, setting them down. Seb looks at his meal, and then at me.

"I know it's chicken again, but I went with what I had in the house, and cooked a recipe I'm familiar with."

His brow furrows. "Are you saying you cooked something that looks and smells this good, and you did it from things you had in your fridge?"

"And the cupboards, yes."

He shakes his head, although he's smiling. "I'm impressed."

"The chicken is stuffed with goat's cheese," I say. "And it's cooked on a bed of spinach and cherry tomatoes, served with parmesan potatoes."

"I didn't think I was hungry for food until you said that."

I giggle and watch as he starts eating, closing his eyes the moment he begins to chew.

"Is it okay?"

"Okay? It's fantastic." He takes a second mouthful, and then a third, while I join in, and then he puts down his fork, sipping his wine.

"Could your wife cook?" I ask, although I don't know why, and he stares at me for a second, slowly replacing the glass on the table.

"She's my ex-wife, and yes, she could." He reaches over, taking my hand in his. "Before you ask, you're way better."

"I wasn't fishing for compliments… I mean, you don't have to say that just because…"

"I'm not saying it for any reason, other than that it's the truth. Pippa could cook, but she was only really any good when she was following a recipe. If she'd faced the debacle you had to deal with last night, she'd have thrown everything in the bin and ordered a take-away."

"All I did was improvise, and make a potato salad. It was nothing special."

"Yes, it was."

He leans in, raising my hand to his lips, and kisses my fingers.

"Shall we finish?" I suggest, and he nods his head.

He takes a couple more mouthfuls before he puts down his cutlery again. "Was there a reason you just mentioned my ex?"

"I don't know."

"You're not worried about her, are you?"

"I'm not aware of being worried. Why? Are you worried about Fergus?"

"A little."

"You've got no need to be." He really hasn't, although I don't know how to say that.

"What if I... what if I'm a disappointment?"

I smile, reaching for his hand, which he gives me. "I don't think that's possible. You're already so much more romantic than he ever was."

He smiles. "No-one's ever called me that before."

"What? Romantic?"

He nods his head and we both start eating again, although we hold hands at the same time, managing with just our forks. "I've never been renowned for having a softer side."

"You surprise me."

"I hope so. Surprises can be good in relationships. I don't think it pays to let things get boring, do you?"

"Probably not. Although I'm not sure I like surprises that much. They've always tended to backfire."

He grips my hand a little tighter. "Not my kind of surprises."

I've suddenly lost my appetite, and I put down my fork, staring across the table at him. He copies me, and then after just a second or two, he stands, holding on to my hand still as he comes around the table and twists my chair, kneeling before me.

He leans in, our tongues meeting before our lips. His kiss is intense, and I shudder as I feel him raise my skirt, and then jump and squeal when his hands connect with the flesh at the top of my thighs.

He pulls back instantly, gazing down at me. "I thought...? Sorry. I mean, if you're not ready yet, you only have to say."

I reach out, tugging at his shirt. "I'm ready, Seb."

He grins, putting his hands behind me and pulling me forward, so I'm right on the edge of the seat. Then he lifts me into his arms and stands up.

"Which way is your bedroom?" he asks.

"Down the corridor."

He walks quickly, straight into my bedroom, and I flick on the light as we pass through the door, looking up into his eyes as he deposits me on the floor beside the bed.

Removing my dress is the work of moments, and he takes a breath before unfastening my bra.

"Oh, my God…" he whispers.

"What's wrong?"

He shakes his head, making me feel self-conscious, and I raise my hands to cover myself, but he pulls them down by my sides, holding them there.

"Don't. Don't hide yourself from me."

"But if you don't like…"

"Don't like? Are you kidding?" He lowers his eyes to my breasts again. "I've never seen anything so perfect in my life."

He doesn't say another word or acknowledge my smile. Instead, he dips his head, running his tongue across my left nipple. I can't hold in my gasp, or the shudder that rocks through my body.

"Do that again. Please?"

"With pleasure."

He repeats the motion, moving from left to right, sometimes gently, sometimes a little harder, and then sucks and nips at me, until I'm quivering, and barely able to stand.

"I need to sit, Seb, before I fall."

He stands upright, smiling down at me. "Why don't we by-pass sitting and lie you down instead?"

I nod my head and he lifts me, lowering me to the mattress, then puts his fingers in the tops of my knickers and, pulls them down, staring at me for a moment before he crawls onto the bed, and pushes my legs apart. He stops on all fours, confusion etched on his face.

"What's wrong?"

"Nothing... it's just I don't know what to do next."

I raise my head, fear rushing through me. "I'm sorry?"

He smiles. "Don't misunderstand. I know what I'm doing, it's just... I'm torn."

"Between what?"

"The need to taste you, and the need to be inside you."

Need? That sounds good.

"If you want to do the latter, you'll have to get undressed."

He nods his head. "Hmm..." He edges backwards, like he's decided to stand and take off his clothes, but then he dips his head at the last minute, running his tongue over that most sensitive spot. My body arches into him.

"Oh, yes... yes..."

"You taste so sweet," he whispers, before he reaches up and rolls my nipple between his fingers and thumb.

"What are you doing to me?"

"Teasing you," he says, flicking his tongue over me repeatedly.

"Why?"

"Because I can."

He stands abruptly, shaking his head, and unfastens his shirt, stopping after two buttons and pulling it over his head, revealing a firm chest with just a dappling of hairs across it. "Why have you stopped?"

"Because I know my limitations."

"And you're reaching them?"

"I'm getting close. I think, before I embarrass myself, I'd better cut to the chase."

I giggle, and he smiles, lowering his jeans and underwear. My breath catches in my throat, but I try to stay calm at the sight of him, and shift back on the bed a little as he crawls up over me.

He leans in to kiss me, but I pull back.

"Oh... don't you want to taste yourself?" he says.

"It's not that. It's just..."

"Just what?"

"Can I ask you something?"

He lowers himself onto his elbows. "You can ask me anything."

"I—I know you and Pippa had sex on your first date, but can I just ask, is that something you've done a lot? I don't just mean before her, but since... always assuming she wasn't your first, obviously."

He frowns slightly and brushes the backs of his fingers down my cheek. "She wasn't my first, by a long way. I was thirty when I met her, remember?"

"Oh, yes."

He smiles. "And I suppose I'd have to say I didn't often hang around."

"I see. What about since your divorce?"

He shakes his head. "I haven't slept with anyone since Pippa and I split up."

I lean back as far as the mattress will allow me. "Y—You haven't?"

"No."

"But that's seven years, isn't it? That's what you said."

"I know. Now maybe you understand what I meant about knowing my limitations."

I smile. "I didn't realise."

"It's not something you forget how to do... just in case you're worried."

"I wasn't."

"Good," he says, leaning in to kiss me. There's a sweetness to his lips, and I put my arms around him, raising my hips, feeling his arousal pressing into me.

"I hope it hasn't been too tortuous for you, having to wait so long," I say as he raises himself above me, and he grins, pressing in to me, making me gasp at the intrusion.

"It's been worth every minute."

Chapter Fourteen

Seb

I meant it when I said I know my limitations, and I'm getting close to them. Really close.

I guess any man would be, though, with the woman he loves thrashing and screaming through her second orgasm. I thought her first would finish me, but I held on, and now… now she's coming apart beneath me, her body writhing and contracting.

The thing is, I want more.

Or maybe it's that I don't want this to end.

That must be it… because I don't.

I want to stay here, and keep doing this, every single minute of every single day, for as long as I live.

Anna calms, catching her breath, and opens her eyes, looking up at me.

"Oh my goodness," she says, grinning. "That was…"

"Amazing." I finish her sentence for her. "But I'm not done with you yet."

Her eyes sparkle and she parts her legs a little wider. "I can't do that again, but don't let me stop you from…"

"You think you can't do it again?" I say, teasing her, leaning in and kissing her perfect lips.

"I know I can't."

I shake my head, raising myself above her again.

"Now, there's a challenge I can't resist."

She puts her hands on my biceps, holding them there. "I mean it, Seb. I've never been able to have more than one orgasm at a time before. Not... I mean..." She stops talking and shakes her head. "Two was more than I ever expected. Three would be impossible."

"No, it wouldn't."

I pull out of her and kneel back, then flip her over onto her front, which makes her giggle.

"What are you doing now?" she says, turning her head so she can speak.

"Wait and see."

I raise her hips off of the bed, just slightly, nudging her legs apart, and enter her again, smiling as she sighs out her pleasure. So much for 'impossible'.

Leaning over her, I change the angle, and as I plunge into her again, she gasps, looking over her shoulder at me.

"What was that?"

"Me. What do you think it was?"

"But it felt so..." I do it again, slightly harder. "Oh, God..."

"Still think you can't come again?"

Her body shudders beneath mine and I smile, knowing it won't take much longer, and watching as she tips over the edge.

"Seb..." Her scream fills the room. She clutches on to the bedding, and I can't hold back a second longer. I might have told Anna I hadn't forgotten what to do, but I must have forgotten something... because I'm not aware of having ever felt anything like this before. There's no control to this. None whatsoever. I've lost my mind, my body... my heart. It's all hers. Every little piece of me is entirely hers.

I struggle to breathe, coming down from the highest of highs, and lower myself a little further, tipping us both onto our sides, her back to my front, and my arms tight around her. My hand finds her breast, and I knead gently, tweaking her divine nipples.

Anna chuckles. "What is it about you and my breasts?" she says, still a little breathless herself.

I kiss the back of her neck. "I told you. They're perfect. They're exactly the right shape. And I love the way your nipples react to the slightest touch."

She twists around slightly, so she can look up into my face. "Thank you."

"It's my pleasure, believe me. Would you…?" I stop talking, wondering if I'm asking too much.

"Would I what?"

"I was going to ask if you'd mind me drawing you."

"Drawing me? What for?"

"For myself," I say, to set her mind at rest. "I'm not about to put a picture of you on public display, but I'd really love to try and capture you, just as you are now… if you'd let me."

"You promise you won't show it to anyone else?"

"Never." I kiss her just briefly. "You're mine."

She smiles. "In that case…"

"You don't mind?"

"If it's what you want."

I smile and kiss her again, slowly pulling out of her. To my surprise, I'm still aroused, but I ignore that for now. Time is of the essence if I'm going to get this sketch right.

I shimmy off of the bed and look down at her perfect prone figure as she lies back on the bed. "Don't move a muscle. I've got a sketch pad in my coat. I won't be a moment."

I don't wait for her reply, but rush through the house to the front door, rummaging through my coat until I find my sketchbook and pencil. Jasper looks up at me from his basket, a confused expression on his face, but I don't have time for conversation, so I just smile and hurry back to Anna, who's exactly where I left her, lying across the bed, her legs parted, her skin flushed.

"Do you want me to lie here, just like this?" she says, looking up as I enter the room.

"Not quite."

I put down my pad and pencil on the end of the bed, and kneel up, adjusting her position just slightly, so one leg is more bent than the other, her back is arched, and she's turning her head, looking in my direction.

"Perfect," I whisper.

"It may be for you, but it's not the most comfortable position in the world," she says.

"I'll just do a rough sketch for now. It won't take long."

I settle at the end of the bed, flipping through the pad until I reach a blank page, and take a breath as I gaze down at her, before putting the pencil to work.

"Tell me what you've been thinking about today," she says, with a hint of a tease in her voice.

"You."

I glance up and lean over, adjusting the position of her left leg.

"What about me?"

I smile, focusing on the sketch. "I've been thinking about our kisses last night," I say, tilting my head. "And about making love with you."

"Was it a disappointment?" she asks, more seriously this time.

"No. Far from it." She smiles. "Try to keep still, sexy."

"I'm not sexy," she says, her smile fading.

"Yes, you are. You're the sexiest woman I've ever seen."

"Do you mean that?" She turns her head completely, looking at me, and I stop drawing.

"Absolutely. We promised we'd tell the truth, and I am."

Her smile returns, and without any prompting from me, she puts her head back where it's meant to be, so I can return to my drawing. I have to smile myself, and after a second or two, she twists just slightly and says, "What are you thinking to make you smile like that?"

"Just how unfounded your insecurities are."

"I'm not insecure."

"Oh? Really? I am."

She turns again, and I stop drawing. "Why? I told you, you've got nothing to worry about. You're everything I've ever wanted, Seb… and more."

I lean over, kissing her lips. "Thank you. That's the nicest thing anyone's ever said to me."

"Then stop worrying."

I think any man would worry in my shoes. But I feel a little better for that, and once she's in position again, I get back to the sketch.

It doesn't take long to complete, and when it's finished, I close the book. "I'll work it up properly later," I say, putting it down alongside the pencil.

"No." Anna sits up, grabbing my arm. "Let me see it. Please?"

"Okay, if you want." I grab the book again, flipping it open, and turn it around. "It's only rough, so don't expect miracles."

She glances down, a gasp leaving her lips, and then raises her eyes to mine. "It's very flattering, Seb. I don't really look like this."

"Yes, you do."

She raises the book, glancing at it again, and shakes her head. "Did you ever draw your wife?" she asks, surprising me.

"I thought you weren't worried about her."

"I'm not. I'm just asking a question."

"Okay. In that case, I'll give you an answer. I drew her a couple of times."

"Nude?" she asks.

"Yes."

"How do I compare?" she asks, lowering the book and gazing into my eyes.

"You're head and shoulders above her."

She shakes her head. "That doesn't make sense, Seb. You told me you were attracted to Pippa because of how she looked. That means she must have been beautiful."

"She was. I'm not going to deny it. But I have to say, for someone who says they're not worried about my ex, or my past, and who claims not to be insecure, I'd love to know where this is all coming from. I admitted to feeling insecure about Fergus…"

"Even though you definitely don't need to be?" she says, interrupting me.

"Yes. You were with him for twelve years. I'm bound to feel like the new kid in town. I'd understand if you felt the same about Pippa… only you say you don't."

"Because I don't. Not really. It's just that you made a point of telling me that Pippa was tall, and slim, and beautiful, and…"

"And that bothers you?"

"Of course it bothers me. If you must know, I thought you were incredibly insensitive to say that."

"Why? It's the truth. Besides, you told me Fergus had the physique of a builder. I knew what you meant by that, and that I could never hope to compete, but…"

"You don't have to," she says, shaking her head. "I'd forgotten I'd said that. It wasn't very sensitive of me, either. I'm…"

"Don't you dare say sorry." I interrupt her inevitable apology as she looks up at me, her eyes glistening, and I take the sketchbook from her, glancing down at it before I turn it around and hold it out to her. "Look at the picture again. Tell me what you see."

"I see a naked woman lying on a bed," she says, looking up at me with a puzzled expression on her face.

I turn the book around, paying more attention to the sketch this time, to the lines of her perfect body, her rounded breasts and hips, her shapely legs, and divine face.

"Do you want to know what I see?" She shrugs her shoulders, and although that's not a 'yes', I'm going to tell her, anyway. "I see a beautiful woman whose eyes make me want to fall into them… who has skin which is so soft that lying in her arms is like being cradled in silk." I point to the picture. "Your face will haunt my dreams, Anna, and your body… it's like nothing I've ever seen, in real life, or on canvas. You make me want more… and more…" I throw the book to the end of the bed, rolling her onto her back and settling between her parted legs as I kiss her. "And so much more…"

I open my eyes to find Anna still in my arms, and I kiss her gently. I'm not trying to wake her. At least, not yet. I'd rather just lie with her for a while.

I was right. Her skin is like silk, and I might as well enjoy it while I can, so I pull her a little closer, unable to stop the smile from forming on my lips as I recall last night, and all the things we did and said.

It was as much of a shock to me as it was to Anna that I managed to make love with her a second time, but I think we both needed the reassurance of it… of knowing it hadn't been a one-off. It definitely wasn't, and if anything, the second time was better than the first. I certainly wasn't as nervous about it, but Anna had told me I had nothing to worry about – twice – by then.

She seemed more relaxed, too, and her orgasms were louder and longer than before, which was gratifying.

Afterwards, once we'd got our breath back, I'd fully expected that we'd fall asleep in each other's arms, and was surprised when she planted a brief kiss on the tip of my nose, got out of bed and started getting dressed. Initially, I panicked, until I remembered we were at her house, and she couldn't possibly be leaving.

"Um… where are you going?" I asked, sitting up in bed.

"I've got to take Jasper for a walk." She looked down as she fastened her bra.

"Can I come with you?"

She smiled, tilting her head. "If you want to."

I knelt up, crawling across the bed to her. "Of course I want to."

I got dressed myself then, and we went out into the living room. Jasper seemed surprised once again, but hid it well, leaping to his feet the moment Anna reached for his lead, which made me chuckle.

"He won't know what to make of this," she said as she opened the door and took my hand.

"He'll just have to get used to it." She looked up at me and smiled, then led me out through the door, which I closed behind us.

The walk itself was quite refreshing, and to be honest, I don't mind doing anything, as long as I'm doing it with Anna. We held hands the whole way, while Jasper trotted ahead of us, sniffing at lampposts, and glancing back every so often as though to check we were both still there.

We'd only been out for twenty minutes when he spun around and headed for home, which made me laugh.

"He often does that," Anna explained, as we fell into step behind him. "Especially at this time of night. It's like he knows he needs the exercise, but he'd rather just get back to bed."

"I can understand the sentiment."

Her eyes sparkled, the innuendo not lost on her. "I'm sure you can."

I put my arm around her then, and she nestled against me, which felt lovely.

The walk back didn't take long and once Jasper was settled in his basket, I helped Anna with her coat, hooking it up alongside Jasper's lead.

She turned then, looking up at me, and rested her hands on my chest. "Is something wrong?" she asked.

"No."

"Then why have you still got your coat on?"

"Because I don't want to make assumptions, Anna. You might not be ready for me to stay the night, and I'm dressed now, so…"

"I'm ready for you to stay the night," she said, silencing me as she reached up and pushed my coat from my shoulders.

I chuckled, taking it off properly and hooking it up, before she took my hand and brought me back to the bedroom. We undressed each other and got into bed, and although we didn't make love again, we kissed for a while, until the need for sleep became too great, and we snuggled down in each other's arms.

That's the last thing I remember, other than a feeling of sublime happiness, which hasn't diminished with the dawn of a new day.

I lean in and kiss her again, taking a little longer over it this time, and smiling when she opens her eyes.

"Hello," she says, a perfect smile forming on her lips.

"Good morning."

She moves closer and I wrap my arms around her, relishing that soft, warm feeling of her body pressed against my own.

"What time is it?" she asks.

I glance at my watch, which I didn't bother to remove last night. "Ten past seven."

"Oh, my God…" She pulls away from me and I let her, smiling as she stumbles out of bed. She looks glorious, even if she is panicking. "I've got to shower, get dressed, walk the dog, and have breakfast… and be at work by eight-thirty."

I kneel up and clamber to the edge of the bed, grabbing her hands. "Would it be easier if I stayed and tried to help, or if I left and let you get on with it?"

She bites on her bottom lip, her eyes dropping downward and widening when she notices my arousal.

"I hate to say it, but it'll probably be better if you leave. That way I can't be tempted."

I reach out, my hands on her hips, as I pull her close. "Does that mean you would be, if I were here?"

She puts her arms around my neck. "Of course," she says, leaning in even closer until our lips meet, our tongues clashing in an instant. "Why do you need to ask? You can't still be feeling insecure… surely."

"Not as much as I was, no."

She tilts her head, gazing into my eyes. "Please don't. You're so much more than he ever was. I promise."

"That's good to know." I dip my head and kiss her, although she pulls away again almost immediately.

"What am I doing? I don't have time for this."

I laugh, kneeling back, and she looks down again, letting out a sigh. "I'll get out of your hair," I say. "But can I see you tonight?"

She nods her head, grinning. "Do you want to come here again?"

"It's probably easier. If you come to my place, you'll have to come back to walk the dog."

"I could bring him with me, I suppose…"

I shake my head. "I don't know how my landlord would feel about that." Her face falls and I reach out, taking her hand. "I can find out, though, if you want?"

"Okay. But for tonight, you'll come here?"

"You couldn't drag me away."

She chuckles and I kneel up again, pulling her into a hug, which becomes a kiss. Within seconds, we're breathless, and she's writhing against me, before she pulls back, shaking her head.

"We have to stop," she says.

"Okay. I'll go."

"I wish you didn't have to."

"I don't have to. I can join you in the shower, if you like?"

"Oh…" She sucks in a breath. "That sounds good."

"But may not be conducive to you getting to work on time?"

"Probably not."

I stand, looking down at her. "Don't worry. We can shower together later."

"You're sure?"

"I'm positive," I say, bending my head to kiss her, but keeping it brief. "What time shall I come over?"

"I'll text you when I leave work, shall I?"

"Okay."

She smiles up at me, and opens her mouth, like she wants to say something, but then clearly remembers the time, and turns away, rushing to the bathroom.

I sit on the edge of the bed, smiling as I hear the shower start, and I pull on my underwear and jeans, shrugging on my shirt and fastening it before I quickly make the bed. It seems like the least I can do, as I helped to make it such a mess, and once I'm done, having found my sketchpad on the floor in the process, I head out of the bedroom and past the bathroom.

"See you tonight, Anna," I say, loud enough for her to hear me.

"Have a good day." Her reply makes me smile. I might be returning to my own home, but this feels so domesticated, which is maybe why I pause before I leave and clear the table. We didn't do it last night, and I can't leave it all to Anna. So, I quickly stack everything beside the sink, hoping it helps, and then I leave, resolving that my first job of the day will be to call the letting agents. I want Anna and I to spend more time together – to spend all our time together, if the truth be told – and that means I need to find out how Sean Clayton feels about dogs.

I climb out of the shower, wrapping a towel around my hips and shaking the water from my hair. It wasn't such a good idea to call the agents first, after all. Aside from the fact that it was too early when I got back here, my priority was a shower and a change of clothes… not to mention breakfast. Anna and I didn't finish dinner last night, and given everything we did instead of eating, I think I'm allowed to be a little peckish.

I'm also allowed to be a little surprised. At least, I think I am. After all, considering where we started off, who'd have thought we would end up like this?

Come to that, who'd have thought I'd ever want to share my life with a woman again, or find love a second time around? It seems beyond belief that I could find such happiness, or love even harder than before, but I know it's real. The memories are too fresh.

There's a lightness in my heart, too, but before I get carried away by it, I need to get on, and standing in the bathroom daydreaming isn't helping.

I quickly dry off and wander into the dressing room, gathering up some clothes before sitting on the bed and pulling on a pair of socks. Underpants follow, then jeans and a bright blue polo shirt. I can change later, before I go to Anna's, although I don't think she'd mind if I went there dressed like this. I smile, wondering how long I'll keep my clothes on tonight, and chuckle as I get to my feet. *Not too long, I hope…*

My tummy's rumbling with hunger, so I make my way downstairs to the kitchen, put on the kettle and slice some bread, placing it under the grill, while I prepare the teapot. I like my morning rituals, and besides, it helps kill some time. The agents' office doesn't open until eight-thirty, so I've still got a while to go yet.

Like most of my meals, breakfast is simple enough, comprising toast and marmalade, with two cups of tea, and once I've eaten, I check the time. It's eight-thirty-four, and I pick up my phone from the countertop, and look up the agents' number, dialling it.

It rings and rings, and I'm about to give up when a man answers, which is unusual. Normally, the phone is answered by a woman, with a slightly nasal voice.

"Hello?"

"Hi. This is Sebastian Baxter. I…"

"Mr Baxter? Is there a problem?"

"No. Not as such."

"Oh. It's just the office has only just opened. I assumed…"

"Sorry. I needed to ask a question."

The man sighs. "I see." I half expect him to say, 'And it couldn't wait?', but he doesn't. He doesn't say anything at all, and after a few seconds, I decide to fill the silence.

"I was wondering whether Mr Clayton would permit me to have someone to stay, if they were bringing a dog with them."

"A dog?" he says, with a tone of voice that would be more appropriate if I'd asked permission to open a crack den on his client's property.

"Yes."

"I doubt it," he scoffs. "Mr Clayton is very particular about his home. Some of his furniture is very valuable, know you? He wouldn't like the idea of a dog running around, scratching and chewing at things, making a mess and so forth."

"Jasper doesn't chew or scratch," I say, defending Anna's dog. "And I'd appreciate it if you'd ask Mr Clayton, rather than deciding for him. Perhaps you could tell him that the person concerned is my girlfriend. Her name is Anna Goddard, and she works for the solicitor whose offices are above yours. She has a four-year-old spaniel, not a puppy, and both of them are completely house-trained."

"Very well. I'll contact Mr Clayton and get back to you."

He hangs up, huffing, and letting me know he's not pleased. I suppose, when all is said and done, I'm not his client. Sean Clayton is, and as such, he probably doesn't care too much about my opinions. Even so, I didn't like his tone, and I'm too old to be lectured.

I'm also busy, and I clear away the breakfast things, loading them into the dishwasher before I make my way up to the studio.

I can't help worrying now that, in letting my temper run away with me, I might have ruined Anna's chances of coming to stay here. I know she won't come without Jasper, but the idea of her having to leave every night doesn't appeal. Obviously, I can stay at her place, and while there's nothing wrong with her flat, it's so much nicer here. There's more space, the views are spectacular, and as I sit at my drawing board, I wonder how Anna would feel if I asked her to move in here… always assuming Sean Clayton agrees, of course.

Is it too soon?

Of course it is.

But is that a reason not to ask?

I pull my phone from my back pocket, flip it over and go to my contacts. Anna's name is right at the top, and I connect a call.

I'm not going to ask her right now. 'Will you move in with me?' is a question that's best asked face-to-face. But there's no harm in making sure she got to work on time, is there?

The call goes straight to voicemail, which doesn't surprise me in the slightest. Anna's a very professional woman. She wouldn't have her phone switched on during working hours, and I smile to myself, waiting for the recorded message to finish before I start speaking...

"Hi. It's only me. I just wanted to make sure you got to work okay. I've spoken to the agent, and he's going to call Sean Clayton and ask how he feels about having a dog in his house. He was concerned about Jasper being house-trained, and I kind of lost it with him. He was being particularly pompous at the time, and I think I ended up telling him you both were. Sorry about that. Anyway, I'll catch up with you later, when I've got more news." I pause for a second, desperate to say 'I love you', even though I can't. I say, "Take care," instead, and hang up.

I glance around as I put down my phone, wondering what to do.

I might be busy, with deadlines to meet, but until I hear from Rodney that the client is happy with the sample I've provided, there isn't much point in starting any of the other illustrations on that job. I could tidy my studio, but that doesn't appeal... and I can only think of one other thing I can work on. Not that it'll be work.

A smile touches my lips as I get up and run down the stairs, rummaging through my coat pockets until I find my sketchpad, and take it back up to the studio with me.

I flip through the pages, stopping in my tracks when I reach the sketch of Anna.

"God," I whisper. "I'm a lucky man."

I really am, and I stare down at the simple pencil drawing as I walk back around to my seat. I sit for a while, just staring down at it, and then grab my phone again. There's no point in calling, but I can text her...

— Hi. It's me again. I'm just looking at the sketch I drew of you last night, and I take back what I said. You don't make me want more. You make me want everything. S xx

With nothing else to do, I grab some paper, tape it to my drawing board, and sit back, studying the sketch, just as my phone rings.

I flip it over, hoping to see Anna's name, and sigh out my disappointment when I see the agents' number at the top of the screen.

"Hello?" I say, answering promptly.

"Mr Baxter?"

"Yes."

"It's Mr Liddicoat here. We spoke earlier?"

"Yes."

"I just thought I'd call to let you know, I've been in touch with Mr Clayton." Already? That's a surprise.

"I see. And?"

I'm suddenly nervous, worried about Anna and what I'll do if the answer is 'no'.

"We communicate by e-mail, and I wasn't sure how long it would take for him to come back to me, but he replied straight away, so I'll forward his message on to you, if that's okay?"

I'm not sure why he can't just read it out, or tell me 'yes', or 'no', but I confirm my e-mail address and we end the call.

It takes a few minutes, but the message comes in, and I click on it, sitting back as I read…

'Dear Mr Liddicoat,

Thanks for getting in touch.

Ordinarily, I'd probably say 'no' to having a dog at the house, but as it's the tenant's girlfriend, I don't feel I can object. After all, who am I to stand in the way of true love?

SC'

I chuckle and lean back, looking up at the ceiling.

It feels as though the road has been cleared. I can ask Anna to move in, and while I'm almost certain she'll say I'm out of my mind, she won't be wrong, will she? Because I am. I'm completely crazy about her. I'm in love with her, and that's what I'm going to tell her.

I go to the messages app on my phone, returning to the one I just sent to Anna, and type out another.

— *__Hi. Guess who? I just heard from the agents – and Sean Clayton himself – and he's happy for Jasper to come here… with you, of course. We can leave our arrangements as they were for tonight, but maybe we can talk about the future? Can't wait to see you. S xxx__*

I don't expect an immediate answer. Anna's working, so I doubt I'll hear from her until lunchtime. Even so, I can't stop smiling as I put down my phone and pick up a pencil, returning my attention to Anna's sketch…

I love my job at the best of times, but when I'm drawing a picture of the woman I adore, it's easy to lose track of time altogether. That said, I'm struggling to get her feet quite right. I didn't put them into the rough sketch and I'm regretting it now, because the angle is proving tricky. I'm thinking about burying them beneath a throw or cover, instead of spoiling the effect with lop-sided ankles, when my phone rings and I pick it up, absent-mindedly staring at the drawing in front of me.

"Hello?"

"Hi, Seb."

It's Rodney, and I put down my pencil, although I don't take my eyes from the sketch of Anna.

"Hi. How are you?"

"I'm okay. How are you?"

"Never better." That's the honest truth, although I don't think I'll elaborate.

"That's good, because I'm just calling to let you know the client is happy with the sample illustration you sent through."

"So I can go ahead?"

"You can."

I'll admit to feeling a little relieved by that. It's always worrying when you start working on a new project, and now this initial phase is out of the way, I can get on.

"Okay. I'll make a start straight away."

"Great. Let me know if you hit any problems, won't you?"

"I will." Although I can't see what problems I'll have. None that Rodney can help me with, I shouldn't think. The job itself is reasonably straightforward. In fact, my biggest problem is that I'll have to stop work on Anna's drawing, and probably leave it to one side until this job is completed.

It's a shame, but there's nothing to be done, and I end the call with Rodney and get up, standing back a little to study my morning's work. It's looking good, although it's far from complete and maybe I can use the enforced pause to decide what to do about Anna's feet…

I smile, shaking my head, as I carefully remove the paper from my drawing board and carry it over to the desk at the side of the room. This might have been Sean Clayton's writing desk, but I find it handy to store my work when I want to keep it flat and out of the way. I place a piece of card over the top of the paper to stop it from curling at the edges, and then return to my drawing board again.

I've already decided that the best course of action with this brief will be to work through the illustrations in order, which means the first one is going to be of an orang-utan. I've got some reference pictures, and I tape them to the top of my board, along with a large sheet of drawing paper, and settle down to work…

*

It's my tummy rumbling that makes me look up, and I'm surprised to find the light has changed, and that when I check my watch, it's gone four o'clock.

I've got a lot done since Rodney called and although I could work on, hunger and thirst get the better of me, and I grab my phone and leave the studio, going down the stairs and straight into the kitchen.

Once the kettle's boiling, I open the fridge, grabbing some grapes, and a block of cheese, before I check my phone, frowning at it. There's no word from Anna yet, and although I assume she must still be at work, I place a call to her, which rings and rings, and then goes to voicemail. I can't see the point of leaving another message, but I can text her.

— ***Hi. I haven't heard from you all day. Is everything okay? S xxx***

I put my phone down, finding a knife to cut some cheese, just as the phone beeps, and I snatch it up from the work surface, flipping it over.

— ***No. I can't see you.***

The message is definitely from Anna, but I don't understand. What does that mean?

— ***You can't see me tonight? Why not? Has something happened? Are you all right? x***

I know I'm bombarding her with questions, but I'm confused. I'm also scared, and I don't care if she knows it.

— ***I'm not talking about tonight, Seb. I'm sorry, but it's over.***

I stare at the screen, numb from head to foot. She's sorry?

I connect a call to her, but it rings five times and then goes to voicemail. She's not taking my calls. For crying out loud. What's going on?

I go back to my message app.

— **What's happened, Anna? Why are you doing this?**
— **I can't tell you that.**

Is she serious? She tells me it's over, but won't tell me why? And I'm just supposed to accept that, no questions asked? I don't think so. I call her a second time and after the fourth ring, just as I'm getting ready for her voicemail again, she surprises me by answering, although she doesn't say a word. The silence is deafening, but it's a silence I have to break.

"Anna? Are you there?"

"Yes." Her voice sounds distant, reserved... nothing like her usual self.

"I don't understand. What did I do wrong?"

"Nothing. You didn't do anything. It's not your fault."

"Then why are you breaking up with me?"

"I already explained. I can't tell you."

"I thought we promised to be honest with each other. You said you were falling for me. But you can't have been if you can do this."

"Yes, I can."

"Then explain it."

"I can't."

"Why not?" She doesn't say a word, and once it's obvious she doesn't intend to, I shake my head. "How is this honest, Anna?"

"It's not. I know it's not, but it's best if you just forget about me... about us."

"How the hell am I supposed to do that?"

"I don't know, but it's for the best. Believe me."

"Why should I? Why should I believe a word you say?" I hear what sounds like a sob, my heart cracking. "I'm sorry. Please don't cry."

"I'm not." *You could have fooled me.*

"Can I come over? Can we talk?"

"No." Her reply is too quick, too loud. It takes my breath away. "I've got to go out."

"Where to? I can meet you."

"Please, Seb… there's no point. Can you… can you just stop?"

"Stop what?"

"Trying so hard."

"I think we're worth trying for."

There's a definite sob, which stabs at those cracked pieces of my heart. "I'm sorry," she says, and the line goes dead.

I stare at my phone for just a second and then hurl it from the kitchen into the living room. Fortunately, it lands on one of the couches, but that doesn't help the way I feel.

It's like nothing I've ever experienced before.

Sure, I felt broken when I discovered what Pippa and Dom were doing behind my back, but this is so much worse. I know that's because I don't understand it, but how can I ever hope to when Anna won't talk to me? She's shut me out with no hope of the future I've been dreaming of, and no clue why. While I've been planning to ask her to move in with me, she's been… she's been what? I've got no idea what she's been doing. What can she have been doing in the few hours since I left her this morning? Everything was fine then. I know it was. So, what's changed?

I sit at the island unit, only to stand straight up again, pacing the floor instead, unable to settle.

Nothing makes sense.

Nothing feels right.

And no matter what she says, I can't forget about her, or stop trying.

I rush through the living room, grabbing my phone from the sofa, and then picking up my keys as I run out of the door, straight to my car. I take two attempts to turn it around, but that's because I'm not thinking straight, and then I head off down the track, turning onto the main road, towards the village.

I know Anna made it clear she didn't want to see me, but I'm not walking away this time… not without at least knowing why.

The pub car park is busy, but I find a space and pull into it, locking the car and walking out onto the harbour. I take a moment, just to breathe, and then turn, heading up Church Lane. In no time at all, I'm at Anna's flat, and I ring the doorbell. I fully expect her to slam the door in my face, so I'm prepared, my foot on the threshold already… except she doesn't answer.

I ring again.

Still, she doesn't answer, so I knock.

"Anna? It's me, Seb," I call, loud enough that she'd hear, even if she was in the bedroom.

Eventually, I take a step back, looking up at the building.

She's not at home.

Okay, so I don't know for sure that she was at home when we spoke earlier, but it felt like she was. She said I couldn't come down and see her. She didn't say she wasn't in. I remember her saying she had to go out, though. That not only suggests she was at home at the time, but that she's gone somewhere else while I've been thinking and pacing the kitchen floor and driving down here.

Where can she have gone to?

Maybe to take Jasper for a walk?

I walk down onto the harbour, craning my neck and even standing on tiptoes, although how that will help, I don't know. I might be tall, but Anna isn't. She'd be swamped by the people strolling along, and I'd never be able to spot her… not in a million years.

I check my watch again. It's only just gone five o'clock. That's odd. What was she even doing at home when I called? She should still have been at work then…

Did something happen at the office?

Should I go and see her boss?

What would I even say to him?

I shake my head. That's a non-starter, although I suppose there's no reason for me not to wait for Anna to come back. She'll have to, eventually.

I turn, glancing up at the pub behind me and wondering if I should wait in there, rather than outside her house. It might be wise, considering how upset she was. The last thing I want is to cause a scene or embarrass her. I can come back in an hour or so and see if she's home then.

I take a step forward, but stop again. Do I really want to sit in the pub where we had our first two dates… in the place where I so nearly messed it up with her? Do I want that reminder? I don't think so.

Where else can I wait, though? There's the café, but I could use a drink… other than coffee or tea. I suppose there's always the hotel. Anna's brother is the manager there, of course, but I'm not about to trouble him with my woes. That would be worse than discussing them with her boss. Even so, there's nothing to stop me from sitting quietly in the bar.

I set off down the harbour, dodging passers-by, trying to fathom what can have happened to make Anna behave the way she has. She seemed so happy last night… and this morning, too. I know I didn't imagine that. It wasn't just the look in her eyes, or the smile on her lips. She invited me back. She said she wanted to shower with me. How did we get from her wishing I didn't have to leave, to 'we're over'?

I turn the corner into Bell Road, crossing the street and pausing by the wall at the hotel entrance, pushing my fingers through my hair and tipping my head back to stare up at the cloudy sky. It matches my mood perfectly, and I let out a sigh. Why can't I work this out? It can't be over. Making love with Anna was so perfect… so different…

"Oh, shit…" I mutter the words out loud, my blood chilling. Of course it was different, and not just because it had been so long.

I didn't use a condom.

I lean against the wall, lowering my head.

How could I have done that to her?

How could I have been so inconsiderate?

It explains…

I push myself off the wall again, because in reality, it explains nothing.

Anna's a grown-up, just like me, and if that was the problem, surely she'd have spoken to me about it… even yelled at me about it. She didn't seem to notice last night, any more than I did, but if she worked it out this morning, or some time during the day, she didn't have to break up with me, and refuse to talk.

Sure, I've been a fool, but it's nothing we can't get through together. It's nothing we can't…

I startle at the sound of a door opening, and look up, my heart stopping when I see Anna coming out of the doctor's office, opposite the hotel. She's as white as a sheet, shrugging her jacket on over the top of her work clothes, and for a moment, I'm frozen to the spot, just watching her slowly make her way to the gate, open it, and then close it softly behind her as she steps out onto the pavement.

"Anna!"

She looks up as I call her name, shock registering on her face.

"H—How did you know I was here?"

"I didn't." I step forward off of the pavement and onto the road as she shakes her head.

"Don't, Seb… please," she says.

"Don't what?"

"Don't come any closer."

"You're kidding."

"No." She raises her voice and I stop in my tracks, even though I'm still standing in the road.

"Anna, what's wrong?" I ask, trying to control my fear.

She stares at me for a second, then shakes her head and without another word, she takes off toward the harbour, running as fast as she can.

I'm rooted to the spot, although I jump out of my skin at the sound of a male cough, and I turn to see Robson Carew, the village doctor, standing by his garden gate, his hands in his pockets. He must have witnessed that scene from his window, and he steps forward.

"Are you okay, Sebastian?" he asks.

"No."

I complete my crossing of the road and join him on the other side. "Can I help?" he says.

"I don't know. I was talking to Anna, and…"

"I know. I saw."

I push my fingers back through my hair again. "I don't get it, Doc. She and I, we're… that's to say we were…" I stop talking and take a breath. "She broke up with me."

He frowns. "She didn't mention that you were seeing each other."

I nod my head. "Why would she when she so clearly doesn't want me anymore? It's not her fault, Doc. It's mine. I screwed up."

"What makes you say that?"

I move a little closer and lower my voice. "We slept together for the first time last night, only I—I forgot to use a condom, and I guess she…"

He holds up his hand, nodding his head. "I suggest you stop talking, Sebastian."

"Sorry." I step back again.

"Don't apologise. That's not what I meant. You know you can tell me anything, and I'll treat it in confidence. It's just that things aren't always what they seem."

"They aren't?"

"No." It's his turn to move closer. "I can't tell you why Anna came to see me, not even to confirm or deny anything. She's my patient, too, and I can't break her confidence, any more than I could break yours."

I look up into his worried face. "What can you tell me?"

"Just that you need to speak with her."

I let out a sigh. "I wish I could, but how can I when she won't even give me the time of day?"

He places a hand on my upper arm, to reassure me, I think. "Keep trying. Be sympathetic. And don't beat yourself up too much."

He gives me a smile, and while I'd like to be able to read something into that, and his words, I'm not sure what to think… about anything.

Chapter Fifteen

Anna

I haven't stopped crying for days.

Okay, so that moment in the shower on Monday morning didn't make me cry. It made me panic. My one solace was that Seb had already left, calling to me as he did. I'd stuck my head out from the shower, and raised my voice, telling him to have a good day, and then settled back under the water, feeling a little achy, but very happy and satisfied, for all of about two minutes.

Time wasn't on my side, so I got on with shampooing my hair, and then grabbed the soap from the dish on the side to wash… and that was when I found it.

I ran my fingers over it, again and again, just in case I'd made a mistake, even though I knew I hadn't.

It was impossible not to panic.

I shut off the water and leapt out of the shower, my body shaking, uncertain what to do.

Calling someone seemed like the best idea. But who? I had no means of telling the time in the bathroom, but I doubted it was seven-thirty yet. A look at my phone in the bedroom confirmed that to be true, which meant I had to wait another hour for the doctor's surgery to open.

Even so, I couldn't just sit and do nothing.

I had to talk to someone... someone who wasn't Seb. He'd want to come back, and I couldn't face him.

So, I called Stephen.

"Hello. Is something wrong?" he said, clearly surprised to be hearing from me at that time of the morning.

"Y—Yes," I said, still reeling, as I sat on the edge of the bed, wrapped in a towel, my hair dripping.

"Anna? What's happened?" I could hear the concern in his voice, and it cut through me.

"I—I've found a lump."

There was a very brief silence, then he cleared his throat. "Okay. There's no point in panicking yet." I felt like telling him it was too late. That horse had already broken down the stable door and was running wildly around the paddock. "You need to know what you're dealing with first."

"I know, but I can't even phone Doctor Carew for another hour."

"Really? I thought the surgery didn't open until nine."

"No. They changed the hours about a month ago. They open at eight-thirty now."

"I didn't know that."

I wasn't sure why we were discussing something quite so trivial, but I suppose it helped to kill time.

"What do I do?" I asked, sounding as desperate as I felt.

"Find things to keep you occupied. Are you dressed yet?"

"No. I was in the shower when I found the lump, and now I'm sitting in the bedroom, wrapped in a towel."

"Then get dressed, take Jasper for a walk, have something to eat, if you can. And once you've spoken to the doctor, call me back."

"Okay."

I hung up, and did exactly as he'd said, getting dressed for work, like it was an ordinary day. After that, I went out into the kitchen, noticing the dishes had been stacked by the sink. Seb must have done that, and I swallowed down my tears. It was a simple gesture, probably done to make my life easier, but I couldn't think about that… or him, so I took Jasper for a walk. I was on automatic pilot the entire time. If you were to ask me who I saw, or what Jasper did during that walk, I couldn't tell you. All I could think about was how it had felt at that moment in the shower, and what it might mean…

When I got back, it was still only eight-twenty, so I made a cup of tea, which I knew I wouldn't drink, and I sat at the table, watching the minutes tick by on my phone until they reached eight-thirty.

Then, with shaking hands, I connected the call, grateful that the line wasn't busy, and the receptionist answered straight away.

"I'd like to make an appointment with Doctor Carew, please."

"He's very busy today," she replied, and my heart sank.

"It's quite important."

I heard her tapping on a keyboard. "He's got a slot at five o'clock this afternoon, if that's okay?"

"That's fine."

I'd rather have had something sooner, but at least I wasn't faced with the prospect of waiting overnight. I gave her my name, and hung up, wondering how on earth I was supposed to get through the next eight and a half hours.

By working, probably. I was already running late, and I poured away my untouched cup of tea and headed for the front door, just as my phone rang. It was Stephen, and I answered straight away.

"I thought I was going to call you," I said, opening the front door.

"I know, but I couldn't wait any longer. How did you get on?"

"I'm seeing the doctor at five this afternoon."

"That's good. Do you want me to come with you?"

I was tempted to say yes, but he could hardly hold my hand, could he? "No, it's fine. I'll call you when I've finished with him."

"Okay, but if you need to talk before then, just ring me, or pop into the hotel."

"I—I will." My voice was cracking up, and I ended the call. I needed to pull myself together, if I was going to get through the day, and I stared at my phone for a moment or two before switching it off. I couldn't face the idea of him checking up on me every five minutes, and I think I'd already worked out that the best thing for me to do was to focus on work… or anything other than my five o'clock appointment.

Ben didn't even notice that I was a few minutes late, because he was on the phone with Mrs Green. It wasn't anything major… or I don't think it was. He came out and explained, but I only heard every other word. Once he'd finished, and I knew I'd got his attention, I asked if it would be all right for me to leave a little early.

"I've got a doctor's appointment," I said, deciding on the truth, but knowing he'd be the last person to ask for any further explanations.

"That's fine."

"I'll work through my lunch break to make up for it."

He shook his head. "There's no need. Not after all the extra hours you put in last week."

He went back into his office then, but I'd already made my decision about lunch, and that's exactly what I did. Other than taking Jasper for a quick walk, I worked right through, burying my head in files and letters, so I didn't have to think.

Ben came out at just after four, checking his watch as he went through the filing cabinet on the far side of the room.

"Don't you need to leave soon?" he said.

"Not for another half hour or so."

He turned around, clutching the file he'd been searching for in his right hand. "Why not head off now? You've done more than enough today, and you're looking a little pale."

I felt sure I was, and although I'd have preferred to stay at work for the extra thirty minutes, I couldn't really argue with him… not without explaining myself in more detail, anyway.

"Th—Thanks," I mumbled, gathering my things together, as he went back to his office.

"See you tomorrow," he called out, and I sighed, attaching Jasper's lead to his collar.

He seemed pleased to be going home early and trotted down the stairs beside me, out onto the harbour. I could have taken him for a walk, but I wasn't in the mood, and I steered him home, much to his confusion. He looked up at me, tilting his head as I opened the door, and then he came and sat on the sofa beside me when I flopped onto it.

I stroked his head as he rested it on my leg, and then I remembered my phone, pulling it from my handbag. The moment I switched it on, it started beeping. Jasper's ears twitched, and I stared at the screen, my heart sinking when I saw there were two text messages from Seb, and also a voicemail. Could that be from him, too? Or from Stephen?

I sat back, feeling guilty. Was Seb the real reason I'd turned my phone off?

I couldn't be sure, but it appeared he'd been trying to contact me all day, and I'd been ignoring him.

I decided to listen to the voicemail first, in the hope it might be from Stephen… except it wasn't. I put it onto speaker, and the moment I heard Seb's voice filling the room, tears welled in my eyes and my heart splintered.

"Hi," he said, sounding cheerful. "It's only me. I just wanted to make sure you got to work okay. I've spoken to the agent, and he's going to call Sean Clayton and ask how he feels about having a dog in his house. He was concerned about Jasper being housetrained, and I kind of lost it with him. He was being particularly pompous at the time, and I think I ended up telling him you both were. Sorry about that. Anyway, I'll catch up with you later, when I've got more news." There was a moment's pause, and I shook my head, wondering if things like that mattered anymore, and then he said, "Take care," and the line cut out, the automated voice asking if I want to save the call. I disconnected it, unable to decide, and returned to my text messages, reading them in order.

The first one came in just a few minutes after his voicemail…

— ***Hi. It's me again. I'm just looking at the sketch I drew of you last night, and I take back what I said. You don't make me want more. You make me want everything. S xx***

Oh, God…

Why? Why did he have to say that? Especially about that sketch. The last thing I needed was a reminder of that… or of the things he'd said, and the things we'd done.

Tears blurred the words on my phone, but I blinked them back, and looked at the second message, which he sent not long after the first.

— ***Hi. Guess who? I just heard back from the agents – and Sean Clayton himself – and he's happy for Jasper to come here… with you, of course. We can leave our arrangements as they were for tonight, but maybe we can talk about the future? Can't wait to see you. S xxx***

Future?

What future?

It didn't feel as though I had one, and I put down my phone just as it rang. I thought it might be Stephen and picked it up, half expecting him to berate me for turning it off all day, and let out a yelp of surprise when I saw Seb's name at the top of the screen.

There was no way I could speak to him. No way on earth, so I let it ring out, knowing he could leave a message if he wanted.

It seemed he didn't want to, though, and instead, he sent another text, which came in just seconds later.

— Hi. I haven't heard from you all day. Is everything okay? S xxx

Nothing felt like it was 'okay' anymore, and although I'd stayed silent all day, I knew I had to tell him something. The only logical explanation in my head was to tell him it was over between us. After all, how could I face him again, with his words so fresh in my mind, knowing I'd always be a disappointment to him?

I wiped away my tears as I typed out my response.

— No. I can't see you.

Unsurprisingly, he replied straight away, making it clear I should have been more precise in my wording.

— You can't see me tonight? Why not? Has something happened? Are you all right? x

So many questions, and there was only one answer. No matter how much it hurt to type it…

— I'm not talking about tonight, Seb. I'm sorry, but it's over.

I tried hard not to cry, jumping out of my skin when my phone rang.

"Oh, God… Seb." It was him again, but how could I talk to him? What was I supposed to say?

I waited for it to stop, and Jasper, seeming to sense my unrest, shifted closer and stared up at me as my phone beeped yet again.

— ***What's happened, Anna? Why are you doing this?***
— ***I can't tell you that.***

How could I? How could I tell him the truth? He'd feel obliged to help – or try to – and yet I'd know deep down that helping, staying and supporting me would be the last thing he'd want. He'd made that very clear already.

The phone remained silent, and I closed my eyes for a second, just as it rang.

It was Seb... again.

I glanced at Jasper, who seemed to frown at me, and then look at the phone in my hand, and although I knew he couldn't possibly understand, there was something in that gesture that made me feel guilty enough to answer, even if I couldn't say a word.

"Anna? Are you there?" Seb's voice sounded so strong, and for a moment, I was tempted to tell him everything, and beg him to come over... just to hug me.

"Yes." I was surprised by how pathetic I sounded.

"I don't understand," he said. "What did I do wrong?" I could tell how hurt he was, just from the tone of his voice, and couldn't help but remember all his insecurities... no matter how unfounded they were.

What could I say, though? I couldn't tell him the truth, so I just said, "Nothing. You didn't do anything. It's not your fault."

"Then why are you breaking up with me?"

"I already explained. I can't tell you," I said, willing him not to make things harder than they already were.

"I thought we promised to be honest with each other. You said you were falling for me. But you can't have been if you can do this."

"Yes, I can."

"Then explain it."

"I can't."

"Why not?" I couldn't reply to him, so I stayed silent, until he eventually said, "How is this honest, Anna?"

"It's not. I know it's not, but it's best if you just forget about me… about us."

"How the hell am I supposed to do that?" he asked, raising his voice just a little.

"I don't know, but it's for the best. Believe me."

"Why should I? Why should I believe a word you say?" That hurt, although I couldn't blame him, any more than I could stop the sob from escaping my lips. "I'm sorry," he said. "Please don't cry."

"I'm not." I was, but I didn't want him to know.

"Can I come over? Can we talk?"

"No. I've got to go out."

"Where to? I can meet you."

"Please, Seb…" I was begging him. "There's no point. Can you… can you just stop?"

"Stop what?"

"Trying so hard."

"I think we're worth trying for."

I couldn't hold back, hearing him say that, and I cried openly. "I'm sorry," I whispered, and desperate to end the call, I hung up.

None of that was what I wanted, and hearing him say all those things nearly broke me, but what else could I do? I certainly couldn't tell him the truth and watch everything I'd ever dreamed of falling apart around me. Not again.

Doing it my way felt like I was in control… at least, that was what I told myself.

Although as I got ready to go to the doctor's, I felt about as out of control as I think I've ever been in my life.

I left Jasper at home, and with sweating hands and a churning stomach, I made my way along the harbour and up Bell Road to the doctor's office. Fortunately, there was no-one else before me, his previous patient having already left, so he showed me straight into his room, where I sat at the end of his desk.

"How can I help, Miss Goddard?" he said, sounding as kind as ever.

"I—I've found a lump." It seemed best to get to the point, and he nodded his head, edging forward.

"Okay. Can you show me where?" I pointed, and he nodded again. "It's probably best if I give you a quick examination, and we'll take it from there."

He was doing his best to sound reassuring, but I struggled to stop shaking, even as I undressed behind the curtain.

The examination was brief, although I couldn't help noticing the expression on Doctor Carew's face, as he touched and pressed against me, and then stepped back, letting out a deep sigh.

"Put your clothes back on, and we'll have a chat," he said, and my heart sank.

"You can feel it too, can't you?" I said, sitting up.

He smiled. "We'll talk in a minute."

I got dressed, fumbling with my bra, and not bothering to tuck my blouse into my skirt. Then I pushed back the curtain, draping my jacket over my arm, and joined him at his desk, where he was typing something into his computer, although he stopped straight away, giving me a sympathetic look.

"There's definitely a lump there," he said.

"I thought so."

He moved a little closer. "I'm going to refer you for an urgent appointment at the hospital."

"Urgent?" I repeated the word in a hushed whisper.

"Yes. But you mustn't panic. This is just routine."

It didn't feel routine to me. "And what should I do while I'm waiting?"

"Try not to worry," he said, smiling. "I know that's easier said than done, but do your best to keep busy. Find things to take your mind off of it."

I nodded my head, wondering if that was possible. Until then, I think I'd hoped I'd imagined it, but having it confirmed by the doctor made it so much more real.

I got up again, as there was nothing more to say, and he saw me to the door, although I let myself out, closing it behind me as I shrugged on my jacket.

I felt like I was in a dream – or a nightmare, I suppose – and I walked to the gate, unaware of putting one foot in front of the other, let alone what I was going to do next.

"Anna!"

I jumped, looking up as I stepped out onto the pavement. The voice was familiar and my heart both stopped and skipped a beat when I saw Sebastian leaning against the wall by the hotel entrance.

I had no idea what he was doing there, but I couldn't face him.

"H—How did you know I was here?" I asked. It seemed like a logical question, being as only me, Stephen, the doctor and his receptionist had been aware of my appointment.

"I didn't."

I was beyond confused, which was only made worse when he pushed himself off the wall and started across the road, heading straight for me. Instinctively, I shook my head, the words, "Don't, Seb… please," escaping my lips and a frown forming on his face.

"Don't what?"

"Don't come any closer." I needed to keep some distance between us, for both our sakes.

"You're kidding," he said, his confusion obvious.

"No." I raised my voice, and he stopped dead, right where he was, in the middle of the street.

"Anna, what's wrong?"

I stared at him, unable to answer, and then shook my head again, and turned, running as fast as I could towards the harbour.

I couldn't see a thing for the tears streaming down my cheeks. No matter how much I loved him, I couldn't face him. I had to get home… to feel safe again, and I fell through the door just minutes later, making Jasper scamper to the back of the house in fear.

"It's just me," I called out and after a few moments, he came back and sat beside me on the sofa, nestling against me while I cried.

I half expected Seb to knock on the door, and although I would have welcomed a hug, seeing him was the last thing I needed. Still, there was someone else who I knew would hug me, and I pulled out my phone and called him straight away.

"Anna? How did it go?" My brother's voice had never sounded so good, and I took a deep breath and blinked back my tears.

"The doctor agreed there's a lump," I said, trying to sound matter-of-fact.

"I'll come over."

"It's…" He'd already hung up, and I sat back, feeling relieved. At least I wouldn't have to be alone.

The doorbell rang less than ten minutes later, and I dragged myself off of the sofa to answer it, removing my coat at the same time.

Stephen looked down at me, and pulled me into his arms, holding me close while I cried onto his jacket.

"Should you be here?" I asked eventually.

He frowned down at me, guiding me back to the sofa, where he sat us both down, side by side.

"Where else would I be?"

"At work. It's Ed and Nicki's wedding this weekend, isn't it?"

"Yes. But Laura's got everything organised. And in any case, I thought you could use the company."

"You're not wrong there." I smiled up at him as best I could.

"Do you want to talk about it?" he asked, and I shook my head.

"Not particularly, although I'd love to know how Seb found out where I was."

He frowned, and I realised my mistake, no doubt born of having too many other things to think about.

"Who's Seb?" he asked, tilting his head, and I decided to tell him.

"He's the man who was rude to me… the artist on the harbour. Remember?"

"Yes, I remember him." His frown deepened. "But what's any of this got to do with him? I thought you didn't like him."

I shook my head. "That was all a misunderstanding. He's not the monster I made him out to be."

"Does that mean what I think it means?" He smiled, his eyes twinkling with a hint of mischief. "Are you two together now?"

"We're not anymore… but we were."

His smile faded. "Oh. You broke up?" I nodded my head. "When was that?"

"Earlier today."

He leant back, his frown returning. "After you found the lump, or before?"

"After, of course."

"Why 'of course'?"

"Because I don't want to be a burden to him."

"But you don't know that you will be. There might be nothing wrong, and even if there is, surely it's as much his choice as yours." He moved closer again, taking one of my hands in both of his. "You're going to need someone to help you get through this. Even waiting for the appointment won't be easy."

"Are you saying you won't be there for me?"

"Of course I will," he said. "But if you've found someone special, then you should be with him. He'd want you to."

I shook my head. "No. No, he wouldn't. He's not like that. He was married before, and… well, let's just say, he made it clear he doesn't like women who can't stand on their own two feet."

Stephen sighed. "I doubt he was talking about a situation like this… unless his former wife had cancer?"

I hated the sound of that word. It was the first time anyone had mentioned it, and I pulled away from him. "No, she didn't, but I don't want to talk about it anymore."

"Okay… but I'm just going to say, I think you're wrong."

I didn't agree with him about Seb, but he was right about everything else. The last two days have been horrendous.

I hadn't realised how hard waiting could be. But I suppose I'm not just waiting, am I? I'm waiting in ignorance of what the future holds.

It's only been a couple of days, and I'm already at my wit's end.

I can't think about anything else, other than the storm cloud that's hanging over me.

Although at least I know when my appointment is now.

They phoned me this morning just before I left for work. That felt ominous in itself. I'd expected a letter, not a phone call… and hearing from them in that way made it feel even more important. More of an emergency.

My appointment is next Wednesday.

Which means another week of waiting…

Another week of getting through each hour of the day, one at a time, trying to pretend I'm okay, when I'm not.

Seb has called and sent countless messages since Monday afternoon, begging me to talk to him, asking why I'm being like this. I can't explain… obviously, and I'm sure he'll give up, eventually. He'll stop asking… stop caring. Start hating. That's how it goes, isn't it? That's what I said to Stephen when he asked why my phone keeps beeping all the time. He didn't agree with me on that, either, but I told him it's for the best.

I'm not sure it is, but for now, I read each message, over and over, wishing things could be different.

Wishing Seb could be here.

Even though I know he can't. Because, if he knew the real story, he wouldn't want to be.

And having to go through that would break me.

Fortunately, I have Stephen, and he's been incredible.

When I called him at lunchtime to let him know I'd heard from the hospital, he said he'd come over after work… and he did.

In fact, he's only just left, having told me he'd arranged with Laura that she would cover for him next Wednesday, while he comes with me to the hospital.

"You'd didn't tell her why, did you?" I said, panicking that the news might somehow get back to Seb.

"No. I just said you had a hospital appointment. That was all."

I nodded my head, feeling relieved.

As far as I'm concerned, the fewer people who know, the better. If Seb ever found out, I'm sure he'd pity me, and I think I'd rather anything than that. I think I'd even prefer his hate…

Chapter Sixteen

Seb

I haven't slept properly for the last two days. All I've done is snatch an hour or two, here or there, when exhaustion has overcome me and I've nodded off. The rest of the time has been a living hell.

Deadlines or not, I can't function. I can't work.

Even finishing the sketch of Anna hasn't helped. I thought it would. I assumed it would be a kind of therapy; something that would make me feel closer to her, but all it's done is remind me of what I'm missing, and how much I love her. Now it's finished, I've framed it, and hung it in my bedroom… where it reminds me every time I look at it, that I can't let her go.

Except, I can't seem to keep hold of her, either.

Doctor Carew told me to speak to her, but how can I?

I've sent dozens of messages, and she hasn't replied to a single one. She won't take my calls, either.

It's like she's cut me off completely… and I still don't know why.

I've thought about going to her house on numerous occasions, but I've talked myself out of it, mostly because I'm scared she'll reject me. There's also a part of me that will never forget the look in her eyes just before she ran away from me on Monday afternoon. It was bordering on fear, and I don't like the idea that she was scared of me. I don't know why she'd feel like that, but it's the last thing I want for her.

The problem is, I can't carry on like this.

I can't keep staring at a blank sheet of paper, missing her.

I get up from my drawing board and wander into my bedroom, sitting on the bed and staring at the sketch of Anna.

"Why?" I whisper, studying her naked body. "Why won't you explain it to me?"

She stares down at me with that sultry smile on her face… the one she was wearing on Sunday night, and something snaps inside me.

I have to know what changed.

I can't keep living in ignorance of why my heart has to be broken for a reason I can't even begin to understand.

I leap up off of the bed and run from the room, straight down the stairs, grabbing my keys as I pass, and slamming the door closed behind me before I sprint to my car.

I'm shaking with fear, but I manage the drive, parking at the pub, and taking a deep breath before I get out of the car.

It's only a few paces back to Anna's flat, but they're long enough for me to decide against knocking on her door. I'll admit that's partly out of anticipation that she'll slam it in my face, but it's also because I don't want to hassle her.

I glance across the road, recalling the last time I came here to try to put things right between us, and I cross over, standing in exactly the same place, my back against the wall. She'll have to come out eventually, even if only to walk Jasper, and while I wish I'd thought to pick up my coat, I don't care how cold I get, or how long I have to wait.

I have to know...

It's getting dark. My hands are starting to numb in the chill evening air, and I'm wondering if she walked Jasper before I got here, when suddenly the door opens. A man comes out, and my heart sinks.

Can it be that simple?

Can history be repeating itself?

I squint through the evening gloom, trying to see him more clearly, and then he turns, as the door closes, and I recognise him.

It's Anna's brother.

I remember him from when the two of them met in the street, and I jumped to conclusions about her.

I'm not jumping to conclusions now, though.

"Excuse me..." I call out, running across the street, and he turns to face me.

"Yes?" He peers at me, then tilts his head. "Are you Seb?"

I stop in my tracks, one foot on the pavement, the other still in the road.

"I am. How did you know?"

"Because Anna told me about you."

"She did?" I'm not sure if that's good or bad.

"Yes."

His answer doesn't help.

"How did you recognise me? We've never met."

"No, but she pointed you out to me." He nods his head, like he's confirming something to himself. "You've been texting Anna, haven't you? I wondered if you'd try to see her."

"She hasn't replied to me. I didn't know what else to do."

"You could've knocked."

I shake my head. "I didn't want her to feel pressured."

"What do you want?"

"To know what's going on. To understand why she broke up with me... and, more than anything, I want her back."

I never thought I'd say anything like that to another human being, let alone a man I don't know, but I'm beyond pride.

He smiles, and without another word, he turns around and knocks on Anna's door. My mouth is suddenly dry, my palms sweating, and my heart is trying desperately to patch itself together so I can breathe.

"Who is it?" I hear Anna's voice from inside the house, my stomach flipping over. It's been so long.

"It's me," her brother says.

She opens the door, her eyes alighting on him, and then, after just a second, landing on me. A gasp leaves her lips, and she glares at her brother.

"What are you doing?"

"I found Seb outside. He needs to talk to you… and you need to talk to him."

She shakes her head. "No, I don't."

He moves closer to her. "Yes, you do."

"Stephen, this is none of your business." Her voice is firm, and for a moment, I wonder about leaving… or at least offering to.

"Maybe not, but you're bloody miserable, Anna, and I think Seb is, too. You have it within your power to change that for both of you."

"You think?" she says, narrowing her eyes at him.

"I know. Being with Seb won't stop you from being scared, but at least you'll be able to share it, and that's half the battle."

She hasn't looked at me since that first glance, but I can't take any more of this, and I step forward. "For God's sake, Anna. Will one of you please just tell me what the hell is going on? What's making you scared? And why are you so determined to shut me out?"

Stephen takes a breath, tilting his head at his sister. "Are you going to tell him, or shall I? Because leaving him in the dark is unfair… and unkind, and that's not who you are."

Anna deflates, her shoulders dropping and her diminutive frame shrinking even further before me. "Okay," she says. "I'll tell him."

"Do you want me to stay, or go?" Stephen offers, and my fear ratchets up a notch.

"You can go."

"Because you're angry with me?" he asks.

Anna takes a moment, and then says, "No. Because this is personal."

He nods his head, smiling. "Okay. Call me if you need me."

She doesn't reply, and he glances quickly at me before he turns and leaves.

Once we're alone, the atmosphere between us changes in an instant. It's brittle… like the slightest word, or look, or touch could break it, and break us.

That said, I'm already broken, so I figure I have nothing to lose, and I step inside the house, closing the door.

"Anna?" I say, looking down at her as she leans back against the wall. "What's wrong?" She stares into space for a moment or two and I move closer. "Is this because I forgot to use a condom when we made love? Is that what you're worried about? Because…" Her eyes dart up to mine, her confusion silencing me.

"F—Forgot what?" she asks.

"To use a condom. Didn't you realise?"

"No."

"Neither did I until Monday afternoon. I'm sorry, Anna. I assumed that was why you were at the doctor's… why you split up with me."

She frowns. "You thought I'd break up with you over something like that?"

"I couldn't think of anything else. You'd seemed so happy. You'd made me so happy. What else was there?"

"If it had just been that, I'd have spoken to you about it."

"Just?" I say, moving closer still.

"Yes… compared to…" Her face crumples, tears falling onto her cheeks. I reach out, longing to hold her, but it feels wrong, and I let my hands fall again.

"Talk to me, Anna. Please. Tell me what's wrong."

She looks up at me, trying to compose herself, and failing, as she opens her mouth, closes it, and then blurts out, "I—I found something."

"You found something?"

She nods her head. "Yes. A lump."

The word is only whispered, but it fills the room, stopping my heart and everything around it.

"Where?" I ask and she looks down, then raises her left hand, touching it to the side of her breast. That fear I felt before is ramped up a hundredfold, and I step closer, so we're almost touching. "Is that why you went to see the doctor?"

"Yes. I've got an appointment for a mammogram next Wednesday."

"Okay. I'll come with you."

She frowns, blinking back her tears. "No."

"Why not?"

"Because we broke up."

"For reasons I still don't understand, Anna. Why would you do that?"

"Because of what you said," she says, wiping her tears with the back of her hand.

"I said a lot of things. Was it something specific?"

"Yes. Y—You told me… you told me you liked my breasts."

"I know. Because I do."

She nods her head. "Exactly. You kept telling me over and over how perfect they were. You even drew a picture of them."

"And?"

She frowns at me, as though I'm being dense. "And if I end up needing surgery, they won't be the same, will they?"

I take a half-step back. "Is that it? You told me we were over because you won't look the same if you need surgery? Is that what you think of me? You think I'm so shallow, I'll stop loving you because of that?"

She bites on her bottom lip, staring up at me. My words went over her head, I think. Not that it matters. Words like that ought to be important, but for once, there are bigger things to deal with. I'm about to say something along those lines when she pushes herself off the wall, standing upright and looking into my eyes. "It's not just that."

"What else is it, then?"

"You said you liked your wife because she was independent."

"What of it?"

"Well… if I've got cancer, I'm going to be sick for some time, I imagine. I'll need…"

"You'll need me."

She shakes her head. "You like self-sufficient women… ones who don't rely on a man. That's what you said."

"Then I was wrong."

"You're only saying that because…"

"I'm saying it because it's true, Anna. I know what I said about Pippa, and I meant every word. We lived separate lives, and I liked that, because it was what I wanted from her. But you were right, that's not a marriage. It's just two people who happen to share a house and a surname… and I want so much more than that with you." She sucks in a breath, and I smile down at her. "Do you know, when I first met you, I had you down as an independent woman, who'd reject the kind of man who made any effort to help, and who'd probably laugh if he tried to behave in a gentlemanly manner. I thought if a guy opened a door for you, you'd probably slam it in his face. Only, you're not like that at all. You're gentle, and kind, and funny, and unlike anyone I've ever been with before, you make me want to be a gentleman."

Her face softens. "You are, Seb."

"Only with you."

She shakes her head. "That's all well and good, but if I need a mastectomy, you won't want me anymore."

"There are an awful lot of 'ifs' going on here. If you have cancer. If you need a mastectomy. If hell freezes over and I stop loving you…" Her mouth drops open and she blinks hard.

"If you stop…?"

"That's the second time I've said it, Anna. I think you missed it the first time around."

"I think I must have done. Sorry."

"Hey… don't apologise. You've got a lot on your mind." I reach out and cup her face with my hand. "I'll give you another 'if', shall I? If you think I'm going to let you break up with me and go through this on your own, you don't know me at all."

Chapter Seventeen

Anna

I lean into Seb's hand, relishing his touch.

Did he really just say all that?

He must have done, because his words are still ringing in my ears, and he's waiting…

The problem is, I can't seem to talk.

My mouth won't open, my voice won't work.

"It's okay," he says, edging closer. "I know how this feels."

I don't see how that's possible, and I move away, his hand falling to his side, which makes him frown.

"How can you?"

"Because I found what I thought was a strange-looking mole on my back last year."

"Oh, God…" I feel awful now, and step closer again. "Was it…?"

He shakes his head. "No. My immediate thought was skin cancer, though. I used to love working outdoors whenever I could, and in the summer, I'd rarely bother to cover up, or use a sun cream of any kind."

"Is that why you have a tan?" I ask, and he smiles.

"Yes. I was one of those people who thought it couldn't happen to him... until it did."

"But you said it wasn't cancer."

"No. It was something unpronounceable. But just the process of finding out was enough to wake me up to taking more care. I can remember how scared I was when I first noticed it, and what it felt like to wait for the tests and the results. It was terrifying." He sighs, cupping my face with both his hands this time. "It was nowhere near as terrifying as this, though."

I look up into his eyes. "I—I can't even think about anything else. It's in my head the whole time."

He nods. "I feel the same, now I know. I just wish you'd told me sooner."

"So do I." I really do. I feel like such a fool for keeping it from him.

"Can I... can I hold you?" he asks, stammering over his words.

"I wish you would."

He lowers his hands to my back, wrapping me up and pulling me in to him. I didn't think it would be possible to feel safe again – not until I knew the answers to all my questions – but as he holds me tight against his chest, I have to admit, I don't think I've ever felt so safe in my life.

"It'll be okay," he whispers as I fight my tears, and I lean back, looking up at him.

"You don't know that, Seb."

"Yes, I do."

I shake my head. "What if it's..."

"Whatever it is, we'll fight it together. Okay? Just don't push me away again."

I lean against him, my arms around his waist, and I whisper, "I'm sorry."

"It's okay. But I'm really not that shallow, you know?"

I look up at him again. "I know. It's just…" He shakes his head and I stop talking.

"It's probably my fault for making such a big deal about your breasts in the first place, although they are…"

I reach up between us, placing my fingers over his lips to stop him from speaking. "Please don't say anything more."

He pulls my hand away. "They're perfect," he says, finishing his sentence and breaking my heart. I step back, although he won't let me go. "Why are you trying to pull away from me?"

"Because I don't want to hear it, Seb. I don't want to hear how perfect they are, when they might not be, if…"

"There you go with those 'ifs' again."

"I know, but I have to face it. I have to accept that I might be different."

"No, you won't. You'll still be you, and in my eyes, you'll still be perfect. Nothing will change, just because a part of you has been removed, Anna."

I stare into his eyes, needing to see the truth. "Do you really mean that?"

"Yes. I can't lie to you. I love you."

I really want to say those three words back to him. I even open my mouth to do so, but I bite them back. It seems unfair to speak of loving him, when I don't know what lies ahead. It's better to wait and see… I think.

"When did you realise you'd gone from falling to loving?" I ask instead.

"I don't think I was ever falling," he says with a smile. "Not really. I think I just fell. I only said I was falling because it was what you'd said, and I didn't want to rush you into love."

I hadn't expected that, and I nestle against him, relishing the strength of his embrace. "In that case, when did you realise you were in love?"

"I think it was when I felt so bad after walking out on you at the pub."

I look up at him. "Don't you normally feel bad when you're so mean to someone?"

"I don't know. To be honest, I'm not sure I've ever been that mean to anyone in my life. But it wasn't just because I felt abnormally guilty for treating you so appallingly. It was because I suddenly realised how much I cared about you. I didn't know your story then, but I knew I didn't want you to be the person I'd imagined. I wanted you to be better than that. It was important. That's why I persevered."

"So you knew before we made love?"

"Definitely." He sighs. "Speaking of which, there's something we need to talk about."

"Oh?"

He nods his head. "I realise you've got other things on your mind, but were you really unaware that I hadn't used a condom on Sunday night?"

I have to smile. "I was too busy enjoying myself to notice anything." He manages a smile, but it doesn't hide the worry in his eyes. "It's okay, Seb. I'm on the pill."

His face clears in an instant. "You are? But I thought you wanted to start a family with Fergus."

"I did, but we hadn't reached the decision. I'd been on the pill since we first got together."

"His idea or yours?" he asks, raising his eyebrows.

"His, needless to say. He didn't want the inconvenience of another child... not that I knew that at the time. Obviously, if he hadn't been a lying, manipulative cheat, I might have stopped taking it at some point, so we could have a baby, but that never happened."

He nods his head. "So we're okay?"

"Yes."

I hear his sigh of relief, which is a little disappointing, although with everything else that's going on, I really can't think about that now.

"What do you need?" he asks, his question surprising me.

"In what way?"

He tilts his head. "I don't know. Can I run you a bath? Get you a coffee? Give you a massage? What can I do? Do you need me to walk the dog?"

I shake my head. "No, it's fine."

"It's not fine, Anna. Nothing about this is fine. It's scary. I get that, and I want to help, if you'll let me."

"Thank you."

"Don't thank me. Just tell me what you need."

"A bath would be lovely."

"Okay." He steps back.

"And if you could walk Jasper for me?"

"Of course. Anything else?"

"I don't think so."

He leans down, kissing my forehead. "If anything comes to mind, just say." I nod my head and he leads me to the sofa, sitting me in the corner. "Is that comfortable?"

I look up at him. "Please don't make me feel like an invalid."

"I'm not." He crouches in front of me. "I just want to take care of you, Anna."

"Okay... but don't use too much cotton wool."

He smiles. "I'll do my best."

The bath is lovely and soothing, although even the soft bubbles and warm water can't do much to ease the worries floating around my mind.

No matter how good it feels to have Seb here – and it does feel good – I can't escape the fear that his words won't count for much if things go wrong. It's easy to sound supportive when everything is theoretical, but what will he do if it becomes real?

Or am I doing him an injustice?

He said he loves me, and I should believe him, shouldn't I?

I should trust him, too… no matter how hard it is.

"I'm back." His voice rings out through the flat and I sit up. Have I really been in here that long? He said he'd take Jasper out for an hour, and I guess my fingers are a little prune-like.

I climb from the bath, just as the door opens, a waft of cool air filtering into the room, along with Seb.

"I really wish I'd brought a coat with me," he says, rubbing his hands to get warm.

"You should have said. I wouldn't have asked you to take Jasper out, if I'd realised."

"It's okay." He smiles at me, reaching for a towel and wrapping it around me before he pulls me in to his arms. "I can warm up with you."

I snuggle against him as he rubs my back, drying me off, and I look up into his eyes. "I'm sorry."

"What for?"

"Breaking up with you. I should have had more faith."

He smiles. "I can't contradict you on that, but let's forget about it now, shall we? We've got more important things to think about."

I let out a sigh. "Yes, we have."

"Hmm… you need to decide whether you want fish and chips, or chicken and chips. I wasn't sure what you'd feel like, so I got one of each."

"You mean you've bought us dinner?"

"Yes. So, what's it to be?"

They both sound enticing, and I give it a moment before I say, "Chicken and chips, I think."

He nods his head, planting a kiss on the tip of my nose. "Okay. You finish drying off and I'll fetch your robe from the bedroom."

He disappears, returning within moments, carrying my pale pink, fluffy bathrobe, which he holds onto while I finish drying my legs. Then I drop the towel to the floor, turning around, so he can help me put on the robe, which he does, resting his hands on my shoulders and pulling me back in to him, kissing my neck just gently.

"You go and sit down. I'll be there in a minute."

I'm not about to argue, and I make my way through to the living room, where Jasper's curled up in his basket, having clearly enjoyed his walk.

"Do you want to use plates? Or eat out of the paper?" Seb asks, and I turn to find him standing in the kitchen.

"Plates, I think."

He nods his head, smiling, and fetches a couple from the cupboard, dishing out our take-away, and bringing it over.

"Let's see if we can find a movie," he says, grabbing the remote control from the arm of the sofa as he sits beside me and hands me my dinner.

"You think we'll agree on what to watch?" I turn, putting my feet up, and smiling at him.

"Of course."

He flicks through, stopping when he reaches *When Harry Met Sally*, and pressing 'play'.

"You want to watch a romantic comedy?" I'm surprised, and he turns to me, grinning.

"I do tonight."

"And you actually expect me to sit through that scene in the diner with you?"

He grins now. "You bet I do." I can't help laughing, which feels like a miracle in itself, and as the movie starts, he leans over. "I love to hear you laugh."

"Don't get too used to it."

"I won't. Now, eat your dinner before it gets cold."

I smile, nodding my head, because I can't think what else to say, and we both tuck into our chips.

Chapter Eighteen

Seb

I open my eyes to the early morning sun, with Anna in my arms, and although I know I should probably wake her, I can't. She looks so peaceful, and yet I know the moment she awakens, the reality of her situation will come flooding back to her.

Yesterday was such a rollercoaster, and although she's still got a long road ahead of her, at least she won't be travelling it alone. Not anymore.

We're back together, and I'm not going anywhere.

I think she understands that now.

She gets that this is about more than sex and looks, and trivial things like that. It goes a lot deeper, and I think she realised that when we came to bed last night.

Or maybe it was before… once we'd watched that infamous diner scene in the film. As Meg Ryan started moaning, her sole purpose being to prove that a man wouldn't know a fake orgasm from the real thing, I felt Anna shift in her seat. A quick glance at her told me she was studying her plate of food rather than the TV screen, and as the scene progressed, Meg Ryan's pretend orgasm growing in intensity, I could feel the embarrassment pouring off of Anna. Once it was all over and the older woman sitting nearby had asked for whatever Meg Ryan was having, I leant in and whispered, "Are you okay?" It seemed better not to make light of things.

Anna turned and looked up at me, nodding her head. She paused for a second and then said, "Has that ever happened to you?"

"What?"

"Has a woman ever faked it?"

"Not that I'm aware of, although I suppose Pippa might have done, bearing in mind she loved Dominic more than she loved me. Why do you ask?"

"No reason." She looked down at her plate again, although I could see the blush on her cheeks and I nudged in to her.

"Tell me." She turned her head, and I could see something in her eyes that made me wonder. "Are you saying you've faked it?" I asked, and her blush deepened, answering my question even before she nodded her head. "With me?"

"God, no." She looked so shocked at the suggestion, I couldn't help smiling.

"You faked it with Fergus?"

She nodded. "Not all the time, but like I said to you the other night, I'd never been able to have more than one orgasm at a time… not with him. I think it might have had something to do with how difficult things were when we first started seeing each other. It was always so rushed and sometimes I used to fake it, just to… sorry, are you okay with me talking about this?"

"Of course. If you want to talk about it, go ahead."

She smiled then, just slightly. "I used to fake it just to get it over with."

"Did he notice?"

"He never said anything if he did. I hoped it would be easier once we were living together, and sometimes it was."

"But not every time?"

"No. He couldn't always wait for me to get there... so I faked it then too, pretending we'd got there together, so he wouldn't feel bad." She looked back at the television screen. "I shouldn't have done it, should I?" she said.

"Why not?"

"Well... it was dishonest."

"Dishonest? Compared to everything Fergus did to you, I don't think you need to beat yourself up over faking a few orgasms, out of consideration for his ego, Anna." She turned back and smiled at me. "Just don't fake anything with me... okay? I'm not saying my ego isn't as easily bruised as the next man's but I'd rather you talked to me if I'm getting it wrong. Okay?"

She nodded her head and let out a sigh, then picked up a chip from her plate and fed it to me.

It felt like we'd cleared the air a little... and while Anna faking it with her ex didn't matter in the grand scheme of things, having her tell me that story made it clear she felt relaxed enough to say anything, and in light of what had happened, that felt important.

We finished our meal, watching the movie, and I cleared the plates, although when I returned, Anna was sitting on the edge of the sofa.

"I'm sorry, but I'm too tired to stay up."

"That's okay." I switched off the TV. "You don't need to apologise." I helped her to her feet and looked down into her upturned face. "If you're thinking of suggesting I leave, then let me tell you, that's not happening."

"But I..."

"I don't have any expectations, Anna," I said, holding her close. "I'm happy just to stay here and sleep with you. That's all I ask."

"Y—You mean you don't want...?"

"Of course I want to make love with you, but I can wait."

She looked up at me, her eyes glistening. "Thank you."

"You've got to stop thanking me."

"Why? I'm grateful."

"You have nothing to be grateful for." I brought her to bed then, surprised by how quickly she fell asleep, although I was relieved, too. At least she felt comfortable enough to sleep on me, and I loved her even more for that.

Of course, it hadn't escaped my notice that Anna hadn't said she loved me, but to be honest, I didn't mind. I still don't.

She's got a lot going on, and I'm happy with where we are. I'm in love, and she's still falling… and that's just fine with me.

She snuffles and shifts against me, letting out a sigh as she opens her eyes and looks up at me.

"Hello," she whispers.

"Hello." I lean in and kiss her, just briefly, on the lips. "It's only just gone six. We've got time for a cup of tea, if you'd like one?"

"That sounds lovely."

I slide my arm out from under her, sitting up on the edge of the bed before I stand and turn around. Anna gazes up at me, and then lets her eyes wander south, sucking in a breath when she realises how aroused I am.

"Just ignore it," I say, and she looks up at my face again.

"How can I?"

"Easily. I'll take it to the kitchen with me."

She giggles, which is music to my ears, and I make my way around the bed. "I'm sorry," she whispers, making me flip back around again. "I wish I could…"

I return to her, sitting on her side of the bed, and take her hand in mine. "So do I, but I told you last night, I can wait. However long it takes. I happen to think you're worth it."

She shakes her head like she doesn't believe me, her eyes dropping again. "I didn't realise you'd be so…"

"Hard?" I say, finishing her sentence.

"Yes."

I lean in, kissing her. "Of course I'm hard. I've just woken up with you beside me. What else would I be?" I stand, gazing down at her. "Doesn't mean we have to do anything about it."

There's a look of regret in her eyes, but I ignore it for both our sakes, and make my way through to the kitchen, where I put the kettle on, and stand back, searching the work surface, and then the cupboards for a teapot. I know it's early, and I'm sleep deprived, but I honestly can't find one anywhere, and once the kettle's boiled, I give in and return to the bedroom.

"Where's your teapot, Anna?" I ask, as I go into the room, where I find she's sitting up in bed.

"Teapot? I don't have one."

"You don't have a teapot?" I stand beside the bed, staring down at her. "How to you make tea?"

"The same way most people do… by putting a tea bag in a cup, pouring in hot water, leaving it for a while, then squeezing it out and adding milk and sugar as required."

"Oh, dear God. I need to educate you."

I shake my head as she opens her mouth to speak, but I hold up my hand and return to the kitchen, finding the tea bags, and breaking all my rules as I pour boiling water over them in two matching navy blue mugs, neither of which is made of bone china.

"What do you mean, you need to educate me?" Anna asks as I carry the cups back into the bedroom, setting them down beside the bed, and sitting alongside her.

"I need to show you how to make tea properly… in a pot, with tea leaves, a strainer, and bone china cups."

"The result's the same, isn't it?"

"No, it's not."

She raises her eyebrows. "If you say so, dear."

I laugh, unable to help myself, and sip the tea, trying not to grimace.

"Why don't I take Jasper for a walk while you have a shower?" I suggest, deciding that drinking the tea at its hottest is probably the best idea. The heat might at least dull my taste buds.

"Are you sure you don't mind?"

"Not at all. Then I'll make some breakfast, and you can call your boss."

She frowns, sitting up a little. "Call my boss? What for?"

"To let him know you won't be coming in to work."

She shakes her head. "But I need to keep busy, not sit here going quietly insane. And besides, I don't know whether there's anything wrong yet. It feels pathetic to call in sick when I can't be sure I am."

"Okay, but I think you should tell him."

"Tell him what?"

"That you're having the tests, if nothing else. You're going to need some time off, and I don't think it would hurt if he knew why… just in case."

She stares at me for a second or two and then nods her head. "C—Can you be there with me?"

"Of course I can."

I swallow down some more tea and get to my feet, finding my clothes, and putting them on the bed.

"I'm so glad you're here," Anna says, turning slightly, so she can watch me dress.

"So am I."

I made us coffee to have with breakfast, unable to face any more tea, and although we only had toast and marmalade, I've never enjoyed a breakfast so much. That was entirely because of the company, and I have to admit, I could get used to watching Anna across the table every morning.

Her boss was just as sympathetic as I'd expected him to be. He offered her as much time off as she needed, and even though she declined, I know she was grateful, and relieved, to have told him.

Before I left her at work, I reminded her to call if she needs me, and then I kissed her, keeping it brief.

"I'm gonna go home and take a shower, but I'll come back around twelve-thirty. We can have lunch together."

She smiled. "That sounds lovely."

I kissed her again, and left, retrieving my car from the pub, where it had been all night, and driving home. My emotions were in a turmoil of fear, relief and longing, but I kept them in check, getting on with what needed to be done.

That started with a call to Rodney.

"You won't like this," I said once we'd exchanged a few pleasantries.

"Like what?"

"Do you remember saying I should let you know if there were any problems with this job?"

"Yes." He sounded wary, and he had every right to.

"I need you to negotiate an extension to the deadline."

"You're right. I don't like it. The client's going to like it even less." He sighed. "What's happened?"

"Nothing's happened." I had every intention of working. Like Anna, I knew I'd need the distraction. But I wanted to give her as much of my time and attention as I could for the next few days, without the hindrance of feeling a client breathing down my neck. "I don't need long, Rodney. Just a week or two."

"Even so. I'll have to give them a reason."

Having told Anna she needed to be honest with her boss, I realised I needed to do the same with Rodney. Even if I don't work for him in quite the same way, it was unreasonable to expect him to call in favours without telling him why.

"My girlfriend's having tests for breast cancer," I said, the words making my skin chill.

"Oh, God."

"We can't be sure anything's wrong yet, but I want to be there for her, and I feel like I've got enough to worry about without deadlines getting in the way."

"Of course. I'll speak to Louis and see what he says."

We ended the call, and I took my phone upstairs with me while I had a shower. I was almost dry when it beeped, and I grabbed it from the shelf in the bathroom, wondering if it might be Anna. It wasn't. It was Rodney.

*— **Louis says you can have an extra two weeks, but that's the absolute limit. He'd like you to feed him the illustrations when they're finished, rather than waiting until the end and delivering them all at once. Can I say yes to that? R***

Two weeks was more than I'd hoped for, given the urgency of the job, and I replied at once.

*— **You can. Thanks. S***

The pressure felt like it was lifting already, and I put down the phone, finished drying and got dressed.

I spent the rest of the morning researching the animals I was going to have to draw, although I struggled to concentrate, and then at lunchtime, I went to Anna's office and, once we'd given Jasper a quick walk, I took her to the café.

She seemed tired and a little distracted, and after we'd ordered, I took her hand in mine.

"I'll come to your office and pick you up after work," I said, and she frowned.

"You don't need to. It only takes me about a minute to walk from the office to my flat."

"I know, but I think you should come and stay with me… at my place."

"Stay with you?"

"Yes. There's a lot more space, a garden you can sit out in, if you want to, and where Jasper can run around to his heart's content." He was sitting beneath the table and perked up at the sound of his name, although he quickly settled again. "I want to look after you, Anna. Properly."

She tipped her head to one side. "It's not just because I don't have a teapot?"

"No, my darling, I could buy you a teapot if that was the problem. I want you to come and stay because I love you."

Her eyes glistened, and I knew she was close to crying as she nodded her head and whispered, "Thank you."

I wasn't sure if she was thanking me for loving her, or for inviting her to come and stay. Either way, she didn't need to, but I didn't make a big deal of it, and instead we ate our jacket potatoes, gazing into each other's eyes.

My afternoon dragged a little, and in the end, I gave up any pretence at working, changed the sheets on my bed and tidied the house. It might have been more distracting than staring at a blank sheet of paper, but housework has never been my strong point, and I was relieved when Anna sent me a text message to say she'd finished for the day, and I could go and get her.

She looked like she could sleep for a week, and I took her in my arms the moment I saw her.

"Come on. Let's get you home."

She nodded, and let me help her down the stairs and out onto the harbour.

"Where's your car?" she asked.

"I've parked it at the pub, but I thought I'd help you pack a few things and then bring the car around."

She nodded her head, clearly too exhausted for much else, and I helped her inside, letting her sit on the bed, while I packed a bag to her instructions. We needed to bring some things for

Jasper, too, and I carried them to my car, driving it back and parking outside Anna's house, even though it's not strictly legal. She was waiting, and I helped her to the car, putting her bag in the boot, and Jasper on the back seat, before we set off.

She seemed relieved, and when we got back here, I unloaded everything while Jasper explored.

"He can run around the back garden while I cook us something for dinner."

Anna turned to me. "You? Cook? Don't you think I feel bad enough already?"

I could tell she was joking, and I pulled her into my arms. "I love you so much."

"Then don't even think about poisoning me."

I chuckled. "Okay. I'll help you cook. How does that sound?"

"Significantly better."

That's exactly what we did, although Anna struggled to find anything to cook with, and settled on a simple pasta dish, for which I seemed to have most of the ingredients.

"I'll go shopping tomorrow," I said while we ate. "If you tell me what to buy."

Anna agreed to write me a list, and I cleared away, stacking the dishwasher while she fed Jasper.

She was tired, so I suggested we go to bed, and she followed me up the stairs and into my bedroom, where she let out a gasp the moment she saw the picture on the wall.

"Oh, God… Seb." She stood, staring at it, tears rolling down her cheeks, and I put down her bag and went to her, holding her in my arms as she sobbed.

"Please don't."

She shook her head, glancing up at the picture again. "What if I end up scarred… different?"

"Then I'll draw you again, scars and all. I might even get your feet right in that one, so I don't have to hide them under a blanket, and then we'll hang it on the other wall." She stared up at me. "Whatever happens, it won't change a damn thing, Anna. You'll always be beautiful and sexy to me."

She seemed incapable of speech, so I helped her to undress and got her into bed, where I joined her and held her in my arms until she fell asleep.

My bed is significantly bigger than Anna's, but I still wake with her in my arms, smiling when I see she's already gazing up at me.

"Good morning."

"Hello." She smiles back.

"Did you sleep okay?"

She nods her head. "In a bed like this, who wouldn't?"

I turn my head, glancing at the clock. "It's still early. We've got time for a cup of tea, if you want one?"

"Made in a pot?"

"Of course."

She smiles. "In that case…" I kiss her on the tip of her nose and get out of bed, smiling when I hear her sigh. "You're hard again," she murmurs.

"Of course."

I don't say anything else, and neither does she. It doesn't feel necessary today, and instead I make my way downstairs and through to the kitchen. Jasper slept in here last night, and he looks up from his basket as I come into the room.

"Do you want to go outside?" I ask and he gets up, stretching, and looking out of the window, as though he's weighing up his options. I chuckle and grab the keys for the sunroom, opening the doors, and letting him out. He bounds through and races off toward the end of the garden, disappearing among the shrubs. It's all enclosed, so I know he'll be fine, and I go back to the kitchen to put the kettle on, turning around and spying the invitation to Ed and Nicki's wedding on the countertop.

I've already said I'll go, but it's tomorrow, and I don't feel like it anymore.

I wonder if Anna does, and once the tea is made, I carry it up and set it down beside her.

"So… does it taste that much better?" she says, taking a sip, even though it's scalding. She takes a moment as I walk around the bed and get back in, and then she lets out a sigh. "I hate to admit it, but it does. It's cleaner."

"I know." I sip my own, putting my cup down, and settle in beside her. "Just so you know, I've let Jasper out into the garden."

"Okay. I'm sure he'll be grateful."

"He didn't say." She chuckles. "And…"

"And what?" She turns, looking up at me.

"I remembered just now that it's Ed and Nicki's wedding tomorrow."

Her body deflates, and she shakes her head. "I'd forgotten."

"You're allowed. The thing is, I don't think I want to go anymore."

"Neither do I. I know I should be stronger than this, but…"

"Who says you should? If you'd rather stay at home, that's fine. I know I would."

"How are we going to tell them?"

"Don't worry. I'll deal with it."

"Are you sure?"

"I'm positive."

She shifts over, putting her head on my chest and her arm around me. "What would I do without you?"

"You'll never have to know," I murmur, kissing the top of her head, and I feel her sigh, rather than hearing it.

I've already dropped Anna at work, with instructions not to do too much, and to call me if she needs anything. We're going to have lunch together later, but in the meantime, I need to see Ed.

The pub is closed... which is only to be expected at this time of the morning, but I knock on the door anyway, surprised when it opens within seconds, and Ed stands before me.

"Hello. I thought I'd have to wait ages."

He smiles. "I'm getting married tomorrow. There's a lot to do."

"I'm sorry to disturb you, but that was why I called."

"Oh?"

He steps outside, looking up at the clear blue sky. "Yes. I'm sorry, but Anna's not very well, so we won't be coming to the wedding."

"We?" He frowns. "You mean the two of you are together?"

"Fortunately for me, she's a very forgiving woman."

He nods his head. "Then you're a lucky man."

"I know. I'm just sorry for messing you around at the last minute like this."

"That's okay. If she's not well..." He stops talking and tilts his head. "It's nothing serious, is it?"

"It might be."

He moves a little closer. "I thought so. I've seen that look before."

"What look?"

"The haunted one you've got in your eyes. I used to see it when I looked in the mirror."

"I'm sorry?" I don't have a clue what he's talking about.

"My first wife, Suzannah... she was sick, too. We didn't realise how bad it was, and she kept saying she'd deal with it. Only she left it too late."

"You mean...?"

"She died," he says, nodding his head in confirmation.

"I—I didn't know."

"Why would you? It's not something I talk about very often, and I've been with Nicki since before you moved here, so..." He stops talking and lets out a breath I don't think either of us knew he was holding. "The thing is, if you think it might be something serious, then Anna must…"

"She's already booked in to have the tests she needs," I say, interrupting him. "She's going on Wednesday, and I'm going with her."

"Good." I can hear the relief in his voice. "That's good. Let us know how she gets on, won't you?"

"I'm sure you'll have better things to do. You're getting married tomorrow. Remember?"

"Let us know anyway," he says, and I nod my head.

"I will."

He pats me on the arm before he steps back inside the pub.

I feel a little stunned by that. I didn't realise Ed had even been married before, let alone that his first wife had died, but his story makes me even more determined to be there for Anna… every step of the way.

Chapter Nineteen

Anna

Staying at Seb's place made things easier.

It felt like I'd put my life on hold, because I wasn't living it anymore. I was in a strange paradise, where nothing was quite real.

I've found it very peaceful gazing out across the sea from Seb's bedroom, or the sunroom, and Jasper took an immediate liking to the garden. He's also enjoyed taking long walks in the woods, running wild among the trees, although we always put his lead back on when we get to the headland, just in case.

I may love my flat, but this has been idyllic. I've even been able to make believe everything is okay… or I could until Wednesday.

I woke with a feeling like lead in my stomach, unable to even face one of Seb's perfect cups of tea, let alone any breakfast.

I'd booked the entire day off at Ben's insistence, and in the end, I was glad of it.

The appointment itself was just like I thought it would be. The lady who helped with the mammogram was probably the most considerate person I'd ever come across. She seemed to know how scared I was, and talked me through everything she was doing. That didn't make it any less uncomfortable, and I was glad to get back to Seb, who'd had to wait outside during the procedure. He seemed relieved to see me and came over to take my hand the moment I stepped from the room.

I think we both expected to leave at that point, and were surprised when we were sent to a separate waiting room, and then shown into a consultant's office.

That was scary. It felt very immediate, and every bit the 'emergency' that Doctor Carew had been talking about.

The consultant, who barely looked old enough to shave, let alone to have qualified as a doctor, spoke with a gentle Scottish accent. He glanced up at us both every so often, over the top of his glasses, while he explained that the mammogram had shown 'something suspicious'. That was what he called it, and I felt my blood run cold.

"Suspicious?" Seb said. "What does that mean?"

I was grateful he was capable of speech, because I wasn't.

"It means we need to do further tests, starting with a biopsy." The consultant looked at me and then nodded to a curtained area on the far side of the room. I turned, noticing a nurse for the first time.

"You're going to do it now?" I said, finding my voice, even though it sounded high-pitched.

"Yes."

I glanced at Seb and could tell from the look on his face that he was just as worried by that as I was.

"What's involved?" he asked, turning back to the consultant.

"We'll administer a local anaesthetic, so the area is numb," he said. "And then we'll use a large needle to draw off some tissue from the lump in your breast." He was talking to me, although I only took in every other word.

"Will it hurt?" I asked, and he smiled.

"Not once we've given you the anaesthetic."

Of course. He'd said that already. I felt silly for not paying attention, but he didn't seem to mind.

The nurse stepped forward then. "Would you like some help with getting undressed?"

I wondered why I was being treated with such kid gloves, but I accepted her offer and left Seb in his seat while I went behind the curtain.

Once I was ready, the doctor joined us. He whispered to the nurse, and they fussed over a tray of implements while I stared at the poster on the wall beside me. I was aware of them speaking, sometimes to me, but mostly to each other, and I felt the prick of the needle when he gave me the anaesthetic, although I kept my eyes fixed on that poster. It was about the symptoms of breast cancer, and while the subject matter wasn't ideal, it was better than thinking about the reality of what was being done.

"Okay. We're finished," the doctor said eventually, and I turned to look at him. He seemed older now, and he smiled down at me. "The results will take about a week."

"Do I come back here, or…?"

"They'll write to you."

That felt horribly anonymous, but I nodded my head, and the nurse helped me to sit up, handing me my bra.

I never thought seven days could last so long, but this week has been the worst of my life.

Despite the strange paradise of living at Seb's house, I can't forget the expression on that doctor's face, or the way everything seemed so rushed and urgent… or the fear in my heart when he said the words 'something suspicious'. It was all too real.

I've clung to Seb in a way I'd never have imagined possible. And he's let me. He's been there at every moment of the day and night. Whenever I've needed him, whatever I've asked, he's been there, and he's done it.

He called Stephen for me when we got back from the hospital, explaining what had happened, and then welcomed my brother into his home, letting him stay for dinner, and well into the evening. Stephen was worried, and Seb gave us time to be together. I was grateful for that, and I know Stephen was, too.

He's called me every day since, just to check if I'm okay. I'm not. I'm terrified. But at least I've got Seb and my brother, and I know I'd be lost without them.

On Tuesday morning, when Seb drove me into the village, he parked at the pub, like he usually does, and helped me from the car.

"Let's go to your flat and see if there's anything in the post," he said, taking my hand in his.

"It hasn't been a week yet."

"I know, but it's close enough."

I wasn't sure whether to feel relieved or disappointed when we opened the door and found nothing more than a letter from my bank waiting on the doormat.

It wasn't even anything important, and I consigned it to the pile on the kitchen countertop, throwing the envelope into the recycling bin before Seb took me to work.

Yesterday, there was no post at all, and this morning, I'm feeling even less inclined to check. I suppose that's because it's Thursday. It's officially been more than a week, so there's a greater chance of there being a letter… and I'm scared.

I'm so scared, I can't even get the key in the lock, and Seb has to do it for me, pushing the door open, and sucking in a breath when he sees the envelope on the mat.

He bends to pick it up, and hands it to me, closing the door. Jasper's wandering around, looking for his basket, which is at

Seb's house, and when he can't find it, he sits up on the sofa, like he hasn't a care in the world… if only.

"I—I can't," I whisper. "I can't open it."

"It might not even be from them," he says, sounding reasonable, although I can see the worry in his eyes.

"It's too anonymous to be from anyone else."

"Do you want me to do it for you?" I nod my head and he takes a breath, turning over the envelope before he tears into it and pulls out the piece of paper from inside.

"'Dear Miss Goddard,'" he reads. "'Further to your visit to the Breast Cancer Screening Centre, we can confirm that the sample taken reveals you have a benign cyst…'"

Seb stops talking and throws the letter in the air, lifting me off of the floor and swinging me around.

"It's benign, my darling," he says. "You're going to be okay."

He lowers me to the floor again, gazing down into my eyes, his lips meeting mine. He's held back in his kisses over the last week, but he doesn't hold back now. And I don't want him to. I want to feel alive… and more than anything, I want to tell him the truth.

"I love you," I whisper, between kisses, and he stops, pulling back.

"You love me?"

"Yes… so very much."

He smiles, brushing his fingertips down my cheek. "When did you go from falling to loving?" he asks.

"On the night you tried to poison me."

"That long ago? Really?"

"Yes."

He frowns, like he's confused. "So when you said you were falling…?"

"I was. It was later that night, when I got home, that I realised it was more than that."

"Why didn't you tell me?"

"Because I didn't want to rush you into love, either."

"I can understand that, but why didn't you say something when I did?"

"We had the results hanging over us. It didn't feel…"

"You think the results make a blind bit of difference?" he says, interrupting me.

"Maybe not, but it didn't feel right to say it before. I didn't want you to think I was saying it just because you were taking such good care of me, or because I'm grateful, even though you were, and I am. I wanted you to know it's more than that."

He shakes his head. "I wouldn't have thought that, Anna. And you have nothing to be grateful for. Taking care of you has been a privilege, even if the circumstances haven't been ideal."

"No, they haven't."

He pulls me close, letting out a sigh, then he lowers his lips to mine, his tongue seeking entrance, which I willingly grant as he pulls me into his arms. His moans and my sighs fill the air around us, and he walks me backwards until I hit the wall behind me. He pulls away, breathing hard and staring into my eyes.

"I didn't think it was possible, but I seem to fall a little more in love with you every day… every time we touch, every time we kiss."

"I—I know. I feel the same."

He nods his head, smiling.

"You should probably call your brother, now we know."

He's right, and although I can think of a dozen other things I'd rather do, I pull out my phone and connect the call. Seb doesn't move away. In fact, he keeps me firmly in his arms.

"Hello?" I can hear the fear in Stephen's voice and I can't help smiling.

"We've got the results," I say.

"And?"

"It's benign."

"Thank God for that." He's relieved, that much is obvious, and I can't help giggling. It's a situation that isn't helped when Seb kisses my neck. "We'll catch up later," Stephen says.

"We will, but thank you for everything you've done."

"You'd do the same for me."

"I hope I never have to."

"So do I, Sis. So do I."

We end the call and I let my hand fall to my side, enjoying Seb's attentions as he kisses his way up to my jawline and then to my ear, nibbling at the lobe and then whispering, "Text your boss."

I lean to one side. "To say what?"

"That you're going to be late."

"I can't. I've got no reason now."

Seb shakes his head. "I know that, and you know that… but Ben doesn't need to know that just yet, does he?"

He flexes his hips as he's talking, and I feel his arousal press into me. "I guess not," I say, smiling up at him, and he grins back, watching while I type out a message on my phone, explaining that I'll be a little late in to work.

Ben replies immediately.

— *That's fine, Anna. Take as long as you need.*

I turn my phone around and show the message to Seb, who wiggles his eyebrows, then takes my phone, dropping it onto the sofa beside Jasper as he lifts me into his arms and carries me through to the bedroom.

"It's been a while," he says, lowering me to the floor.

"I know. I'm sorry."

He shakes his head. "You don't have to be sorry. But we've got a lot of catching up to do… starting now."

Chapter Twenty

Seb

Anna was later getting in to work than either of us expected, but I went upstairs to her office with her, just in case Ben said anything. He didn't… not about her lateness, anyway. I gathered he'd just come off the phone with a client of his and had received some good news.

"I've just been talking to Mrs Green," he said to Anna, his eyes alight. "Her husband called her this morning to say he's going to agree to her terms."

Anna seemed shocked, although she unfastened Jasper's lead from his collar and I watched as he sauntered to a basket in the corner of the room. "He did?"

"Yes."

"Have you heard it from his solicitors yet?" she asked.

"No. I'm just going to call them. Mrs Green was adamant, though." He stepped closer, lowering his voice, even though there was no-one else present. "Of course, it makes me wonder what he's trying to hide, but she's happy, and at the end of the day, that's what matters."

Anna nodded her head as Ben went to move away.

"Oh... Ben?" she called, and he turned back.

"Yes?"

"I heard from the hospital this morning."

He clapped his hand to his head. "Oh, heavens... and here I am prattling on about clients." He moved closer again. "What did they say?"

"It's not cancer."

Ben's face lit up. "Oh, but that's marvellous news. I'm so pleased for you." He grinned from ear to ear. "This is turning out to be rather a good day."

He spun around again and trotted into his office, while Anna looked up at me, barely able to conceal her giggle.

"I take it Mrs Green is getting divorced?"

"She is now," Anna said, nestling against me.

I have to admit, that moment brought back memories of my separation and divorce from Pippa, but I wasn't about to say anything. That all felt like something from another life, and I wanted to enjoy the one I'd been gifted.

"Are you okay?" I asked, leaning back a little and looking down at Anna's upturned face.

"Yes. I'll be fine. You'd better go and do some work."

I leant in and kissed her, reminding her I could still taste her, and then I stepped away, walking backwards to the door.

"I'll come and pick you up at about five-thirty?"

She nodded her head, licking at her lips, which made me smile, and then I left, running down the stairs and out onto the harbour.

It occurred to me that Jasper could have come home with me and spent the day at the house, rather than cooped up at Anna's office, but that was something to talk about later.

For now, Anna was right. I needed to work. I might have negotiated an extension to the deadline, but there was still a lot to do, and the sooner I got on with it, the better...

*

I gaze down at the illustration of an orang-utan swinging from a branch and tilt my head to one side. Something doesn't feel quite right, but I'm not sure what it is. I think it's the tree, rather than the animal, but I need a break… and as I've worked relentlessly since getting back here, I feel I'm due one.

It's already gone five o'clock, so I don't have long to wait until I can leave to fetch Anna, and I use the time to clear up the kitchen, checking to see what we've got in the fridge for dinner. It's not exactly overflowing, and it seems the pub might be a good choice for tonight's meal. We've got plenty to celebrate, after all, and we can go shopping tomorrow. I went by myself last time, with a list Anna had prepared, so it'll make a change for us to go together. We can do something normal… at last.

I smile, closing the fridge door just as my phone rings and I pull it from my back pocket, surprised to see Anna's name on the screen. She knows I'm due to pick her up in just a few minutes, so why is she calling?

"Hey," I say, answering. "Is everything okay?"

"I don't know."

"Why not?"

"Because I've just had a call from Doctor Carew. He's asked to see me."

"When?"

"Now."

I can understand her call now, and the fear in her voice. It's replicated by the ice in my veins and the churning of my stomach.

"Okay. I'll come straight down there, and we'll go together."

"I'm so glad you said that."

"I wasn't ever going to say anything else, my darling. See you in five minutes."

"I'll wait out the front."

We hang up, and I pocket my phone, checking the sunroom doors are locked before I rush out of the front, grabbing my keys. As I put them in the ignition, I notice my hand is shaking, and I clench my fists a couple of times, hoping to ease my nerves before I start the car.

The journey to the village takes no time at all, and sure enough, Anna's waiting for me outside her office. It's tricky to park there, as it's right on the corner, so I pull up a little further along and get out of the car, meeting her halfway and taking Jasper's lead from her.

"Are you okay?" I look down into her eyes, seeing nothing but worry reflected back at me.

"I thought it was all over, but I feel so scared again now. What if they've made a mistake? What if the letter was wrong?"

"Then they'd have called you. They've got your number."

"Yes. Of course they have."

"It'll be all right." I say, opening the back door for Jasper to jump in, and then helping Anna into her seat before getting back behind the wheel.

It takes only a matter of minutes to drive to the doctor's office, but as there's nowhere to park, we leave the car at the hotel opposite.

"Stephen won't mind," Anna says as I wind the back window down a little, for Jasper's benefit.

"Should we tell him we've parked here?" I look at her over the top of the car, but she shakes her head.

"He'll realise it's us the moment he sees Jasper."

I nod my head, and join her, taking her hand in mine before we cross the road, and I open the gate to the doctor's surgery, letting Anna walk up the path ahead of me. I'm feeling just as nervous as she is, I think, but I do my best to hide it as she pushes the door open and we go inside.

The receptionist gets up from her desk, coming around to greet us, which isn't normal, in my experience.

"Hello," she says, with a friendly smile, and I smile back, although Anna just nods her head. "I hope you don't mind… I just need to lock the door." We step aside so she can reach the latch. "You're the last appointment of the day, you see."

At that moment, the surgery door opens, and Robson appears. He looks down at his receptionist, whose name I can't remember for the life of me, and gives her a smile, his eyes lighting up. I remember hearing a rumour a while ago that there was something going on between the two of them, and as the receptionist pushes a hair away from her face, I notice the simple white gold diamond engagement ring adorning her finger. Maybe there was some truth in that rumour, then.

"Thanks, Millie," he says, reminding me of his fiancée's name, before he turns his attention to Anna, giving her a smile that makes me feel a lot better than I have since getting her call.

He steps back without a word, and we move into his office, waiting while he closes the door.

"Has something happened?" Anna says as she takes a seat at the end of his desk, and I fetch a spare chair from the wall by the door, putting it beside hers.

Robson walks around his desk, sitting behind it, and shakes his head. "Nothing for you to worry about. I was notified about your test results earlier today, and I wanted to see you to make sure you understood everything and ask if you've got any questions."

I feel Anna's relief and match it with my own, reaching over to take her hand in mine.

"I do, actually," she says, surprising me, and both Robson and I turn to look at her.

"Okay?"

"I wanted to know what happens next," she says. "Does the cyst just go away by itself?"

Robson nods his head. "Usually, they do, but sometimes particularly large ones can be troublesome, so the fluid is drained off."

"And is mine particularly large?"

"Not at the moment, but if it becomes painful or gets bigger, just come back and see me."

"So I need to keep an eye on it for now?"

"That's about the size of it," he says.

Anna nods her head then clears her throat with a gentle cough before she says, "D—Does the fact that I've been on the pill for so long have any bearing on this? Could it have been a cause, I mean?"

Robson frowns. "It's unlikely. Remind me how long you've been taking it?"

"Nearly fourteen years."

He nods. "That's quite a long time…"

"Do you think I should come off of it then?" Anna says before he can finish his sentence.

"That's entirely up to you. If you did, you'd obviously have to discuss other forms of contraception." He glances at me, his lips twisting upwards before they break out into a grin.

"What's wrong?" Anna says, looking from Robson to me and I hold her hand a little tighter, pulling it onto my lap.

"I think the doctor is referring to the fact that, on the afternoon when you came out of here, and I saw you from across the street, I came and spoke to him, and blurted out that I'd forgotten to use a condom when we'd made love the night before. I'd assumed that was why you'd broken up with me, but Robson said I shouldn't beat myself up over it too much."

Robson holds up his hand, and even though she's blushing, Anna turns to him, as do I.

"Obviously, I can't advocate unsafe sex," he says, still smiling and focusing on me. "But in this instance, I knew Anna was on the pill. I also knew why she'd been here, and as far as I was concerned – given the circumstances – it seemed important that you should focus on what really mattered, and forgive yourself for making a mistake."

Anna stares at him for a second, and then turns back to me. "You really said that? You really told him what we'd done?"

"Yes. To be fair, you'd just broken up with me, and I was in shock. Besides, I said it to a doctor, not just a random passer-by in the street."

She shakes her head. "Honestly, Sebastian."

"Oh, God… am I Sebastian again?"

She looks up at me, struggling not to smile. "No, not really."

"So I'm forgiven?"

She nods her head, and Robson coughs to get our attention. The poor man has a life, and we're intruding on it now. "Are there any more questions?" he asks.

"No, I don't think…" I say, sitting forward, about to get up, although Anna stays where she is, and I look down at her. "Is something wrong?"

"I just… I just wanted to ask," she says, focusing on Robson again. "What if we decided I should stop taking the pill? What do I need to do?"

"There are several forms of contraception available. If you want to make an appointment, either on your own, or with Sebastian, we can talk them through."

She shakes her head, which is confusing to both me and Robson, I think. "I'm not talking about contraception," she whispers, so quietly even I struggle to hear her, and Robson has to sit forward. "I'm talking about..." Her voice fades, and although the penny has dropped, it's Robson who gets his words out before I can.

"Talk it over between yourselves," he says, smiling. "If it's what you both want, then come and see me."

"You think it's possible, though?" Anna asks.

"Anything's possible," he says, getting to his feet.

We copy him, although I'm struggling to feel the floor. I'm struggling to feel anything, and while I'm not sure how Anna feels, she's clinging on to me, so I guess maybe she's having difficulties too.

We make it to the front door, and although there's no sign of Millie, Robson opens it and holds it while we pass through.

"Thank you," Anna says, and he smiles.

"You have nothing to thank me for. I wanted to see you for my benefit as much as yours. I've been worried."

I hold out my hand and he offers his in a firm handshake and although I want to tell him we'll be back soon, I can't jump the gun. Anna and I need to talk first.

We make the journey home in silence. I don't want to have this conversation while I'm driving, and it looks like Anna doesn't either. Once I've parked, Anna lets Jasper out of the car and although I half expect him to run around, I guess he's hungry, and he follows us into the kitchen, where Anna prepares him some food, while I wait with growing impatience.

The moment she's finished and his bowl is on the floor, I grab her hand and pull her through to the sunroom, opening the doors to let in some fresh air before I sit on one of the couches, and pull Anna onto my lap, holding her firmly in my arms.

"That was a bolt out of the blue," I say, looking into her eyes.

"An unpleasant one?" She tilts her head, frowning slightly, like she's worried.

"Not in the slightest. I just wasn't expecting you to ask something like that."

"How do you feel about it?" She leans against me, letting out a sigh. "I know you wanted to have children with Pippa, but has that boat sailed?"

"I thought it had, if I'm being honest. When she and I divorced, I thought I'd lost my chance of becoming a father. But I still want it, if I can have it."

She leans up again, pushing herself away from me. "In that case, can I ask why you seemed so relieved when I told you I was on the pill?"

"Why do you think?"

"I don't know. That's why I'm asking."

"It was because you'd just told me you'd found a lump in your breast. As far as we were concerned, we both thought you might have cancer and I couldn't think of anything worse than those two situations colliding, and having to choose between treatment for you, or the life of our baby."

"Of course," she says, smiling again. "That never even occurred to me."

"No, because you knew you were on the pill. I didn't."

"So it's something you want?"

"Yes, it is. Although I think we should temper our dreams with a smattering of reality."

"You're talking about my age, aren't you?"

I nod my head as Jasper runs through from the kitchen, bounding out into the garden. "We have to accept it won't be as easy as it would have been ten years ago."

"Is that a reason not to try?"

"No, but it's a reason to go in with our eyes open."

"I know." She rests her hand against my chest. "The way I'm looking at this is, a few weeks ago, I didn't know you. I didn't think I'd ever find love again, or get a chance like this… so why not grab it with both hands?"

I chuckle, taking her hand and holding it to my lips, kissing her palm and then her fingers, one at a time. "I couldn't have put it better myself… and speaking of grabbing chances, I think you should move in with me on a more permanent basis, don't you? If we're going to make a baby, we need to spend as much time in bed as possible."

"Do we?" she says, trying not to smile.

"I believe that's how it works, and that being the case, I think it would be better if we were living under the same roof."

Her smile fades and she tilts her head, a frown settling on her brow. "I—I don't know, Seb."

"About living with me? Why not?" I lower her hand, although I keep hold of it.

"It's all been so… so quick," she says. "We barely know each other."

"Excuse me? You want me to be the father of your child, but you don't think you know me well enough to live with me? That doesn't make sense."

"I know. It's just…"

"You've been living here for the last ten days. I know the circumstances have been horrible, but haven't you enjoyed it? Don't you like being with me?"

"Of course I do."

"In that case, I…" I stop talking, realising at once what the problem is, and that it has nothing to do with how well we know each other, or the speed with which our relationship has blossomed. "I get it," I say, holding her just a little closer. "You don't want to live with me."

She gasps and tries to pull away, although I don't let her. "I do, Seb. Honestly."

"No, you don't. You lived with Fergus, but it always felt like you were selling yourself short, didn't it?"

"If I'm being honest, yes," she says, shaking her head.

"Exactly. Which is why you want to marry me."

Her brow furrows again, her eyes widening slightly. "That didn't sound at all conceited, or presumptuous."

"Because it wasn't. I was just stating a fact."

"Oh, really?"

"Yes. You don't want us to live together. You've done it before and it didn't work. That's why you'd rather we were married. Am I wrong?"

She hesitates for a second, pursing her lips before she shrugs her shoulders and leans in to me. "No," she says. "You're not. But is getting married such a bad idea?"

"Not in theory."

"And in practice? I know your experiences of it aren't great, but does that mean we can't make it work for us?"

I smile, shaking my head. "We can do anything we want, Anna… and if you want to get married, then we will."

"Really?" She positively beams with excitement.

"Yes, really."

"You're sure?"

"I'm positive. I'll buy you a ring, and you can have a lavish ceremony with all the bells and whistles, and…"

"I don't want any of that," she says, leaning up to kiss my cheek.

"What do you want?"

"I don't want a magician."

"Good. But all you're telling me is what you don't want, and I want to hear about what you do want."

"I want you."

"I'm so glad you said that," I say, smiling down at her as I sit forward, and then stand, lifting her in my arms.

"Where are you taking me?" she says, squealing and clinging to my neck.

"Upstairs. I'll take you out to dinner later, so we can celebrate, but for now, you're all mine."

She giggles and I bend my head, kissing her as I walk through our house and up the stairs, while Jasper runs around the garden, barking with delight.

The End

Thank you for reading *It Started with Jasper*. I hope you enjoyed it, and if you did, I hope you'll take the time to leave a short review.

We'll be back in Porthgarrion soon, with *It Started with Kindness*. This is the story of Anna's brother, Stephen Goddard. Lonely and fed-up, he's contemplating leaving the village, until Avery Watts arrives. Recovering from a nervous breakdown, she's been hired to play the piano in the hotel restaurant for a few weeks, and the two of them warm to each other over cream teas and conversation. The question is, what will Stephen do when faced with her overbearing father, and her imminent departure? Will he fight for her, or will he let her go?

Printed in Great Britain
by Amazon